J.T. EDSON'S FLOATING OUTFIT

The toughest bunch of Rebels that ever lost a war, they fought for the South, and then for Texas, as the legendary Floating Outfit of "Ole Devil" Hardin's O.D. Connected ranch.

MARK COUNTER was the best-dressed man in the West: always dressed fit-to-kill. **BELLE BOYD** was as deadly as she was beautiful, with a "Manhattan" model Colt tucked under her long skirts. **THE YSABEL KID** was Comanche fast and Texas tough. And the most famous of them all was **DUSTY FOG**, the ex-cavalryman known as the Rio Hondo Gun Wizard.

J. T. Edson has captured all the excitement and adventure of the raw frontier in this magnificent Western series. Turn the page for a complete list of Floating Outfit titles.

J. T. EDSON'S
FLOATING OUTFIT
WESTERN ADVENTURES

J. T. EDSON'S
CIVIL WAR SERIES

OTHER BOOKS BY J. T. EDSON

J.T. Edson

DECISION FOR DUSTY FOG

CHARTER BOOKS, NEW YORK

DECISION FOR DUSTY FOG

A Charter Book/published by arrangement with
Transworld Publishers, Ltd.

PRINTING HISTORY
Corgi edition published 1986
Charter edition/March 1988

ISBN: 1-55773-011-3

Charter Books are published by The Berkley Publishing Group,
200 Madison Avenue, New York, NY 10016.
The name "Charter" and the "C" logo
are trademarks belonging to
Charter Communications, Inc.
PRINTED IN THE UNITED STATES OF AMERICA

10 9 8 7 6 5 4 3 2 1

*For Dudley Pope, in gratitude for many hours of
enjoyable reading and for allowing me to examine
the relative documents belonging to the Ramage
family with which to complete this book.*

Author's Note

While complete in itself, the events in this book precede those recorded in *The Code of Dusty Fog*.

To save our "old hands" repetition, but for the benefit of new readers, we have included details respecting to the careers and special qualifications of Dusty Fog, Mark Counter, the Ysabel Kid and Waco, plus some pieces of information regarding the Old West—about which we have frequently received requests for clarification—in the form of five Appendices.

We realize that, in our present "permissive" society, we could use the actual profanities employed by various people in the narrative. However, we do not concede a spurious desire to create "realism" is any excuse to do so.

Lastly, as we refuse to pander to the current "trendy" usage of the metric system, except when referring to the caliber of certain firearms traditionally measured in millimeters—i.e. Walther P-38, 9mm—we will continue to employ miles, yards, feet, inches, stones, pounds and ounces, when quoting distances or weights.

J. T. Edson,
Active Member, Western Writers of America,
Melton Mowbray,
Leics.,
England

DECISION FOR DUSTY FOG

CHAPTER ONE

That Freddie Woods Lady

"Just take a look at this here lime-juicer, Merle, Red!" requested a voice with a Texas accent.

"Why dipsy doo!" responded a second, with the same indication of regional origins and a similar suggestion of the speaker having taken a couple more drinks than was wise. "Don't he just look the bestest riding man you *ever* did see?"

"Sure enough, Bernie," was a third opinion, its tone implying it originated from another slightly inebriated denizen of the Lone Stare State. "Why he's dressed fit to straddle the rough string, even of the B Bar D. But, seeing's how we'ns don't have it along, let's be right neighbourly's is only fitting 'n' proper for good ole boys from Texas and offer him to sit on poor lil ole Blotchy here."

If the subject of the remarks had been willing to accept advice from one he considered to be of lower social standing, or had a fraction of the intellectual superiority giving knowledge of *everything* which he assumed he possessed, he would have realized it was ill-advised to be walking the streets of Mulrooney, Kansas, dressed in such a fashion. However, filled with an over-inflated sense of his own importance, he had rebuffed a suggestion to that effect given by the vastly more experienced desk clerk at the Railroad House Hotel. What was more, having taken a dislike to him, in spite of proferring the sensible suggestion, the clerk had not tried to press the subject and had left him to his fate.

Just past his twenty-ninth birthday, about five foot ten in height, with narrow shoulders and a far from impressive physique, Shaun Ushermale went against normal Western sartorial fashion in several ways. Straggling untidily from beneath a curly brimmed round brown derby hat, his dark hair was longer than considered acceptable in many circles west of the Mississippi River. Set in lines implying his disapproval of everything around him, the thick drooping moustache he had grown failing to conceal its latent weakness, his face was not likely to win any friends.

Although Ushermale always proclaimed an abhorence for such pursuits, because of opposing the politics of the majority

1

who indulged rather than having any real concern for the
quarry, he was clad in a manner suitable for "riding to
hounds" with one of the "lesser" hunts in Great—as it was
then—Britain which did not insist upon the formal headgear
and "pink" jacket for anybody except the master and other
officials. He had on a black double-breasted reefer jacket,
from the high neck of which arose a sweat stained white collar
embellished by a bright red cravat indicative of his opposition
to "capitalism." Fawn riding breeches were tucked into low
heeled black boots which, despite the hotel offering such a
service for its clientele, were long in need of polishing. Even
if this raiment was insufficient to have attracted attention in a
Western town, he was noticeable for something else. He was
not wearing any kind of weapon in view.

If the appearance of Ushermale was Eastern and, more pre-
cisely, English, everything about the trio whose remarks had
brought a sullen scowl to his unprepossessing features was
undoubtedly Texan. In their early twenties, tall, lean, burned
dark by long exposure to the elements, the wide brimmed and
low crowned hats perched at jaunty angles on their heads were
steamed into the style practically *de rigueur* for a son of what
was then the largest State of the Union.[1] What was more,
apart from their distinctive speech, there were other indications to their origins to eyes which knew the West.

Although the tallest had obviously expended some of the
wages he received at the conclusion of a successful trail drive
upon a brown three-piece suit in the latest style to reach
Mulrooney from the East, he showed his superiority to town-
dwellers' convention by dispensing with a collar and tie to
accompany a white shirt with pink stripes. Furthermore, he
still retained his high heeled, sharped toed boots and had a
gunbelt carrying a Colt 1860 Army Model revolver in its open
topped holster on the right side.

Disdaining such an affectation as the town dweller's attire
worn by their companion, the shorter having fiery hair which
accounted for his sobriquet, the other two retained the kind of
clothing experience had proven most suitable for their work.
However, pictures painted by some artists and a myth of a
later date notwithstanding, they had left the leather chaps

---

[1] *Texas was supplanted as the largest state of the Union
by Alaska in 1959.*

which were worn while working cattle in the bed wagon of their outfit.[2]

Loosely tied about the throat, a large multi-hued bandana served several functions. To name only a few, it could offer protection against the sun on the back of the neck, shield the mouth from rising dust when riding the drag of a herd, be drawn up under the eyes as a guard against snow-blindness, do duty as blindfold to quieten down a recalcitrant horse, or provide a sling for a broken arm. There was nothing out of the ordinary about the open necked shirt, either its breast pocket or those of the unfastened calfskin vest offering a convenient place in which to carry a sack of Bull Durham tobacco and the papers to manufacture cigarettes. Sturdy and functional, the Levi's pants had the cuffs of the legs turned up to a depth of about three inches as a repository for small items such as nails when doing chores on foot. The gunbelts they had were not the rigs favoured by men who earned a living by skill with weapons, but allowed them to have revolvers for defensive purposes fairly readily available. Like those of the tallest cowhand, their boots were carved with a star motif to ensure everybody appreciated they were Texans.[3]

While each of the trio had taken a few drinks already, despite the time being only shortly past noon, they were far from being in an ugly mood. Rather they were looking for some amusement to replace another kind which had failed to materialize. They had brought a horse, which had earned itself a well-deserved reputation for resistance to being ridden, to the front of the Winstanley Livery Stable in the hope of meeting members of other ranch crews who would like to try its mettle. None had put in an appearance and, lacking patience as well as being disinclined to spend valuable time doing nothing, they were on the point of going elsewhere to look for takers. Seeing the Englishman approaching, however, they

[2] Provided the herd was of sufficient size, a second vehicle was taken along to supplement the chuck wagon. For information about what was carried in the "bed" wagon and how a herd was driven from Texas to the railroad in Kansas, see: TRAIL BOSS.

[3] Another example of how clothing could establish a man was from Texas is given in: Case One, "Roan Marret's Son," ARIZONA RANGER.

had decided to indulge in a favourite cowhand pastime of baiting a dude. With that in mind, while making the comments, they had moved into a rough arrowhead formation about him.

"How's about it, fancy pants?" inquired the tallest and, by perhaps a couple of years, oldest of the Texans. "Red 'n' Bernie allows's how you can't possibl' ride as good as you look?"

"Why, Merle," protested the redhead. "It was *you* allowed's how he couldn't even get on much less stay astride even a wored-out old crowbait like Blotchy."

"So it was, for shame," the third cowhand supported. "He even said's he'd bet us a drink a-piece all round's you couldn't. So how's about you calling his bluff and winning us them drinks?"

"Certainly *not!*" Ushermale refused, having the resentment of his kind for being subjected to familiarity by men who—despite a pretense of giving sympathy for being exploited by those who employed them—he regarded as being far below his social level.

"Now that ain't what I'd call neighbourly," Bernard "Bernie" Morris warned, his manner taking on an aspect of threat. "Not neighbourly at all."

"It surely isn't," confirmed Aloysius Hendricks, who much preferred the descriptive sobriquet, "Red," also showing an annoyance which was still mainly simulated. "Be they all so unfriendly back to New York, or wherever you come from in the East?"

"I'm *not* from New York," Ushermale replied and, to anybody who knew England, his less than defiant voice had an accent peculiar to the middle class-middle management stratum in the Midlands' region known as "the Potteries" from which he came. Hoping to create the aura of assumed superiority which he had found would quell most people he regarded as being underlings, he continued, "Nor anywhere *you* would consider to be 'in the East' and I've no intention *whatsoever* of riding your horse!"

"By cracky!" Morris ejaculated. "He don't sound like no Down-East Yankee I ever came across."

"No more he does," Merle Thornton asserted. "Fact being, he sounds something like the lime-juicer boss of the Union Jack back home to Bonham County."

"That he do," Hendricks agreed. "'Cepting ole Monocle

Johnny ain't so all-fired hoity-toity and high-toned. Are you from England like he is, fancy pants?"

"Where I come from is no concern of yours!" Ushermale claimed, making the declaration in a whining rather than defiant tone which emphasised his perturbation, and starting to turn around.

For all his belief in possessing great experience of human nature, the Englishman was making yet another mistake!

If Ushermale had treated the encounter in the spirit in which it was commenced by the trio, it would have passed off harmlessly. While they had only intended to have some fairly innocuous fun, with him suffering at worst a bruise or two when thrown from the horse, his behaviour was changing all that. Good natured though they generally were, they resented his attitude and were determined to change it. However, anybody who knew them—or cowhands in general—would have been aware that all the situation required to end it peaceably was for the Englishman to offer to try to ride the animal, or offer to buy drinks as proof of his inability to do so.

Alarmed by the unexpected turn of events, instead of taking such a course, Ushermale was silently cursing the impulse which had led him to leave the safety of the Railroad House Hotel and he looked around in the hope of seeing a member of the town's police force—as he termed it—despite normally expressing the belief that all law enforcement officers were oppressive tools of the upper classes. Although there were several men clad in various ways in the vicinity, albeit none what could be termed close, he could not locate anybody who had on the kind of blue uniforms he had seen worn by police officers during his limited stays in New York and Washington, D.C. Suspecting that none of the men he could see would be sympathetic to his position, also that to do so might provoke the three "Yankees" to attack him as a reprisal, he did not shout for assistance. Instead, as was his invariable custom when he found himself in any kind of potentially precarious situation, he decided flight was the answer.

"I don't know about you boys," Thornton stated, stepping until he was blocking the Englishman's intended departure. "But I reckon its kind of pitiful when a man's ashamed to admit where he comes from."

"And me," Hendricks supported, moving until he would be able to prevent flight in another direction and running a far from flattering gaze over Ushermale. "'Specially when he don't have the guts to get on a harmless lil ole hoss like Blotchy."

"Maybe Englishmen can't ride horses," Morris suggested, despite knowing the one to whom his companions had referred was very competent in all matters equestrian.[4] [4a] "They only dress up like they can."

"I know what's ailing him," the fiery haired cowhand claimed. "Could be, seeing's how *England's* such a pocket-handkerchief sized slab of no account range, they don't need, nor even *know* how to ride hosses there."

"Are you going to just stand there 'n' let Red mean-mouth your country that ways?" Thornton inquired, "Why, was it *me*, I'd get on that ole Blotchy hoss 'n' cut him down to size by proving him wrong."

By making the second suggestion, the tallest of the trio was seeking to prevent the situation from going further than was intended. Knowing how he and his companions would have responded immediately should even a far lesser slight be put upon Texas, he was wondering whether their comments would arouse a similar resentment. He knew the other two did not want to provoke a fight, but neither would back away from one should it begin. However, he was slightly older and more mature than them.[5] Despite having had a few drinks, he had a greater appreciation of the ramifications. Having no doubt

---

[4] *Further information about that particular Englishman, Sir John "Monacle Johnny" Besgrove is given in:* NO FINGER ON THE TRIGGER.

[4a] *Although Sir John Besgrove did not wear such an aid to vision, a popular misconception in the United States all through the Nineteenth Century was that all members of the British upper class wore monocles. This could have been helped to gain strength as a result of a few like the Earl of Hawkesdon, known as "Brit," who did so; see:* RIO GUNS.

Having learned of the supposition, the very competent British criminal, Amelia Penelope Diana "Benkers" Benkinsop wore a monocle as an aid to creating the character she was playing at one period during her visit to the United States in the mid 1870's; see: Part Three, "Birds Of A Feather," WANTED! BELLE STARR. *Further information about the visit is given in:* BEGUINAGE IS DEAD! *and* Part Five, "The Butcher's Fiery End," J.T.'S LADIES.

[5] *In a few years time, Merle's maturity and sense of responsibility caused him to be appointed segundo of the B Bar D ranch; see:* NO FINGER ON THE TRIGGER.

over the result of such aggression, even with bare hands as the Englishman showed no sign of being armed, he was aware that it could result in them all winding up in jail. As their boss, Bradford "Brad" Drexell, had warned them against this contingency, he would be furious if it occurred. Therefore, while disliking Ushermale's attitude, Thornton was still content to let the affair pass off as originally planned provided the other showed signs of willingness to go along with their fun and he was satisfied that his companions would follow his lead.

"Hell's fire, amigo," Hendricks scoffed, when Ushermale did not offer to reply. "I'd bet anything *nobody* from England could get on ole Blotchy 'n' stay there."

"I wouldn't go so far as to say *that!*"

Regardless of their concentration upon their intended victim having rendered the young Texans unaware that anybody else was in the immediate vicinity, the comment which followed Red's scathing remark would have diverted their attention under any circumstances. However, there was an even stronger reason why it should cause them to swing their gaze around so as to confirm what they suspected. Although the words were spoken in a noticeably British accent, albeit one which an ear accustomed to such things would have known to come from higher up the social scale than Ushermale, it was not in the masculine gender.

Striding forward purposefully from where she had been an unnoticed witness to the conversation, the speaker was in her mid-twenties at most and an exceptionally fine figure of a woman. Partially concealed by a wide brimmed and low crowned black Stetson close to Texan in style, her immaculated coiffured hair was coal black. Her regally beautiful face had the rich golden tan of one in good health. She had on a lightweight riding costume consisting of a long and trained grey skirt—from beneath which the toes of well polished brown boots appeared and disappeared with each step—and bodice separate. The yellowish-brown jacket, with a small turned over collar and lapels, was worn open to reveal a white silk chemisette buttoned down the front. Such were the magnificent curves of her close to "hourglass" figure, she contrived to make her decorous attire seem as revealing as the most daring evening gown. Nevertheless, her expression and demeanour implied she was a person with whom, despite it still being basically a "man's world," it would be ill-advised to trifle or take any other kind of liberties.

"Why howdy, ma'am," Thornton greeted, just beating his companions to speaking and performing the gesture—which Ushermale did not make—of removing their hats. "Aren't you that Miss Freddie Woods lady from England's we've been hearing tell about."

"Yes," the beautiful young woman confirmed. "I'm 'that Miss Freddie Woods lady from *England*' you've been hearing tell about."

"There wasn't *nothing* meant to you personal, ma'am," Morris asserted and, also having noticed the emphasis placed on the word "*England,*" sharing the summation of the other Texans that the disparaging references to the country of her birth had not been well received.

"It surely *wasn't*, ma'am," Hendricks confirmed, shuffling his feet in a bashful manner. "We was only joshing the Lime—this jasp—*feller* to see if we could get him to ride—!"

"I *know* what you were doing," Freddie Woods stated, being less annoyed than her demeanour suggested.

Although his interest was less in her as a magnificent example of feminine pulchritude, his sexual inclinations running along different lines, Ushermale found the newcomer as interesting as did the Texans. He was able to identify her accent as that which came so naturally to a class of society he hated for having privileges not accorded to him. What was more, although he had no recollection of ever having met her elsewhere, he felt sure he should, if not know, at least recollect something of interest—even importance—about her. Instead of speaking to try to satisfy his curiosity, he stood in sullen silence and listened to the conversation in the hope that it might supply him with a clue to solve the puzzle.

Although her real name was Lady Winifred Amelia Besgrove-Woodstole and having been raised as a member of the British aristocracy, the beautiful young woman had spent sufficient time observing cowhands from Texas to have come to know their ways pretty well. Arriving at the livery stable to collect the two horses she kept there, she had found none of the staff were present on entering the rear door. Being competent to saddle the animals, but wanting to avoid causing concern for the owner and his employees when their absence was discovered, she had come to the front entrance on hearing voices to tell whoever was there of her intentions.

On seeing and deducing what was happening, Freddie had

formed a far more accurate conclusion than Ushermale over the motives of the cowhands. However, despite the circumstances of her departure from England having made it impossible for her to return in the foreseeable future, she had sufficient loyalty to the land of her birth to resent the comment made by Hendricks, even though realizing what had prompted it. Having formed an accurate estimation of the Englishman's character, she had also decided it fell upon her to uphold the honour of their country.

"It's just that the dude here—!" Merle began apologetically, feeling as discomfited as he often had when confronted with an accusation of some misdeed by the elderly yet fiery schoolmistress of his childhood and to whom he was still in awe, despite the fact he was almost the same age as Freddie.

"So you think *nobody* from England could ride old Blotchy there, do you?" the young woman asked, apparently paying no attention to the attempt at exculpation. "Well, as this *gentleman* clearly doesn't mean to, *I'm* going to have to prove you *wrong!*"

CHAPTER TWO

It is Her!

"*You*, ma'am?" Merle Thornton croaked and, as they too had not envisaged such a contingency, his companions gave similarly startled exclamations.

"*Me!*" Freddie Woods confirmed, nodding emphatically. "And, as I haven't got all day, let's make a start at it."

"*Star—?*" the tallest of the three Texans commenced, throwing a look redolent of alarm at his companions and finding both were standing with mouths dangling open in attitudes of amazement.

"I don't know how it is in *Texas*," Freddie continued as the comment was left unfinished, turning towards the horse. "But back in Merrie Old England, one has to start *everything* before one can do it."

"I'd reckon *one* does, ma'am, just like back home to Texas," Thornton answered. Then, still worried about the possible danger and feeling sure the attire worn by the beautiful woman would not permit sitting astride, he warned hopefully, "But we don't have no side-saddle for you to use."

"That is a *point*," Freddie conceded. Then she dashed the hopes she raised by continuing, "But, it is one *easily* settled."

As she was delivering the second part of her comment, the young woman reached for the waistband of her skirt. Unfastening and opening the garment out, she lowered and stepped from it. Giving vent to startled exclamations, the cowhands watched what was being done in a manner which suggested they could not believe the evidence of their eyes. While the removal of the garment did not bring into view the underclothing their limited experience—gained from studying the pictures in Montgomery Ward mail order catalogues—led them to assume would be displayed, the sight was far from unattractive to their less than worldly gaze. Ending in boots similar to those worn by Shaun Ushermale, Freddie had on black riding breeches which were almost as tight as a second skin and emphasised the full curvaceous swell of her buttocks and shapely legs.

Despite owning and operating the largest saloon in Mulrooney, Freddie always took care not to go against the proprieties and conventions of the population. Therefore, she had come to the livery stable dressed in an acceptable fashion for a "good"—as such things were judged west of the Mississippi River—woman to go riding. However, she had never lost the love for the extra freedom permitted by sitting astride which she had acquired in her tomboy childhood. To allow her to indulge in this, one horse had a side-saddle required by the feminine riding costume and the other bore a low horned, double girthed Texas range rig. Leaving town on the former, once out of sight, she removed the skirt and was suitably attired to change to the latter.

Removing the jacket of the riding costume, Freddie handed it, the discarded skirt and her hat to Bernard "Bernie" Morris. He accepted them so gingerly he might have believed they would burn his fingers. Relieved of the garments, unbuttoning the neck of the white silk chemisette, she strolled to where the horse was tethered to the gate of an empty pole corral. While doing so, she examined it with the gaze of one well versed in matters equestrian.

Having a washy paint colouration of a somehow grubby looking white much be-splotched by irregular patches of yellowish-red, which obviously accounted for its name, "Blotchy," the animal was a less than attractive sight. Standing on cow-hocked legs and seeming ready to fall over at any moment, its conformation was unlikely to have won any prizes for beauty. No more than fourteen hands, weighing slightly under a thousand pounds, its head was "common"—having big woolly ears, big eyes, narrow jaws and a coarse, flabby muzzle indicative of being underbred—and was set on a ewe neck which seemed almost too long for its body. If that was not enough, it was goose rumped and had short, steep croups.

Should Freddie have inquired why such an ill-favoured animal was included in the *remuda* for a trail herd, especially when also possessing the kind of unsuitable temperament which she suspected was the case, she would have been informed this was an accident upon the part of the wrangler. When the facts had become known, being too kind hearted to shoot it, Bradford Drexell had kept it with them in the hope—which failed to materialize—that it could be sold to some unsuspecting buyer along the way.

However, the thought never occured to the beautiful Englishwoman. Instead she was concerned only with the conclusions she had drawn from the examination. They were not of a kind to inspire overconfidence, or a belief that she had a sinecure ahead. Regardless of all the faults, some of them suggestive of speed and agility being lacking, the beautiful Englishwoman's keen and knowing scrutiny established that the paint was wiry and well muscled. What was more, although it had on a well used Texas range saddle, it was not equipped with a conventional bridle and split ended reins. In addition, the adjustable wide brow band of its hackamore's headpiece had been drawn down to cover its eyes and she knew this was done to restrain any tendency to fight against whatever might be required of it.

"I've heard that sometimes a burr, or something just as sharp, gets under the saddle blanket, or in the girths," the Englishwoman commented, although she felt sure the Texans would not have indulged in such a vicious and dangerous trick.

"Any man who'd do *that* to a hoss deserves to have whatever he uses stuck up *his* butt!" Thornton asserted and his companions nodded an equally vehement concurrence. Then he realized he had employed a term unsuitable for the ears of a lady and his manner became apologetic. "Happen you'll excuse what I said, ma'am."

"I agree and you're excused," Freddie answered with a smile. "Now, let's see if somebody from Merrie Old England *can* sit your old Blotchy horse."

"There ain't no call for you to do that, ma'am!" Aloysius "Red" Hendricks claimed, sounding worried. While he would quite happily have allowed Ushermale to get on the paint despite knowing its temperament, or any other man if it came to that, he did not care to subject a member of the opposite sex—especially one so attractive, charming and friendly—to such a fate."'Cause, fact being—!"

"Fact being, he's not *quite* as gentle and harmless as you've been letting on," Freddie finished for the cowhand, but her demeanour showed she was amused rather than annoyed by the attempted deception. "Don't tell *anybody* I said so, but I didn't think for a moment he *was*. But I can't let down the honour of Merrie Old England—." She did not continue, "even if *he* is doing it," but the glance she directed at Ushermale implied the thought was in her mind. "So, come what may, I'm going to give it a whirl, as you colonials put it."[1]

Studying the determination on the beautiful face and noticing the timbre of her voice warned them the Englishwoman would brook no argument, the cowhands accepted the inevitable. Everything about her suggested she knew what was in store for her and felt competent to cope with it. They also were sure, no matter what the result, she would not hold anything that might happen to her against them.

Apart from the single derisive glance she had directed at Ushermale, Freddie gave him no further attention!

What was more, being fascinated by the appearance of the beautiful young Englishwoman and what she was doing, the Texans had also put the cause of the incident from their mind!

For his part, Ushermale was staring at Freddie with an intensity which would have surprised anybody who knew him. However, his thoughts were not upon the most attractive sight she presented in the less than conventional attire displayed by removing her outer garments. Instead, he was even more convinced there was something about her which he should remember. Failing to bring whatever it might be to mind, he suddenly realized the chance he was being presented by her intervention. Having no desire to face the trio again, especially if anything should happen to her while riding the horse, he backed off a couple of steps. His action went unnoticed and, giving a low sigh of relief, he turned to walk away at a swift pace.

Liberating the one-piece reins from the rail to which they were hitched, Freddie asked for the gate of the corral to be opened. After Hendricks had complied with the request, followed by all three Texans and giving no thought to the Englishman, she led Blotchy inside. Accepting Thornton's offer to hold the washy paint, she prepared to mount. Although she had been taught to ride on the somewhat smaller type of saddle used in the United Kingdom, she had come to like the more comfortable rig which had been developed in Texas to

[1] *Like many of her generation and class, albeit perhaps a trifle tongue in cheek in most cases, as it was in her own, Lady Winifred Amelia "Freddie Woods" Besgrove-Woodstole held to the belief that the world was divided into two parts, Great Britain and its colonies, therefore anybody who was not British was considered a "colonial." We subscribe to the point of view, see the dedication for:* KILL DUSTY FOG!

meet the needs of men who spent much of their working life astride a horse.

Before doing anything else, Freddie tested the fit of the saddle to ensure it was secure. However, this did not imply she suspected otherwise. Nor did any of the trio consider it a reflection upon their honesty. Rather they were relieved by watching a precaution each would have followed and they took it as further proof of her competence. Satisfied that all was well, she made ready to get astride the animal. Because of the way in which the rig was constructed being different from those she had used in England, this called for a slightly revised method of mounting.

When riding on the other side of the Atlantic Ocean, Freddie would have grasped a good hold of the mane with her bridle hand. However, using the Texas range rig, there was something available that was even more secure and less liable to arouse the animosity of a recalcitrant animal. Grasping the low horn and the one piece reins of the hackamore with her left hand, she slipped her left foot into the near side stirrup iron and deftly swung into the saddle. Settling herself firmly on the seat, she ensured her feet were positioned securely in the stirrups. When satisfied all was as she wanted it, feeling the horse quivering between her legs and giving warning of its intentions, she issued the order for the blindfold to be cleared.

Thrusting up the browband, Thornton sprang clear!

Nor did the tallest of the Texans move an instant too soon!

Showing an equal appreciation of the situation, the other two joined Thornton in dashing across the corral and climbing to sit on its top rail!

All the head-hanging, passively somnolent seeming posture left Blotchy and, springing forward, it started the kind of rapid bucking which had won its reputation. However, it soon discovered it had a rider of considerable ability on its back and made extra effort to try and dislodge the unwelcome burden. Rearing, plunging with back arched, chinning the moon, crawfishing, fence-worming, jack-knifing and performing every other trick in its extensive repertoire,[2] it went around and around the spacious confines of the corral in an ever growing cloud of churned up dust.

Thrown back and forwards on the saddle, jolted into the air

[2]*Most of the tricks employed by Blotchy are described in detail in various volumes of the* Floating Outfit, Waco *and* Calamity Jane *series.*

and coming down again on the less than yielding leather seat, Freddie needed all her skill to stay with her mount through its violent efforts. She was oblivious of the yells of encouragement being given by the Texans although she sensed they were there. Nor could she spare even a moment to find out how the Englishman was responding to her attempt to uphold the honour of their native land. She did not even notice that, attracted by the commotion, several men and a few women started running from several directions to watch the struggle for dominance which was taking place.

Before many seconds had passed, Freddie's previously immaculate hair was shaken down until she was compelled to toss her head and clear strands from in front of her eyes. Soon freely flowing perspiration washed the acceptable amount of make-up permitted to a "good" woman from her face. Gasping to exhale and replenish her lungs with air, exertion caused her bosom to rise and fall with a vigour which threatened to burst off the buttons of her snugly fitting chemisette.

At last, after several minutes of unremitting effort, Blotchy's struggles slackened. Despite being urged by jabs from the small spurs on the heels of its rider, it made only a token effort to resume the fray. Then, snorting breathlessly and whitened by copiously shed lather, it came to a halt. Slipping from the saddle and swaying with the effect of her exertions, Freddie leaned against its hot flanks and gently patted its steaming neck. As the three young Texans sprang down from the rail and hurried forward, for the first time she became aware that she had attracted a much larger audience. Surrendering the reins to Thornton, smiling at the enthusiastic way in which he and his companions were responding to her victory, she acknowledged the applause from the men and women around the corral with a tired wave of her left hand. Then she looked for the Englishman. Although she had hoped otherwise, she was not entirely surprised to find he was nowhere to be seen.

"Whee dogie!" Morris whooped, turning Freddie's attention from thoughts which were less than flattering to Ushermale. "You took ole Blotchy like General Sam took Santa Ana at San Jac'!"[3]

---

[3] "San Jac": Texans' name for the decisive Battle of San Jacinto on Thursday, April the 26th 1836, in which a greatly outnumbered force of Texans led by General Samuel "Sam" Houston defeated the army of Presidente General Antonio

"O—Or General Grant took Richmond?" the Englishwoman suggested breathlessly, feeling sure the ride she had just completed would make such an otherwise impolitic remark acceptable to the three young Texans.

"He was just *lucky,* ma'am," Thornton claimed and the grins on the faces of the other two indicated that, despite being confirmed "Johnny Rebs" at heart—like him—they had taken no offence at this reminder of a crucial "Yankee" victory in the War Between The States. "In *two* ways!"

"*T—Two* ways?" Freddie inquired, gently rubbing at her throbbing curvaceous buttocks and concluding they had never felt so sore even at the end of a day's hard riding with the Quorn or Belvoir Hunts near her family's home town of Melton Mowbray in Leicestershire.

"His boys'd wide-looped some good Southron sipping whiskey for him to drink," the oldest of the trio explained with a grin.[4][4a] "And, more important, he *couldn't've* done it was the Texas Light Cavalry there to stop him."

"He sure 'nough *couldn't've,*" Hendricks confirmed.

"Amen to that from here to there and back the long way," Morris supported. "Happen you've heard of the Texas Light in the War, ma'am?"[5]

"I've *heard,*" Freddie conceded. "Anyway, *us* Rebs won the *last* battle of the War."

"We surely did, ma'am," Thornton agreed, surprised that an Englishwoman should be so conversant with that particular event from not too long ago in America's past. He was also delighted by the way in which she had said, "*us* Rebs," implying she too was in favour of the South's cause. "Trouble being, the War'd ended a mite afore Colonel Rip Ford

Lopez de Santa Ana and ended his tyranical rule over them. See: OLE DEVIL AT SAN JACINTO.

[4] According to a legend which was already well circulated at that point, on hearing somebody complaining that General Ulysses Simpson Grant was drinking heavily, President Abraham Lincoln replied, "Find out what kind of liquor he's using and give some to my other generals. He's winning battles and they are not."

[4a] More information about the Texas War of Independence is given in the other volumes of the Ole Devil Hardin series and: THE QUEST FOR BOWIE'S BLADE.

[5] For information about the effectiveness of the Texas Light Cavalry, see: the Civil War series.

whipped the Yankees at Palmitto Hill."[6]

Even as the tallest of the Texans was speaking, noticing where he and the other two were continually yet surreptitiously glancing, caused Freddie to look in the same direction. What she saw warned her that she was no longer dressed in a manner suitable for mixed company. Soaked by the perspiration she had been shedding and being emphasised by her heavy breathing, the thin chemisette was clinging even more tightly to the contours of her torso than under normal conditions. As it was the only garment covering them, despite it having ridden up from the waistband of the riding breeches to leave a gap exposing some of her midriff, the nipples of her full firm bosom were now standing out in bold relief.

"I think I'd better have my coat back," the Englishwoman told the Texan to whom she had given the garments she removed before mounting.

"Yes'm!" Morris answered, jerking his gaze away from the twin magnificent protruberances and blushing furiously at the realization that his scrutiny might have provoked the request. "I—I'm sorry!"

"That your horse *lost?*" Freddie queried with a smile, accepting the jacket. Donning and buttoning it, she went on, "And, if *you* are sorry, how do you think I feel?"

"How come, ma'am?" Thornton inquired, also having found the sight presented by the sweat soaked chemisette most interesting and enjoyable.

"I'll be lucky if I can sit down comfortably for a *week*," Freddie claimed and felt gingerly at her rump again. "Which, with that British Railroad Commission arriving this evening, I'll be expected to do more than a little sitting down with them before they leave. Only it won't be half as much *fun* as proving somebody from England could ride old Blotchy."

"You for sure rode him, ma'am," Hendricks praised with almost juvenile enthusiasm, disappointed the jacket was concealing what he had been looking at, despite appreciating the reason for this being done. "How's about you coming and

---

[6] *Because of the slowness of communications at that period having prevented the news reaching the area, the Battle of Palmitto Hill near Brownsville, Texas, was fought on May the 13th, 1865, approximately a month after the War Between The States ended elsewhere. Ironically, it was won by a force of the Confederate States' Army under the command of Colonel John Salmon "Rip" Ford.*

riding the rough string at the B Bar D?"

"Why I'm honoured to be asked," Freddie replied. Then she continued without thinking, "But the OD Connected has first refusal on my services."

"OD Connected," Thornton said, sounding puzzled. "That's Cap'n Dusty Fog's outfit, isn't it, ma'am?"

"It is," Freddie confirmed.

"We hear tell's how him 'n' the rest of Ole Devil's floating outfit're running the law here, ma'am," Hendricks asserted. "And doing a real fine job of it."

"He is," Freddie admitted. "And they are."

"You'd likely know Cap'n Dusty then, ma'am?" Morris asked, sounding as if he considered the acquaintanceship was unavoidable; albeit in the nicest possible way.

"I most certainly *do!*" Freddie agreed. Then realizing what she had said to provoke the questions and the way of which she had answered the last one, she started blushing. To hide her confusion, she continued hurriedly, "I'd better put on my skirt and hat. I must look a *mess!*"

Despite wanting to make the most of the opportunity which he had been granted by attention having been diverted from him to get away from his tormentors, Ushermale had only withdrawn from the immediate vicinity of the livery stable. Still being convinced he should remember the beautiful young Englishwoman from somewhere, even if it was only as a face seen in a picture which for some reason stuck in the memory, he had watched the struggle with Blotchy from an alley a short distance away. Two men wearing the attire of town dwellers had arrived just as the struggle was ending and halted by his side. Ignoring them, he turned to continue his interrupted departure before his presence was discovered and the abuses by the three "Yankees" were resumed.

"Damn the luck, Tom!" the taller of the pair growled, his accent that of a New Englander. "We've missed something's I bet'd be worth seeing!"

"Sure, Bill," agreed the second, whose origins were similar, also looking disappointed. Then he swung his gaze to Ushermale and asked, "Hey, mister, no offence's meant for sounding nosy; but, by the way you're dressed, I'd reckon you're English?"

"I am," the young man admitted warily, wondering if he was to be inflicted by further abuse and preparing to take flight as fast as his legs would carry him if it happened.

"Maybe you know Miss Freddie then?" Bill suggested.

"No," Ushermale denied. "Why do you think I should?"

"Word has it she's a duchess, or some such, from over in England," Bill explained. "So, you being from over there and it being such a little place, I thought's how your trails might have crossed."

"Well, they *haven't,*" the Englishman affirmed shortly. "And, if you'll excuse me, I have to be going."

"Mighty snooty son-of-a-bitch, wasn't he?" Tom commented, as Ushermale turned and hurried away.

"They do reckon some Englishers are," Bill replied. "It's only natural they can't all be real nice and friendly folks like Miss Freddie is. Come on, let's go on over and tell her's she done real good."

"Freddie Woods!" Ushermale muttered to himself as he walked away, remembering the full name of the beautiful Englishwoman which he had heard mentioned by one of the "Yankees" when she had put in her appearance. Taken with the reference to her being a "duchess, or some such," it sparked off a remembrance and suggested why she had struck him as being familiar. "*Freddie Woods* my arse. It is *her.* She's Lady Winifred Amelia Besgrove-Woodstole as sure as I'm born. Dingers will be so *pleased* when I tell him. What's more, with the associates he—*we* have made, we'll have no difficulty in arranging for her to be arrested and held until we can have her extradited to stand trial for murder!"

CHAPTER THREE

It's a *Bomb*!

"Well, Babsy," Freddie Woods said, making a graceful pirouette like a mannequin displaying her wares. "How do I look?"

"Like you *always* look," replied the young woman to whom the question was directed. Her voice was indicative of one who, by tradition, had been born within hearing distance of the "Bow bells" in London. However, although she was employed as the beautiful young Englishwoman's maid, her tone was sincere and not sycophantic. "Ever so good."

"I wouldn't say *always*," Freddie corrected with a smile. "I seem to recollect that when Buffalo Kate and I were—er, *discussing,* shall we call it—our slight *contretemps,* we *both* finished up somewhat *dishevelled* to say the least."

"I wouldn't know nothing about *that*," Barbara "Babsy" Smith asserted, also grinning as she thought of the hectic fist and hair pulling fight between the entire female staffs of the Fair Lady and Buffalo Saloons which brought to an end the feud between them and, strange as it might have struck some people, created a friendly atmosphere in its wake.[1] "'Ginge' and me was pretty *busy* ourselves and we ended up more than just a *bit* dishevelled. In fact, when we woke up, we was *both* in the bleeding *nuddy*."

"I hope this business with the British Railroad Commission works out well," Freddie remarked, putting aside her thoughts of how the battle had ended and turning to the subject which had caused her to select the clothes she was now wearing.

"How can it miss?" Babsy stated rather than asked. "With *you* behind it, ma'am."

"Really, Babsy!" Freddie replied, without much hope of the protest registering. "You give me credit for *far* too much. It wasn't *me* who thought up the idea of running a spur-line from Mulrooney to Canada."

"Perhaps not, ma'am," the maid replied, but without giving the words any noticeable conviction. "But it was *you* who put it into the heads of them's did."

Having replaced the garments removed before dealing with the ill-favoured paint horse, although she would not have ad-

---

[1] *Described in:* THE TROUBLE BUSTERS.

mitted it aloud, the victress of the struggle had decided she
had no desire for further riding that day. Telling the three
cowhands to call in at the Fair Lady Saloon and have one of
her "barmaids"—as she called the women who served behind
the counter—to set them up a couple of drinks on her after
they had attended to Blotchy's needs, she had walked away
acknowledging the praise from the spectators.

Returning to the spacious and luxurious living accommodation she maintained for herself on what she insisted upon
referring to as the "first" floor of the saloon,[2] Freddie had had
a hot bath prepared. Revived somewhat, although her rump
still gave protests against the treatment to which it had been
subjected, she had rested until the time came for her to make
ready to attend an important function in her capacity as mayor
of Mulrooney.

Although completely indifferent over whether she conveyed the "right" impression or not, but knowing it would be
expected of her and by the young woman to whom she was
talking more than anybody else, Freddie had selected a stylish
dove-grey "walking out" dress. Its bodice was cut close to and
enhanced the lines of her torso, while the straight sleeves were
opened from under the elbow to the wrist and revealed the
puffed "lawn sleeves" of a matching silk chemisette. Funnel
shaped, with little fullness at her curvacious hips, the skirt had
a very wide base and concealed the dainty high heeled bootees
which had replaced her riding footwear. Both it and the
sleeves were decorated with ribbon bands. The ensemble was
completed by a light blue "Stuart cap" which was headdress
and cape in one.

In her own way, Babsy presented just as attractive a feminine figure as her employer. Barely over five foot in height,
roughly the same age as Freddie, she had tightly curled blonde
hair taken in a pile on top of her head. Her face was pretty,
with an expression indicative of a vivacious nature and a love
of life. Although she put on different and much more revealing clothes for when working downstairs in the barroom,
being an accomplished and well liked entertainer in her own
right, she had on the frilly white lace rosette-like headdress,
tight sleeved black dress and white apron which was the tradi-

---

[2] Unlike in the United Kingdom, Americans refer to the
part of a multi-story building at ground level as being the
"first" floor.

tional costume for a maid. The attire fitted so snugly, it did nothing to hide the rich curves of her firmly fleshed close to buxom figure.

Possessing a most spirited nature, the little blonde had insisted upon accompanying Freddie into what amounted to an indefinite banishment from England!

Babsy was absolutely loyal to the black haired beauty and knew more about her past life than did anybody else in the United States, including Shaun Ushermale and the man to whom he had referred, but who had not yet arrived in Mulrooney. What was more, she carried the devotion to an extent which no "liberal" of a later generation would have accepted was possible for a "down-trodden and abused wage-slave for the aristocracy" to feel towards a "bullying and snob-conscious upper class" employer.

For instance, ever since commencing their—what had amounted to—flight from England, Freddie had tried to persuade Babsy to address her in a less formal fashion than was expected by others if not herself. Although the little blonde had refrained from saying, "Your Ladyship," except on rare occasions of great stress, she absolutely refused to employ the more democratic, "Freddie" without adding the polite prefix, "Miss."

"You was, 'me lady,' or 'ma'am' back in Blighty," Babsy had declared more than once when reproved for such an insistence upon formality. "And I don't see how it's no different now we're living among' a lot of bleeding foreigners!"

However, there were times—such as at that moment—when Freddie considered her companion-cum-servant had far too much faith in her ability!

"It's a scheme which could prove beneficial for Mulrooney, the United States and Canada, regardless of *who* might have thought it up" the black haired beauty stated. "But not *everybody* might consider it that way."

"Who wouldn't, Miss Freddie?" the little blonde queried, sounding aghast that anybody would disagree with the point of view of her employer.

"There are those who don't want any closer links between the British Empire and the United States. Which is how they'll see the spur-line."

"They must be bleeding barmy!"

"Their kind are, in more ways than one. The trouble is, they have enough money to hire things done which they couldn't have the ability or courage to do themselves."

"I wish Cap'n Dusty hadn't had to go to Hays City with Frank Derringer," Babsy said. "Couldn't the marshal there have just put that bleeder on a train and sent him here without them having to go and say it was him's killed that poor blonde at Mrs. Gouch's and how we want him back to have him hung for it?"

"Unfortunately not," Freddie replied. "Anyway, don't you think the rest of the marshal's office are capable of looking after things?"

"They're all right, ma'am, considering they're not *English*," the blonde admitted, without hesitation and giving what for her was unstinted praise. A suggestion of something more than just ordinary pleasure came to her ever expressive features as she continued, "*Especially* Waco."

"Is that because he's got more hairs on his chest than you have?" Freddie queried with a smile.

"Cor!" Babsy ejaculated, aware of what was meant by the question and showing no signs of being abashed. "Things don't half get around here. You can't hardly sneeze without *everybody* knows. Anyway, ma'am, good as Waco, Mark and the Kid are, I still wish Cap'n Dusty was back."

"So do I," Freddie admitted, but did not continue by saying that her reasons were not entirely due to concern over the current situation in the town. "Unfortunately, he isn't; so we'll just have to muddle along without him. And, from the look of the time, I'd better go and start muddling."

"Can I come too, please, ma'am?" Babsy requested.

"Of course you can," Freddie assented. "I'm sure the Commission would be delighted to meet you."

"Not bleeding likely!" the little blonde declared. "I *know* my place and it's *not* hob-nobbing with quality like there'll be coming off that train."

"How do you like it, Miss Freddie?" inquired the town dweller called "Bill" who had inadvertantly given Shaun Ushermale the clue required to solve the mystery of the beautiful young Englishwoman's true identity. Like her, he was dressed more formally than while at the corral outside the Winstanley Livery Stable. Waving a hand towards where a ten piece brass band in the obviously well prepared uniform of the Mulrooney Fire Department were finishing the tune they had been playing as the west-bound train pulled into the railroad depot, he continued in a voice clearly hoping for an answer in the affirmative, "Did they get it *right?*"

"They certainly did," Freddie Woods declared. "I've never heard '*Rule Brittania*' played better. And I'm *sure* the British Railroad Commission will think the same."

Completing the comment, the beautiful young Englishwoman turned her gaze to the well dressed and prosperous looking men who were disembarking from a private car coupled to the rear of the train. Ten in number, they were a mixture of sizes, builds and ages. She knew four to be American. The largest and bulkiest, still hard fleshed despite leading a far more sedentary life than when he had been making himself a millionaire several times over by constructing railroads and other engineering projects, was Harland Todhunter. It was he who led the others to where Freddie was approaching followed by Bill and several more prominent citizens of Mulrooney.

Aware that some of the Commission had been sent from England to represent the British Government and to decide whether to give financial support for the spur-line already being built northwards from the town, the black haired beauty searched for any who might have known her prior to her enforced departure. Although she failed to recognize any, three in particular caught her eye. It was to them that Todhunter introduced her first. However, the presentations were clearly made in what he considered as order of merit rather than by social precedence.

"Miss Woods, allow me to present Sir John Uglow Ramage."

"My pleasure, ma'am. Pray pardon my rig, but I didn't expect to meet so beautiful a lady."

"Why thank you, Sir John. I'm delighted to meet you."

Carrying the fawn coloured Homburg hat he had removed, Ramage was tallest of the three and looked to be in his late thirties at least. Having adopted sensible attire for travelling, he had on a matching yoked shooting jacket and breeches, dark grey knitted stockings and sturdy untanned ankle boots. He was tanned, clean shaven, with black hair, handsome aquiline features, a good build and a carriage indicative of excellent physical health. Everything about him hinted he was a man capable of getting things done and yet he also exuded a suggestion of possessing a lively sense of humour.

"Lord James Roxton!" Todhunter continued.

"Delighted, my lord."

"Honoured, ma'am and, as Sir John said, please pardon my informal attire."

Lacking perhaps an inch of Ramage's height and some ten years younger, with a clipped mode of speech, Roxton was lean in a wiry fashion. He had taken off a grey Homburg even more rakish looking than that of the other aristocrat to show rusty-red hair and was dressed in much the same way. Flowerpot red from much exposure to sun and wind, rather than having taken a tan, his face was good looking with a crisp moustache and small—somehow aggressive seeming—sharp pointed tuft of whiskers on his projecting chin to emphasise its hawk-like lines. His poise and demeanour was that of one who enjoyed an active existence and had lived hard in his time.

"Sir Michael Dinglepied."

"Sir Michael," Freddie assented, having detected a less cordial note in Todhunter's New England voice.

Compared with his predecessors, the second baronet was far from being a particularly distinguished or impressive figure. About five foot seven in height, in his mid-fifties, he was so thin his sombre black three-piece suit and grubby white shirt hung limply about his frame and, while it was more formal than the attire of the other two, it appeared slovenly by choice rather than as a result of being worn on a long journey. Although surmounted by a veritable mane of grubby greyish-white hair, his face had little more flesh on it than a skull and bore an expression of what he believed was supercilious superiority, but left the impression that he was continually smelling something bad. All in all, he presented an appearance ideally suited to being used in the caricatures which frequently featured on the pages of those British newspapers opposed to his politic ideals.

'Madam," Dinglepied said shortly, removing his black Derby hat with obvious reluctance and hesitating before holding out his bony right hand.

"*Miss,*" Freddie corrected, having waited until the baronet made the first gesture. She restrained her impulse to go on, "I'm not a madam, I'm one of the girls." As she released the clammy and weak grip so different from the virile grasp given by its two predecessors, she noticed that she was being subjected to a searching scrutiny. However, she was not allowed time to give any consideration to this. Instead, the presentation was carried out for the other members of the Commission —all of whom were Canadians, she was informed—and the two American businessmen she had not met previously. Then she continued, "Shall we go to the Railroad House Hotel, where accommodation has been arranged for you?"

"That'll be satisfactory," Todhunter confirmed, after having glanced at Ramage for concurrence. "And I trust you'll entertain us at your place later this evening."

"I was hoping you would ask," Freddie smiled. "In fact, I would have been *most* put out if you *hadn't.*"

Even while speaking, being satisfied that the Canadians could not know anything about her past, the beautiful Englishwoman was thinking of the three men from Great Britain to whom she had been introduced!

Freddie was aware that the first of them was the only member of the Ramage family in living memory to have selected the diplomatic service instead of taking a commission in the Royal Navy; due to his suffering from such chronic seasickness he had accepted it would prevent him performing his duties as a naval officer satisfactorily.[3] Although they had never met, she knew him to be on friendly terms with a favourite uncle on her mother's side and with other relations.

While closer to her age, the beautiful Englishwoman had not previously made the acquaintance of Lord James Roxton. This was not surprising, even though they came from much the same stratum of society. From his childhood, he had accompanied his father on hunting expeditions and, more recently, had carried out explorations of his own into the jungles of South America.[4]

Try as she might, Freddie could not bring Dinglepied to mind. One thing she did know was that it was highly unlikely he had mingled with the Besgrove-Woodstoles or the Houghton-Rands. If the red tie he had on was any guide, he was one of the radicals about whom the men on both sides of her family spoke in less than complimentary terms. In which case, although she could not recollect him as being involved

---

[3] *Sir John Ramage was the youngest grandson of Admiral of the Fleet, the Eleventh Earl of Blazey; details of whose career in the Royal Navy prior to succeeding to the title are recorded in the* Ramage *series of biographies by Dudley Pope.*

[4] *The tradition of hunting and exploration in South America was continued by Lord James Roxton's son, John; see:* THE LOST WORLD, *by Sir Arthur Conan Doyle.*

in any way with the men who had been responsible for her departure from England, she had found his scrutiny vaguely disturbing and decided he was one person upon whom she would be advised to keep a wary eye.

Emerging from the entrance hall of the depot, the English-woman and the new arrivals were confronted by a good sized crowd. In addition to the members of the local community, who were naturally interested in men who could bring a great deal of extra business and prosperity to the town, unofficial representatives of practically all the kinds of transient population were mingling amongst them.

Suddenly, four men thrust forward until clear of the rest of the crowd. Although their skin was Indian dark and what hair showed was black, they had on derby or higher crowned "tall" bowlers hats, two-piece suits of a cheap rough material and shirts without collars such as were favoured in particular by railroad construction workers of Irish extraction when visiting a town for a celebration. That each had a Colt 1860 Army Model revolver tucked into the waistband of their trousers was unusual, though not unknown. However, the knives hanging on their belts were less common amongst men of the kind they were clearly supposed to be. Furthermore, their footwear was not of the heavy and stout variety which was called for by such a form of employment. In fact, two wore what were— like the sheaths of the knives—obviously moccasins of Indian manufacture and the others riding boots.

Regardless of suggestions to that effect, the quartet were definitely not anything so innocuous as gandy dancers up to some harmless form of mischief!

"Death to all capitalist exploiters!" bellowed the shortest of the quartet in a heavily accented voice, swinging his right arm and flinging something black and round toward Freddie's party.

"It's a *bomb*!" Dinglepied screeched, jerking behind the beautiful Englishwoman.

Already having made such a deduction, Freddie could not see how she might be able to escape the detonation which she did not doubt was coming!

CHAPTER FOUR

I'll Cut Her Throat!

If Sir Michael Dinglepied had deliberately sought to create a panic, his screeched out words were coming close to achieving it!

Instantly, pandemonium reigned amongst the spectators!

While there were men present in the crowd who were unflinching in the face of hostile guns, or other hand-held weapons, the danger posed by a "bomb" was a vastly different proposition to their way of thinking. Guided by this assumption, many of them and practically all the women who were assembled gave thought solely to trying to avoid the explosion which they considered to be inevitable. Having that in mind, apart from a few exceptions, they began to scatter like chickens frightened by the passing shadow of a hawk.

Among the party who had emerged from the railroad depot, the reaction was almost as marked!

Hoping to take advantage of Freddie Woods being taller and better built than he was to shield him from the blast, the older of the British baronets behaved in a not untypical cowardly fashion for him by darting to cringe behind her after having announced the missile was a "bomb"!

However, being men of greater moral and physical courage, Sir John Uglow Ramage and Harland Todhunter just as speedily exposed themselves even further by starting to place themselves between the beautiful Englishwoman and the danger!

Two of the Eastern businessmen elected to throw themselves on the ground with arms shielding the back of their heads!

The other American and the three Canadians stood fast, though ready to duplicate the actions of their companions if this was called for!

There seemed just a slight possibility such evasive tactics might not prove necessary!

Showing a complete disregard for his own safety, Lord James Roxton began to lunge forward with both hands rising like those of a cricketer preparing to catch a ball!

Swiftly though the British aristocrat moved, somebody else

was showing an even greater alacrity!

Coming from amongst the scattering onlookers, clearly having reached a similar conclusion about how to deal with the situation and having a shorter distance than Roxton to travel, a masculine figure converged in a sprint with the flying missile!

Just over six foot tall, blond haired and with a body filling out to powerful manhood, the would-be rescuer was no more than in his late 'teens. However, his good looking tanned face had lines suggestive of a maturity beyond his years and was set in grim determination. Sweeping off his black Stetson hat while he was advancing showed he had neatly trimmed blond hair. The rest of his attire, like the headdress, was that of a cowhand hailing from the Lone Star State and wishing to ensure everybody knew of his good fortune in being born and raised there. That he was not currently employed at working with cattle was suggested by the deputy town marshal's badge pinned to the left breast pocket of his dark blue shirt and partially concealed by the near side flap of his unfastened brown and white calfskin vest. For all his youth, he wore a well made brown gunbelt and the twin staghorn handled Army Colts in its low-tied fast draw holsters with the easy assurance of one well versed in their use.

The reason why the young Texan had removed his hat became obvious as he was approaching his objective. Instead of trying to make the catch with his fingers, as Roxton was intending, he swung it so the open bottom of the crown was facing the approaching spherical black hand grenade. What was more, he did not allow the contact with the Stetson to bring an immediate halt to the lethal device's progress. Instead, he started to withdraw it as soon as the first suggestion reached him of contact being made. Bringing them both down in a gradually slowing motion, before looking to find out whether the grenade was to be detonated by an external burning fuse which must be extinguished to render it safe, he swung his gaze around to ascertain what was happening elsewhere.

A single glance was all the blond needed to warn him that, as his interference was not welcomed by everybody in the immediate vicinity, he would be granted no opportunity to defuse the bomb!

The man who had thrown the grenade and two of his companions were reaching for the Army Colts tucked into the waistbands of their trousers!

More massive than the rest, with a thick black beard partially concealing brutal features—and being one of the pair wearing moccasins—the fourth man's right hand was going to the hilt of the big bowie knife sheathed on his belt instead of his firearm!

Although the trio stood their ground, the enormous man began to lumber forward with the speed of a grizzly bear—which he resembled at that moment—charging its prey!

Menacing as the approaching man undoubtedly was, the youngster appreciated he only posed a fraction of the peril!

While such a method of carrying a revolver as was employed by the three men did not offer the speed of withdrawal which the blond Texan knew he could achieve when drawing from his carefully designed gunbelt, he was in no position to make use of his ability to protect himself!

Having been successful in catching the hand grenade without having it detonate, the youngster realized there was no way in which he could dispose of it quickly and still avoid creating the danger he was trying to avert!

However, help of a most effective kind was close at hand!

Another man, a few years older than the youngster, was coming from amongst the fleeing spectators. A good six foot three in height, with a tremendous spread to his shoulders and his torso trimming to a slender waist set upon long and powerful legs, he towered over the majority of them and was a remarkable physical specimen in every respect. His white Stetson, its crown decorated by a black leather band sporting half a dozen silver conchas, was tilted back sufficiently to display curly golden blond hair kept cut short in the accepted cowhand style. Exuding strength of will and intelligence, albeit at that moment grim of visage, his tanned features were almost classically handsome. Although his attire was that of a Texas cattle country fashion plate, all his clothing was made of the finest materials and specially tailored for him. Such an excellent fit could never have come from the shelves of any store. As was the case with the youngster, he had a deputy's badge attached to his tan coloured shirt. His brown *buscadero* gunbelt, carved with a "basket-weave" pattern, carried two ivory handled Army Colts in fast draw holsters and, showing signs of being well maintained, clearly had seen much use. Despite weighing over two hundred pounds, he gave no suggestion of being slow, clumsy, or awkward on his feet. Rather he was moving with a springiness of step and *very* rapidly for one of his great size.

Showing just as quick and accurate an assessment of the situation as the other blond had displayed, the handsome giant took immediate steps to counteract its dangerous potential. Dipping in a lightning fast motion, his right hand scooped the long barrelled Colt from the off side holster. Regardless of the extreme rapidity with which he was moving, proving he was equally well versed in all aspects of making a fast draw, his forefinger remained outside the triggerguard and his thumb did not offer to ease back the hammer which it had coiled around until an instant *after* the muzzle was clear of leather and turning forward.[1] What was more, having brought the single action to the fully cocked condition, he showed an awareness of exactly what he must do before he dare take the chance of opening fire.

Normally when seeing a weapon drawn in such a fashion, a crowd mainly comprised of people with experience in life west of the Mississippi River—such as had foregathered outside the Mulrooney railroad passenger depot—would have shown an appreciation of their peril by either getting out of the possible line of fire, or taking shelter at all speed. Caught up in what àmounted to something close to mass hysteria invoked by overimaginative thoughts of how dangerous the blast from the grenade could prove, the people scattering in response to Dinglepied's shout were failing to adopt such sensible behaviour. In trying to escape, some of them were committing the folly of going behind the quartet responsible for the trouble.

Therefore, instead of swinging the revolver into alignment and firing instinctively while it was still just over waist level —a method which it seemed very likely a man with such a rig would have perfected along with the lightning fast draw—the blond giant continued to elevate it to shoulder level at arm's length. As he was skidding to a halt a long pace ahead of the other Texan, bringing up his left hand to join its mate on the ivory handle, he took rapid aim using the small V-shaped notch in the tip of the hammer spur and the fairly diminutive foresight at the end of the eight inches long barrel.

---

[1] *For an example of just how dangerous failure to take such a precaution could be when making a draw, see:* THE FAST GUN.

Rudimentary though the sights were, when the Army Colt thundered in the massive and splendidly developed Texan's powerful grasp, only slightly over a second after he started reaching for it, they served his purpose. Swiftly though the movement had been carried out, it produced an effect. Struck in the centre of the chest by a soft round lead .44 calibre ball—more potent in its impact than a pointed and harder bullet—which knocked him in a spinning twirl backwards, the man closest to having his revolver clear was prevented from doing so.

However, this was only a partial solution to the youngster's problem!

Despite having successfully caught the hand grenade, the younger Texan realized he had not completely brought its menace to an end. Inverting the Stetson just sufficiently to allow him to see into the crown, he discovered with relief that there was no external fuse burning to the point where its flame would disappear inside to ignite the waiting black powder. However, as his eyes took in the details of the spherical device, he knew it was far from behind innocuous on account of this omission. If anything, it had a greater lethal potential than would have been the case with a burning fuse. For one thing, if his assumption were correct, he could not chance moving it with other than the greatest care.

Doing anything positive to protect himself, the youngster concluded grimly, was out of the question!

However, one hitherto impending threat was removed!

Sharing what could have been intended as profane threats, but which emerged as a rumbling more bestial than human, the largest of the quartet continued to rush onwards undeterred by the shot which had narrowly missed him. However, he diverted his attack to the direction of the blond giant who was perhaps an inch taller, but somewhat lighter due to trimming down more at the waist. Having no time to even recock the Colt, once again demonstrating the possession of considerable agility, the Texan elected to deal with his assailant in another manner.

Stepping clear as the huge clip point blade of the bowie knife was directed in a swinging thrust intended to disembowel him, the blond giant caused its wielder to blunder onwards under the impulsion given to the thwarted attack. Then, as the other was passing, he removed his left hand and whipped around his right arm. To have struck with the barrel could have damaged the Colt, its construction being less rugged than that of the "solid frame" revolvers available. Appreciating this, the blond giant made no attempt to do so. Instead, rotating his fist until the knuckles were pointing downwards, he ensured that the less vulnerable strip of steel frame at the base of the ivory butt made the contact.

Driven with all the force of the blond giant's powerful muscles, the weapon smashed as was intended into the centre of the bearded face of his would-be assailant. Teeth were shattered and blood gushed from the enormous man's mouth. At the same time, his head was slammed to the rear while his body continued to move forward. Stunned by what a later generation would term the "whip-lash" effect of the impact, his body crumpled and he measured his length on the ground with a jarring thud.

Despite having dealt with two of the quartet in a competent and effective fashion, the handsome Texan quickly discovered the threat was still far from brought to an end!

What was more, the danger was now being directed in the blond giant's direction!

Making the most of the respite they had been granted by their enormous companion's reckless attack, the unharmed survivors of the disguised quartet had completed the extrication of their revolvers!

However, having seen the fate of their companions, the pair were no longer thinking of taking revenge upon the youngster for having thwarted their attempted assassination!

Instead, each was making the giant Texan his intended target!

There was, the golden blond realized, no way he could cope sufficiently swiftly with both to prevent one of the pair opening fire upon him!

The need to do so did not arise!

Even as the big Texan was returning his left hand to join the right in sighting the Colt at the shorter of the pair, who he estimated was presenting the greater threat, he saw he could refrain from doing so immediately!

In keeping with her wish to avoid having to "hobnob with the quality" of the party whose arrival she had come to see, Barbara "Babsy" Smith had been standing some distance away at the front of the crowd. Having delayed her departure from the Fair Lady saloon while she donned a blue and white check dress considerably more revealing than her maid's costume, albeit not *quite* bordering on the indecorous, she had only worked her way to the forefront of the spectators—employing tactics for dealing with crowds acquired in her Cockney childhood—in time to see Freddie and the men from the train coming out of the passenger depot. Nor, regardless of her fondness for the blond youngster, as he and his larger fellow peace officer had arrived before she came upon the scene, had she noticed them. If she had, she would have joined them.

As it was, the curvaceous little blonde was standing beyond the quartet when the attack was launched!

Despite being alone, the response from Babsy to seeing the danger which threatened her employer was typical of her!

Letting out a screech of fury which was lost in the commotion going on all around her, the tiny blonde charged recklessly towards the cause of the trouble instead of trying to evade the explosion of the hand grenade!

Paying no attention to the man shot by the blond giant plunging by her while falling, Babsy was equally content to let him deal with his massive assailant!

Launching herself through the air, the little blonde crashed against the thrower of the missile just as he was bringing up his Army Colt to point it at the larger of the Texans. Enjoyable as he might have found being brought into such close contact with the most definitely feminine contours of her torso under different conditions, he experienced no such pleasure at that moment. The impact given by her firmly fleshed curvaceous little body jolted the weapon from his grasp and he was sent staggering with her clinging on to him. While he possessed sufficient strength to avoid being knocked from his feet by the unexpected tackle from the rear, his movements otherwise were seriously impaired. One arm was wrapped about his waist and, guided by feminine instinct, the other hand thrust off his "tall" bowler hat to bury its fingers deeply and most painfully into the mass of shoulder length black hair which had been concealed therein until that moment.

Given succour by the Cockney maid's gallant intervention, the blond giant made the most of it!

As the Colt was swinging into a different alignment apparently of its own volition, with the double handed grip resumed, he once again endangered his own life by taking the brief period required to ensure he did not put at risk any of the harmless by-standers; although "by-movers" might have been a more accurate description of their behaviour. Not being inflicted by any such concern for the welfare of those about him, the second survivor fired. However, less skill was employed in taking aim and, fortunately without finding any other target, the bullet missed its intended mark. Nevertheless, it passed by so small a margin it carved a nick through the ample material of the Texan's left sleeve.

Oblivious of his narrow escape from injury, the blond giant did not grant the man a second opportunity to try to kill him!

Once more satisfied he could do so without putting other people at risk, having recocked the hammer and turning the barrel instinctively yet rapidly, the big Texan depressed the trigger. Again the firing sequence was repeated. Flame erupted from the muzzle of the Colt, followed by what appeared to be swirling white smoke, but which was the result of the detonated powder charge in the uppermost cylinder having been changed into a greater volume of gas and propelling the lead through the rifling grooves of the barrel.

On this occasion, the blond giant's aim proved even more efficacious than his previous effort!

Starting to prepare his own weapon to resume the attack upon the taller Texan, the man was taken in the centre of the forehead by the bullet sent his way. Driving onwards to shatter out at the back of his skull, spinning away his hat to show he too had been concealing long black hair, it stopped his movements instantly. Going over with the weapon still not cocked and flying from his hand, he was dead before his body struck the ground alongside his already felled companion.

Having removed the latest threat to his life, the blond giant gave his attention to the last of the quartet!

Quickly though he moved, the Texan was too late!

Putting into effect a wiry muscular power too great for her to cope with, the thrower of the grenade had already escaped from Babsy's clutches!

However, the little blonde was not so fortunate!

Having attained his freedom, the man did not take flight!

Instead, realizing the danger of doing so, he sought a way to reduce the risk!

Grabbing hold of Babsy before she could avoid him, the man moved around swiftly and twisted her right arm behind her back with his left hand. Dipping down while he was doing so, his right snatched the J. Russell & Co. "Green River" hunting knife from the sheath on his waist belt. Crouching slightly until he was almost hidden by her and raising the eight inches long clip point blade, he swiftly placed its clearly razor sharp edge beneath her chin.

"Let the gun drop!" the man demanded, glaring over his captive's shoulder at the blond giant. His guttural voice had a French timbre and he continued, "Do it, damn you, or I'll cut her throat!"

"Do it, mister!" shouted one of the Canadians, still trying to bring his revolver from the close topped holster in which it was carried. "He's one of *le Loup Garou's Metis* and he'll kill her if you *don't!*"

CHAPTER FIVE

What if it Goes *Off?*

"Don't *anybody* do *anything!*" the blond giant thundered, thumb cocking his weapon and watching the people who had come to a halt on assuming there was no longer any danger of the "bomb" exploding. "Leave it to *me!*"

Regardless of the command—and the words were that rather than a request given to tax paying citizens who helped supply his salary—and despite feeling sure the warning given by the Canadian was valid, the golden blond deputy town marshal did not comply with the demand immediately!

Having served in a similar capacity at another town,[1] although there had been no such incident during his term in office upon which he might formulate a plan of action, the big Texan was aware that he was confronted by a situation which was not infrequently faced by peace officers throughout the world![2] [2a]

Therefore, much as the blond giant liked and respected Barbara "Babsy" Smith, he was aware that to yield to the threat might not save her from serious injury or death!

While unwilling to let the man get away, having been the one who threw the hand grenade, the first concern of the big deputy was for the close to buxom little blonde's safety. Nor did he minimize the danger. Going by what he had heard about those *Metis* who served Arnaud *"le Loup Garou"* Chavallier,[3] [3a] [3b] her captor would have no compunctions over

---

[1] *Told in*: QUIET TOWN.

[2] *How the blond youngster coped with a similar situation at a later period of his career is described in*: Part One, "The Campaigner," WACO RIDES IN.

[2a] *How a modern day Texas sheriff dealt with a "hostage" situation is recorded in*: Part One, "Hostages," THE LAWMEN OF ROCKABYE COUNTY.

[3] *The Metis were a race evolved in Canada as a result of marriages between voyageurs—boatmen and traders generally of French-Canadian origin—and women of the various Indian tribes with whom they came into contact. The name had its origination from a corruption of the French word, "metissage," meaning miscegenation*

[3a] *"Le Loup Garou," the Werewolf.*

using the J. Russel & Co. "Green River" knife. What was more, the man would continue to use her as a shield as long as he considered necessary. However, something could easily happen to frighten him into ripping the razor sharp edge of the blade across his captive's throat. Or he might kill her as a reprisal for the thwarted assassination attempt if he should be allowed to keep her until he was satisfied he could effect his escape.

One thing was to the good, the Texan told himself!

The little blonde maid was behaving in a most commendable and desirable fashion!

Not that the blond giant had expected otherwise!

Being possessed of an impulsive nature which—when added to her intense devotion and loyalty to those whom she considered worthy of receiving it—had led Babsy into the *very* dangerous predicament and not for the first time in her life. Nevertheless, quick tempered and high spirited though she undoubtedly was on most occasions, she possessed sufficient good sound common sense to realize struggling would only make her extremely perilous situation worse. On the other hand, although she was standing perfectly still in the painful grasp the man had upon her, the blond giant knew she would be ready and willing to do anything which might be required of her. He could also count upon her to wait until finding out what action this might be.

Appreciating the situation and knowing how best to cope with it were *vastly* different propositions!

Competent a marksman as the big Texan knew himself to be, especially when employing the double handed hold as an aid to aiming, he was disinclined to chance using the Colt 1860 Army Model revolver under the prevailing conditions. Crouching behind the captive's buxomly curvaceous little body, despite looking over her shoulder, the *Metis* offered him too small a target for him to contemplate hitting it without accepting the risk of the bullet striking her first. On the other hand, he was equally unwilliing to carry out the order by dropping his weapon.

The matter was taken out of the giant's hands in no uncer-

[3b]*Further information about Arnaud "le Loup Garou" Chavallier, although we inadvertantly called him "Cavallier" is given in:* THE REMITTANCE KID *and* THE WHIP AND THE WAR LANCE.

tain fashion!

In fact, despite having sought to create the impression that he was going to deal with the situation unaided, the big deputy had anticipated this might prove the case!

Sounding whiplike in comparison with the bark made by an Army Colt, a rifle cracked!

Clearly, being to the left and on the side away from the railroad depot instead of in front, the user of the repeater—a category indicated by the very rapid and easily recognizable double clicking sound of the mechanism being operated to replace the discharged cartridge case with a "live" bullet from the magazine—had not found the crouching posture of the *Metis* too great an impediment to aiming in the only manner which would turn the tables upon him.

Arriving in the *Metis'* left temple, the bullet ranged onwards to burst out at the other side in a spray of blood and flying fragments of destroyed brain and shattered bone!

Having her captor killed almost instantaneously brought an end to the little blonde's ordeal!

Because the flying lead found the point on the anatomy of Babsy's captor at which all his automotive instincts were immediately rendered inoperative, he was prevented from carrying out the threat he had made regarding any attempt to save her. Not only did the unexpected impact jerk him away from her, due to the destruction of the brain's left lobes—which controlled the movements of the body's right side—but he was prevented from raking the blade of the knife across her throat. Instead, he was pitched to the right and the weapon went away from its position without its edge touching her flesh.

Staggering forward involuntarily on being liberated, the little blonde's face was white under its make-up. She gave the impression that her knees were weak and her legs were shaking underneath her. Making an effort of will, she managed to keep a firm grip on her emotions and contrived to hold down a surge of something close to hysteria caused by the relief at having been saved. Nevertheless, she was wobbling uncertainly on her feet and felt there was a danger of collapsing.

Twirling away the long barelled Army Colt with a similar speed to when it was being drawn, the blond giant caught Babsy by the shoulders as her legs were beginning to buckle. Supporting her sturdily curvaceous weight erect with no discernible effort, he scooped her into his arms and held her pressed gently against his chest. Knowing she would not wish to let others see her disturbed frame of mind, he kept her face hidden from the people who were converging hurriedly from all sides for the few seconds she required to regain her composure. That the weakness was only momentary was proven by her response at the end of the brief period.

"Leave off, luv!" the little blonde requested breathlessly. "You're squeezing all the bleeding wind out of me!"

Complying with a good grace to what people who did not know Babsy would have considered a lack of gratitude, the blond giant released and lifted her gently to set her down at arms' length. Directing a wink his way to prove she had not meant anything so ungracious by her comment, which he already knew, she turned her gaze in search of whoever had fired the shot which saved her from her captor.

Lean and wiry, particularly in comparison with the golden blond, the man responsible for the rescue was some three inches shorter. So glossy it seemed almost blue in some lights, the hair beneath his Texan's style Stetson hat was black as the wing of a Deep South crow. Indian dark, unless one looked at his curiously coloured red-hazel eyes which gave a hint of a *vastly* different character, his features were handsome and seemed almost babyishly innocent. They offered little suggestion of what his age might be, except for a hint that he was almost certainly a few years older than he looked. Less costly than that of the big deputy, every item of it being black, his garb—except for his sharp toed boots having low heels more suitable for walking than riding—was of the style practically *de rigueur* for a cowhand from the Lone Star State. He too had a badge of office on the left breast pocket of his shirt. At the right side of his gunbelt, a Colt Dragoon Model of 1848 revolver hung with its plain walnut butt pointing forward in a low cavalry-twist draw holster. On the left was sheathed a massive ivory hilted James Black bowie knife.

"Blast it, Babsy-gal!" the black dressed Texan greeted, his melodious tenor voice implying he was delivering a rebuke. He had been prevented from intervening earlier, thereby removing the need for the maid to tackle the shortest of the *Metis*, by the fleeing people milling about in front of him. However, he had taken the earliest opportunity to deal with the situation and felt sure that, apart from being frightened a little, she was no worse for the experience. Gesturing with the Winchester Model of 1866 rifle grasped by its foregrip in his right hand, he went on in a similarly aggrieved tone, "I've *allus* told you's how you're too *small*."

"We don't have our boots stuffed full of horse muck when we're little in England, to make us shoot up like weeds same's you blokes from Texas do," the buxom blonde answered with apparent wrath. "Anyway, what's me size got to do with *anything?*"

"Way that jasper was hiding behind you," the Indian dark deputy replied, somewhat ambiguously considering his previous comment. "Mark couldn't draw a bead on him and I had to *waste* a bullet doing it."

"I'll buy you a bleeder to replace it, see if I don't!" Babsy promised, albeit with the words sounding more in the nature of a threat. Knowing no open thanks were required, or expected, she turned an equally wrathful looking glare at the blond giant and went on in a similar vein, "And *you* don't know your own bloody strength. Not content with grabbing me so hard you've probably bruised my shoulders, you nearly squashed me ribs in hugging me."

"I didn't know there was any other way of doing it," the big deputy answered, his baritone voice indicative of one who had received a better "schoolhouse" education than the black clad Texan.

"Well, my girl!" Freddie Woods put in, having hurried forward followed by most of the men she had met from the westbound train. Sir Michael Dinglepied was one who abstained, as was Lord James Roxton, albeit with a far more commendable reason. However, the hug she delivered to the little blonde belied words which a "liberal" would have expected from one of her status when addressing an "underling." "Don't you *ever* do *anything* like *that* again. You gave me such a *fright*. I thought I was going to need a *new* maid."

"I won't *never* do it again, me La—*ma'am!*" Babsy promised as seriously as if she believed the rebuke had been genuine. "In fact, if we can put the clock back a few minutes, I won't even do it *this* time."

"You're beginning to think like a *Texan!*" the black haired beauty accused, sounding as if she could conceive nothing worse.

"Blimey, am I?" the maid ejaculated, showing well simulated distaste. "I'm going to have to watch *that!*" Having delivered the sentiment, she swung her gaze to the youngest of the deputies. He was standing with Lord James Roxton at his side and she demanded with apparent heat, "Why don't you get shut of that bleeding thing in your titfer afore it goes off and spoils me hair-do?"

"That means in your hat, old boy," the aristocrat interpreted, realizing he had forgotten the existence of the hand grenade in the subsequent excitement. He spoke in a clipped fashion, yet conveyed the impression that he found the entire situation boring. "And getting rid of it isn't such a *bad* idea after all, although I don't think there is any danger of it going off *now.*"

"I wouldn't count on *that,*" the blond youngster contradicted. His tanned face was showing the relief which had come after the strain he had been under while watching the little blonde in danger and being unable to do anything to help her. Swinging his gaze back to the Stetson he was holding and extending it gingerly towards the Englishman, he went on, "I don't know where they got this son-of-a-bitch, but it doesn't need no burning fuse to touch it off unless I miss my guess."

"Good god!" Roxton snapped, losing his languid posture for an instant as he looked down. "You're *right,* old sport. And, providing you don't think it presumptious of me to make a suggestion before we've been formally introduced, I think *we* would be *advised* to do *something* about it."

"They call me 'Waco'," the youngster drawled, giving the only name he had ever claimed as his own.[4]

"'Mongst other things," the black clad Texan put in. "Mostly *worse* and *always* deserved."

"Which I conclude's introduction enough," Waco continued, as if the interruption had not been made. "And seeing's how I've been sort of thinking along those same lines myself."

"Then shall *we* get it done?" Roxton suggested.

"Here?"

"Do you fancy taking it somewhere else?"

"Well, now you come to mention it, *no!*" the youngster admitted. "I don't take kind to *walking* no place, no time. Which goes 'four-bled' at least, happen that's the word, when I've got a bomb in 'me titfer.'"

"I'm *inclined* to agree," the lean aristocrat declared, then

---

[4]*Information regarding the background and special qualifications of Waco, including why he knew only one name, is given in:* APPENDIX FOUR.

waved a languid gesture which encompassed a circle about him. "But having all these people around could prove—um —*restrictive,* shall we say?"

'Happen they'll back off a ways, asked polite,' Waco drawled, also glancing at the onlookers who were closing in talking excitedly amongst themselves. "How's about it, *amigo?*"

"All right, *everybody!*" boomed the blond giant, the second comment having been directed his way. His voice and demeanour were those of a man expecting to be obeyed without hesitation or question. "Back off *pronto!*"

"Which same means right *now,*" supported the black clad deputy in a tone which implied he too would brook no objections from *anybody.* "Fact being, starting ten seconds back!"

"*That's* what you call asking *politely?*" Roxton inquired, despite noticing that the command was starting to be obeyed without protest and quickly, even by the members of his party, two of whom in particular he would have expected to object to being subjected to such cavalier treatment from men they were likely to consider to be of a lesser social standing.

"You should hear Dusty on occasion," Waco answered with a grin. "He can get practical' *rude* when he's so minded."

"Lumme!" Babsy said to Freddie, while the two young men were speaking, pointing what was clearly an accusatory finger at the black clad deputy. "You don't mean's how I'm starting to *think* and *talk* like what that there Lon does?"

"I've noticed you do on occasion, but it isn't something one likes to *mention,*" the black haired beauty replied, then looked at Waco and Roxton. "Are you going to try to deal with that thing?"

"The thought had crossed our minds, dear lady," the aristocrat replied.

"But it might go *off!*" Babsy pointed out in some alarm.

"In that case," Roxton drawled, once again sounding as if consumed by ennui. "Bury me at Barton Stacey, Ogben Saint George, Ogben Saint Andrew and Winchester. You might even save a bit for Shepton Mallet. But, as I went to Oxford, don't let Cambridge have any."

"I'll see it's done," Freddie promised, then swung her gaze to the blond youngster. "And have *you* any last requests?"

"Yes'm," Waco replied. "Cepting I want to die all old 'n' ornery, in bed with my boots *off.* There's just one thing, though."

"And what might it be?" the beautiful Englishwoman asked.

"*When* this son-of-bit—lil ole thing—goes off and blows me to lil bits," the youngster obliged, still sufficiently in control of himself despite being fully aware of the situation's danger to make the correction to the definition. "Don't *nobody* say, 'That's him all over.'"

"And *when* it happens to me," Roxton continued. "I'd be just as *obliged* if you'd refrain from saying, 'Pull yourself together, man.'"

"I wish I'd *never* asked!" Freddie asserted, realizing how such comments helped to relieve the tension and finding it a comfort herself as she was all too aware of the peril which the two young men would be facing while trying to render the grenade harmless. "Come on, Babsy. Let's leave them to their *fun.*"

"Yes'm," the little blonde replied and also contrived to conceal her concern. "Me stomach's turning over from all them *jokes!*" Nevertheless, there was some hint of it as she continued, "Good luck!"

"Well, old boy," Roxton said, when everybody else had withdrawn to a safe distance with the blond giant and the black clad deputy dragging along the still unconscious massive bearded man. "Shall I carve, or will you?"

"It's *my* hat's'll get mussed up should anything go wrong," Waco answered. "So I reckon I'd sooner do it."

"As you will, old thing, as you will, the aristocrat assented. "Hand over your 'titfer' and see what you can do."

CHAPTER SIX

Dusty Isn't Going to Like It

"I suppose *this* is hardly the time or place to *ask,* old thing," Lord James Roxton remarked, after having glanced around to ensure everybody else had withdrawn to a safe distance. He carried on, continuing to behave in what seemed to be the disinterested fashion of one making casual conversation. "But you *do* know how this little blighter *works?*"

"Just so long it's like them I've seen back home to the OD Connected," Waco claimed, eyeing with considerable disfavour the spherical black object reposing in the crown of his Stetson and somehow conveying a suggestion of evil against the white lining. "Dusty brought a couple of 'em back from the War and it *looks* like they do."

"That's a *comfort,*" the British aristocrat declared, also looking down at the hat he was holding with both hands by its wide brim. "It's not that I don't have *complete* faith in you and all that, but I didn't know you had things like this over here in the colonies."

"You don't find 'em in your friendly neighbourhood general store. I'll have to come right out and 'fess up truthful true," the blond youngster answered, still studying the device in the hope of discovering if it differed in any external fashion from the Haynes "Excelsior" Percussion Grenades to which he had referred.[1] "And I wish this son-of-a-bitch *wasn't* here at all."

"But you *can* deal with it?"

"Sure—Only—!"

"*Only?*"

"Happen I'm *wrong,* don't let on to my *amigos* such was so!"

"I *won't,* trust me," Roxton promised, as soberly as if he

---

[1] We have been unable to find details regarding a Haynes "Excelsior" Percussion Grenade being acquired by any member of the OD Connected ranch's crew, or even being used during the War Between The States. However, a contemporary device, the Ketcham's "Four-Pounder" Grenade, which operates upon a different and somewhat safer principle, is employed in: THE COLD AND THE SABRE and COLD DECK, HOT LEAD.

believed he would be unaffected by the explosion if the grenade was detonated so close to him. Having considerable experience in dangerous situations, even though he was willing to concede none had offered such a great element of personal risk, he was aware that such an apparently light-hearted and inconsequential conversation helped to relieve the tensions at such a moment. "Shall we find out whether you're right or wrong, old thing?"

"Why not?" Waco drawled without any too discernible concern, albeit showing what anybody who knew him well would have recognized as being considerable emotion.

Saying the words, the blond youngster reached into the hat and lifted the device with great care in both hands.

Made of black cast iron, clearly formed by two separate pieces which had been screwed together, the exterior of the grenade was in the shape of a ball with a ridge around the middle and had a diameter of two and a half inches. This was no different from the "Excelsior." However, the present example bore a shine suggesting it had been manufactured more recently than the War Between The States and—particularly as it was no longer being produced by the original designer, having been considered too unsafe for general issue—it showed none of the evidence of having been a 'battlefield purchase', acquired as loot, like the pair he had seen previously.

The excellence of the condition, Waco told himself silently, implied somebody else had made the device since the War and there could be modifications he knew nothing about in the construction!

In fact, the grenade might even operate upon a completely different principle!

"Would you reckon to twist to the right, or the left, *amigo?*" the youngster inquired, holding the grenade firmly with the tips of his left thumb and fingers.

"Dunno, old thing," Roxton replied and, despite his aura of seeming ennui, a close acquaintance would have realized he was under a similar strain to that of the Texan. "My folks were *never* militarily inclined, nor even jolly old sea dogs like Ramage's family, so I've never even *seen* anything like it."

"Then why're you standing here?" Waco inquired with justification, although his tone was curious rather than annoyed.

"Well, old boy," the British aristocrat answered. "I thought you'd look rather *lonely* standing here by yourself."

"I wish I *wasn't* standing here, by myself or with you, pleasant-like though your company be," the youngster admitted wryly, grateful for the moral support he was receiving and adding to the liking and respect he had already formed for the Englishman. "So why don't I just put the damn thing down some place and we'll light a shuck. Babsy's got a lil friend called 'Ginger' as's close looking to her's two peas in a pod, 'cepting their hair's different colour. We could take you along and present you all right and proper to her."

"What a *splendid* idea, old thing," Roxton enthused, darting a quick and far from disapproving glance to where Barbara "Babsy" Smith was standing in the forefront of the crowd with Freddie Woods, Sir John Uglow Ramage, Harland Todhunter and the other two deputy town marshals. "I'd say 'yes' to it like a shot, but all these good people are standing around waiting for the little fellow there to blow us up and it would be *such* a shame to disappoint them."

"We *couldn't* do *that!*" Waco admitted, ignoring the perspiration which was trickling down his forehead. "It wouldn't be *right* at all!"

While the latest part of the conversation was taking place, alert for the slightest indication that he could be doing something wrong, Waco started to twist the upper half of the sphere slowly in a clockwise direction. It moved just a fraction, then halted and resisted his further efforts. Reversing the direction his right hand had been taking, continuing to grip the lower section firmly in his left, he met with a momentary refusal. Then, as he intended, the movement was commenced anti-clockwise.

Feeling the motion stick, the youngster stopped his hand's pressure!

After only a brief pause, without halting his suggestion about going to introduce the English aristocrat to Babsy's friend, Ginger, the youngster started the turning motion again. Although nothing was discernible on his face, as he had suspected there could be some means employed to prevent the device from being dismantled after it was primed ready for use, he experienced a surge of relief when the upper section started moving without the effect which would have taken place had his supposition proved correct. He was less concerned when a second and third brief obstruction was encountered.

"Aw shucks!" Waco said in well simulated annoyance, lifting away the liberated upper section of the outer casting. "Looks like we're going to *disappoint* these good folks after all."

"You Yankees just don't have any *sporting* spirit at all," Roxton replied, but he too was unable to entirely conceal the relief he was experiencing.

"Look here, *amigo,*" the youngster said, with what appeared to be the serious demeanour of one imparting information of the greatest importance. "I know you haven't been over here in the *colonies* for long. But, happen you want to stay on here all happy and peaceable, don't you *never* call no *Texan* a *Yankee.*"

"An error of *some* magnitude, I suspect?" the aristocrat queried.

"You *could* say that," Waco confirmed. "I was raising fourteen summers—and winters too, comes to that—afore I even knowed's 'god-damned Yankees' wasn't all *one* word."

"I thought that thing was like grenades I've seen in Europe, with a burning fuse to set it off," Roxton breathed, losing all his suggestion of dry levity as he watched the latest developments. "So I was going to catch it with my bare hands!"

"I'd thought on them self-same lines," Waco admitted. "Only I remembered them I'd seen back to home just in time and concluded using my hat'd be safer's it'd make for a *softer* landing."

While speaking, the youngster and Roxton were studying the result of the former's efforts!

The removal of the cover had exposed the means by which a Haynes "Excelsior" Grenade operated!

While limited in its radius of lethal effect, the device would have killed, or maimed, several of its intended victims if it had been allowed to land!

Certainly neither Waco nor the Englishman would have survived if the grenade had exploded while it was being opened!

A second cast iron sphere, which had fourteen nipples covered by brass percussion caps spaced evenly all around it, was within the outer shell. When thrown and striking a solid enough object, one of the detonators was certain to receive a blow of sufficient force to cause it to perform its function by setting off the waiting charge of black powder. When the explosion came, both inner and outer cases would shatter into many pieces and spray their immediate surroundings with the effect of what a later generation would call a "fragmentation" bomb.

However, the grenade held by Waco differed in one important respect from those made by Haynes during the War Between The States!

Three slender wires had been attached around the centre line of the inner sphere and they were rested in tiny grooves positioned on the top of the outer two-part globe's lower section, around which the "male" thread of the screw was carved. Waco concluded the slight protruberances of the wires had caused the brief hesitation while he was turning and, regardless of the momentary concern he had experienced on the first occasion, he appreciated why they had been added. Instead of the inner sphere being free to move around within its outer casing, thereby adding to the risk of a premature explosion, it was held clear until a definite impact buckled one or more of the comparatively fragile supports and allowed the nearest percussion caps to make the required contact.

"Well, it's done now, anyway," Roxton claimed, after Waco had handed him the upper section of the outer sphere and carefully lifted out the inner, still potentially lethal, inner globe to remove the percussion caps from their respective nipples. "Let's go and apologise to all these good people for not having blown ourselves up.

"I hope that youngster of yours knows what he's doing!" Harland Todhunter commented in a hoarse voice, watching Waco and Roxton with a fascinated gaze. "For *their* sakes, I mean of course."

"Don't worry none about *that*," the handsome blond giant replied, the remark having been directed at him. Despite the even timbre to his voice, feeling the hand which Freddie Woods had grasped involuntarily being squeezed, he was given added confirmation of his supposition that she was sharing his well concealed anxiety. "The boy knows what he's doing *most* times."

"I don't when he ever *has,*" the black clad Texan put in, but his manner suggested he too was more concerned for the youngster's safety than was implied by his words. "You just tell me *one* time."

"The day he stopped taking *your* advice," the big blond replied, glancing at the unmoving shape of the enormous bearded man at his feet. "How's about you earning your wages by getting the doctor to look this jasper over. I want to apologise most humble for whomping his lil ole pumpkin head so hard when he wakes up."

"It looks as if everything is all right," the millionaire stated, after the black clad Texan had strolled away with the Winchester Model of 1866 rifle across the crook of his bent left arm. Watching Waco and Roxton walking in the direction of his party, he turned his gaze back to the blond giant and continued, "And, if you don't mind me saying so, you and your men have done a *very* good piece of work, Captain Fog."

"I agree whole-heartedly," the beautiful Englishwoman declared, having snatched her hand free on realizing who she had grasped in her anxiety. Waiting until the expressions of similar sentiments from the men around her had ended, she went on, "However, Harland, this is Mark Counter. Captain Fog is away on business."

"My apologies, sir!" the burly millionaire offered immediately, running his gaze over the gigantic muscular development of the golden blond Texan. "I naturally assumed—!"

"Shucks, Dusty isn't anywheres near so good looking as I am," Mark Counter replied, having been subjected to the same error of identification on more than one occasion. However, as he did not have a jealous bone in his gigantic frame and had the greatest respect and liking for his absent *amigo*—born of dangers shared and out of each having saved the other's life more than once—he had never felt resentment when such a misconception occurred.[2]

"Your ma—*friend* in black is the Ysabel Kid, of course?" Todhunter asked, although the words came out as more of a statement of fact. "I've heard how well he can handle a rifle and the shot he made to save this young lady certainly proved it."[3]

"I'm mortal ashamed to admit I even *know* him," the blond giant drawled. "But he's the Ysabel Kid." Then he swung his gaze to where Waco and Roxton were approaching and greeted

---

[2]*Details of Mark Counter's background and special qualifications can be found in:* APPENDIX TWO.

[3]*Information regarding the background and special qualifications of the Ysabel Kid are recorded in:* APPENDIX THREE

them with what strangers might have considered a lack of gratitude and cordiality. "You took your own good time."

"I'd've been back sooner, only this gent was asking me for directions to some place's we could take Babsy and Ginger for a drink," Waco claimed. Then he swung his right hand and tossed something towards the little blonde. "Here, honey. *Catch!*"

Responding instinctively, the little blonde did as she was requested. On looking at the object she had caught and finding it to be the reassimilated black grenade, she let out a screech like a scalded cat. However, indicative of her strength of will and presence of mind, realizing the youngster would not put her at risk in any way, she was just able to restrain her equally instinctive impulse to throw away what was certain to be a now innocuous device.

"You silly bleeder!" Babsy restricted herself to retaliating in a just slightly less than ear-splitting screech. "You *wait* until—!"

"You pull all the hairs off his chest, gal!" Mark suggested and reduced both the girl and his *amigo* to blushing confusion.[4] Then he became serious as he swung his attention to the men who were crowding around to offer congratulations. "I reckon we'd best make for either the Railroad House, or the Fair Lady, gents. This business need some talking over."

"Make it *my* place," Freddie suggested with a smile. "You can have the main side room, as there isn't a big poker game going on in it and I can *always* use the business."

"Your place it is, dear lady!" Ramage decided and, with the exception of Sir Michael Dinglepied, who had stood silent in the background ever since he had decided it was the safest thing to do, the rest of the men gave their concurrence. "Lead on, please."

"I've heard some about that Arnaud Chavallier jasper, although we've never had any fuss with him and his bunch either here or while we were running the law up to Quiet Town in Montana back a spell," Mark Counter declared, after the party had transferred to the room offered by the beautiful

---

[4] *What is meant by the reference to hair on the chest is. explained in:* Chapter Eight, 'Waco's Education', THE TROU-BLE BUSTERS.

Englishwoman and were seated around its big green baise covered table. "But how does he get mixed up in this, Colonel French?"

"It wouldn't do his ambitions any good for this spur-line to be built, or to have any other kind of better relations between Canada and the U.S.A.," replied the tall, well built and good looking middle-aged man who had made the identification of the attackers outside the passenger depot. "For all his prattle about improving the lot of the *Metis,* he's like the British and French so-called 'liberals' who support him and want chaos as a means of helping him gain complete control over them without being willing to follow a democratic process in the attempt to get it."

"I thought Louis Riel was the leader of the *Metis?*" one of the American businessman asked.

"He should be," Colonel George A. French replied, giving no indication if he noticed the vicious scowl directed his way by Sir Michael Dinglepied when he had spoken in such a derogatory fashion about "so-called 'liberals.'" "It's always been my opinion that Chavallier and not Riel was the instigator when he summarily tried and executed Thomas Scott for speaking out against him. Basically, he was a fair minded man and only wanted to do good for his people. *Le Loup Garou* only wants to do good for himself."

"Were you expecting trouble from him?" Harland Todhunter inquired.

"I *always* expect trouble from his kind," French asserted. "But this shouting about, 'Death to all capitalist exploiters' is a new wrinkle. Their usual cry is, 'Give the *Metis* land of their own and the right to govern it"; which really means, 'and *we* will govern it regardless of whether they want us to or not".'

"Could be they didn't want us to know they were *Metis,*" Mark suggested. "They were dressed as gandy dancers, 'cepting for the two wearing moccasins, and keeping their hair hidden. So that jasper was told to yell what he did to make us reckon they was just ordinary anarchists."

"That's possible," French conceded, nodding approvingly and deciding the blond giant had formed a shrewd assumption. "Some of the better kind of *Metis* and the decent whites who support them and believe they have some genuine grievances which should be granted redress wouldn't take kindly to learning they were trying to stop the spur-line reaching our intercontinental railway. They know how much benefit can accrue from it."

"You'd have some dealings with the *Metis,* I believe, George?" Sir John Ramage remarked.

"*Some,*" the Colonel agreed. "And, before you ask, I don't recognize any of the four."

"Perhaps the one who you captured will tell you who they are and what they were up to, Mr. Counter," another of the American businessmen suggested, the bearded man having been carried to the jailhouse by members of the crowd acting on the blond giant's orders and no report having yet arrived as to his condition.

"Going by what I saw him trying to do and know about his kind," French put in before Mark could reply. "Even if he knows anything worthwhile, which I *doubt,* he *won't* answer any questions."

"There're *ways* of making fellers talk," the businessman asserted and darted a knowing glance at Mark. "Aren't there, Mr. Counter?"

"Not the kind you mean," the big deputy said coldly. "Least-wise, not in an office run by Dusty Fog!"

"N—Nothing *personal* meant, I assure you!" the businessman declared hurriedly, startled and not a little alarmed by the vehemence of the response to his hint that some form of torture should be employed to produce a solution to the mystery.

"I'd like to know where they got that *"bomb,'"* Waco put in, throwing a less than complimentary glance at Dinglepied as he too employed the incorrect designation for the device. "Or do those *Metis* always go in for things that *fancy,* Colonel?"

"I've never known them to use grenades," French replied. "Although they seem to have a source of supply for other weapons. I'm going to see if I can find out where they come from as soon as I get home."

"And I'll telegraph Cousin Solly down to the U.S. Marshal's Office in Topeka to see what his bunch can find out," Mark promised. [5] [5a] [5b] "Thing being now, though, Colonel. Do

---

[5]*Neither the efforts of Colonel George A. French nor the office of the United States' Marshal at Topeka, Kansas, were able to discover who was the supplier for the arms in the possession of* Arnaud le Loup Garou *Chavallier. However, it*

you reckon those four was all of them, or do we have more to look out for?"

"There could be more," French answered. "Do you have any idea if they have white 'liberal' supporters in your town?"

"Nope," Mark confessed, then his gaze went pointedly to the youngster. "Least-wise, we don't know *yet*. But *somebody* can forget any notions he might have about going out drinking and carousing with two certain young ladies and a gent from England. 'Cause Dusty isn't going to like it when he hears what's happened in his bailiwick and he's going want to be told when he gets back if there's like to be more to come. Fact being, he's going to want to know what's been done about finding out the what 'n' when of all of it."

"Trouble with Dusty is he was *spoiled* as a button," the blond youngster informed Lord James Roxton, to whom he had eventually been introduced formally and had accepted the suggestion that they took Babsy Smith and Ginger to "see the sights" that evening. "Which being, he's mighty set on *allus* having his wantings happen and, *me* being the cream of the marshal's office, I'm going to have to go around 'n' about to see he gets 'em."

"If you're the *cream*, I can only thank the Good Lord that

was later established that many came from Ernst "die Fleisher" Kramer, a dealer in illicit weapons based in Chicago, Illinois, some details of whose career are reported by inference in: THE DEVIL GUN and THE WHIP AND THE WAR LANCE, also at first hand in: CALAMITY, MARK AND BELLE and Part Five, "The Butcher's Fiery End," J.T.'S LADIES.

[5a]In May, 1973, Colonel French created what a later generation would term a "para-military" law enforcement force which was to be called the "Canadian Northwest Mounted Rifles." However, due to the Government military body operating close to its border with Canada—wishing to maintain the spirit of co-operation he had established with various peace officers while visiting America—he substituted the word, "Police" for "Rifles" and this was accepted as a satisfactory compromise by both countries.

[5b]In spite of his experience outside the Mulrooney passenger depot and with other peace officers in the United States besides the town marshal's office at that town, Colonel French continued to retain his close-topped holster and had the same kind of rig supplied to the men under his command.

the rest of us're the skimmed milk," Mark growled. "So you light a shuck and start pouring out some of that cream, or you'll be showing the sights to the blister end of a shovel."

"He outranks *me*, you know," Waco told the young British aristocrat, albeit with his attention focused upon the blond giant ready to evade physical reprisals.

"I *understand*, old boy," Roxton sympathised. "And, as you're going to be unavoidably otherwise detained, I'll take the ladies to see the sights without your invaluable—or would it be *un*-valuable—assistance, invaluable as that would be."

"Oh my Lord!" Freddie Woods ejaculated, having been invited to remain during the discussion. Sharing what could only be described as a look of revulsion between Waco and Roxton, she continued, "Here's *another* one starting to think and talk like a *Texan*!"

CHAPTER SEVEN

We've *Got* the Bitch!

"Did *you* know what was going to happen at that place they called a railway station?" Sir Michael Dinglepied demanded angrily, almost as soon as the main entrance to his suite at the Railroad House Hotel was closed by the bell-hop who had carried up his less than elegant or excessive baggage.

"Certainly not!" Shaun Ushermale denied, with what might have been righteous indignation. However, having heard of the incident, past experience should have warned him to expect the question with its suggestion of being close to an accusation. Although he and the baronet were on more intimate terms than merely those of employee and employer, having the suspicious and petty-minded nature of their kind, neither trusted the other—or any of their associates, for that matter—to any noticeable degree. Showing he considered such an attitude was widespread, he continued in an aggrieved fashion, "And if that fellow you sent me to see was aware of it, he never mentioned anything to *me*. But then, I don't suppose he *would*."

Having remained with the rest of the party from the west-bound train until the end of the meeting at the Fair Lady Saloon, learning enough to suggest there may be other people in Mulrooney already working towards the same end that he hoped to achieve, Dinglepied had come to occupy the accommodation rented for him by Harland Todhunter. On his arrival, he had found Ushermale waiting in the suite.

The young man had been sent ahead in his capacity as confidential secretary to make contact with somebody they had been assured by an associate of their persuasion in Washington, D.C., would be sympathetic to their ideals and render whatever local information and assistance they might require. He was returning from visiting the sympathiser when he had been accosted by the three cowhands outside the Winstanley Livery Stable and had received his first sight of the beautiful black haired Englishwoman.

Having made good his escape from the trio's unwelcome attentions, the young man had been disinclined to leave the safety of the hotel. Instead, he had remained in the suite he had occupied as was authorized by Todhunter—who knew nothing of the true reason for him coming ahead of the rest of the party—on reaching Mulrooney. Nor had hearing of what happened caused him to leave what he considered to be sanctuary. He had been told by the reception clerk, who came upstairs to supply the information as being of interest to him, that nobody in the party he was expecting had been injured and he had declined the suggestion that he might want to go to find out whether his employer needed any assistance.

On coming together, the memory of the incident at the Mulrooney passenger depot and the response it elicited from the baronet momentarily caused both him and his secretary to forget the important news each had meant to impart!

Seeing the sullen droop which came to Ushermale's lips, Dinglepied reminded himself—as he had on previous occasions when some contretemps threatened their relationship—of the danger causing resentment could create for him. The young man knew enough about his private affairs to ruin his career and perhaps even cause him to be sent to prison if provoked into disclosing the details to the wrong people. With that in mind, he decided to pass on some information which he felt sure would heal the breach and return them to the *status quo*.

For his part, Ushermale was equally wary of antagonizing his employer. While he was in possession of various facts which rendered betrayal less likely to happen, he was all too aware of how vicious and malicious the baronet could be if aroused. Having no desire to face the consequences of his past misdeeds, not all of which were minor, he felt a diversion would not come amiss. Fortunately, he believed he had the means to bring this about.

"Do you know who I've seen?" Dinglepied and his secretary said in the same breath.

"I've seen that damned Lady Winifred Besgrove-Woodstole!" the baronet announced, after he and Ushermale had paused and stared at one another for a moment.

"I *knew* it was h—!" the secretary began, furious that his surprise had been destroyed. However, wishing to create the impression of possessing more information than was the case, he revised his comment. "I saw her before *you* did!"

"I didn't know you'd seen her in England, so you'd be able to recognize her," Dinglepied countered, unwilling to even share the credit for the discovery.

"Of course I did!" Ushermale lied, equally disinclined to concede guesswork rather than personal knowledge had produced his recognition. "She was always running around the West End with the rest of those idle, useless dregs of so-called Society."

"Anyway," the baronet said, so excited by the thought of what the discovery entailed to remember that Lady Winifred Besgrove-Woodstole had only rarely visited London and, on those widely spaced occasions, never mingled with the type of young aristocrats to which his secretary referred. "We've *got* the bitch!"

"How do you mean?"

"A warrant was sworn for her arrest."

"So I heard," Ushermale admitted, but did not sound enthusiastic over the knowledge.

"If she is taken back," Dinglepied said, with the kind of important patience often shown when a less than intelligent child is being given an explanation of something it should already understand. "She'll stand trial for *murder!*"

"There's not the *slightest* chance she'll be found guilty and hang," Ushermale answered, sounding disappointed in spite of his frequent claim to abhor the infliction of capital punishment regardless of how serious an offence had warranted it. "You know how those damned Tories and the rest of those upper class parasites stick together."

"She might not hang, or even be found guilty, with the kind of jury who'll be picked to try her," the baronet admitted, also showing he found the prospect far from appealing. However, he brightened a trifle as he went on, "But the scandal of her trial will do tremendous damage to the Tory Party, no matter what the verdict. It could even divert attention from poor dear Laurence. He's *suffered* so much, having to live in exile since that aristocratic bitch killed poor Gerald and Tommy."

"There's *one* problem though."

"What is it?"

"We will have to get the bitch to England before she can be tried."

"That won't present any problems," Dinglepied claimed. "Uncouth and barbaric as these damned Americans are, with the pressure we can have brought to bear by our associates in Washington and New York, they'll be willing to have her arrested and held for extradition."

"Who's going to make the arrest?" Ushermale inquired, delighted to have information overlooked by his employer.

"They must have a police force, even in this god-forsaken hole," the baronet answered, noticing the response and wondering what he had missed. "In fact, I *know* they do. Three of its detectives were at the railway station and save—*stopped* the poor fellows who were trying to assassinate Todhunter and his cronies."

"Oh yes, they have a police force all right!" the secretary conceded, having discussed his "narrow escape" at the livery stable with the desk clerk and received a fair amount of information when complaining about the lack of official protection he was afforded. "And, from what I've been told, she has them all wrapped around her little finger like her kind do the police in England. They'll *never* arrest her."

"Then we'll get somebody who *will!*" Dinglepied asserted. "Perhaps the chap you've been to see will be able to help us on that."

"Unless he was *lying,* he should be able to," Ushermale admitted, but he clearly had reservations on the possibility. "According to him, he has all kinds of useful connections." Knowing his employer to be parsimonious by nature, he paused before continuing with a thinly concealed relish. "But he says they'll all need *paying* for whatever we want them to do."

"Don't they *always?*" the baronet whined, having a reluctance to part with his own money under any circumstances; although always willing to accept payment for his services. "Go and talk to him—!"

"Why not have him fetched here?" the secretary suggested, having no liking for the prospect of leaving the safe confines of the luxurious hotel after his experience earlier in the day.

"The less people know about him working for us the better!" Dinglepied claimed, with justification considering what he was hoping to achieve. "So *you* can go and see him without *me*. Doing things like that is why I've brought you over here with me."

"Dear Lady Winifred,
I can understand that, for obvious reasons, you might not wish to spend too much time in conversation about a certain matter *with the other British members of the Commission for which I have the honour to be*

*chairman. However, I would deem it a pleasure and a
privilege if you would come and meet me behind the
Railroad House Hotel this afternoon at half past one so
we could have a private chat. I'm sure your family in
Melton Mowbray would be delighted to receive information at first hand about your recent activities and I
will be delighted to supply it on my return to England.
You may rest assured, upon my word of honour as a
gentleman, that I will not disclose your whereabouts to
anybody else.*

Yours sincerely
Sir John Uglow Ramage, Bart."

Standing clad in brief black lace underwear—which established beyond any shadow of a doubt her Junoesque contours
were provided by nature and needed no artificial assistance—
matching silk stockings, supported by scarlet suspender
straps, and high heeled red pumps, Freddie Woods lowered
the letter after having read it through twice and frowned.

"Who did you say brought this, Babsy?" the black haired
beauty inquired.

"Bertha reckoned it was a bloke who could be a gandy
dancer," the close to buxom little blonde replied, referring to
the senior "barmaid" on duty downstairs.

"Not somebody from the Railroad House?" Freddie asked,
glancing from the envelope in her left hand to the sheet of
paper it had held and knowing both were the kind supplied in
every room of the use of their guests by the management of
the establishment to which she had referred.

"No, ma'am," Babsy answered. "I asked Bertha about that
and she said the geezer told her the porter from the hotel give
him the price of a drink to fetch it over. Is something wrong?"

Freddie did not reply for a moment!

Although Sir Michael Dinglepied had not accompanied
them, the rest of Harland Todhunter's party had returned to the
Fair Lady Saloon the previous evening after having settled
into their respective accommodation at the Railroad House
Hotel. They had agreed with the suggestion from the black
haired beauty that, to coin a phrase she had acquired from
military members of her family, no "shop would be talked in
the Mess" and the business which had brought them to
Mulrooney was not mentioned. However, on being asked his
intentions, Lord James Roxton had asserted that he would stay

with the others and postpone the "seeing of the sights" in the company of Babsy and Ginger until Waco would make up a quartet.

Only one slight discordant note had marred the pleasures of the evening!

When asked why she had come to live in the United States, by the American businessman who had antagonized Mark Counter during the meeting in the side room, Freddie had treated him as she had predecessors who showed a similar unwelcome interest in her private affairs. There had been such a chill in her reply, "For my health, *sir!*" that he and everybody else present had refrained from displaying further curiosity. Nevertheless, despite having a thoroughly good time in the company of a different—somewhat more cultured—quality than was usually her lot since starting to run the saloon, she had been more relieved than sorry when they had taken their departure. What was more, because of the reason for her departure from England and having elected to adopt a vastly different way of life under an assumed name in the United States, she had concluded it might prove inadvisable to meet the members of the British Railroad Commission on a social basis unless there were also some of the Canadians or Americans present.

That morning, there had been no chance of Freddie meeting any of the party she had welcomed at the railroad depot. Being aware that she was going have a fair amount of her time devoted to them throughout the visit, she had occupied herself in making preparations to do so. She would be accompanying them in her capacity of mayor of Mulrooney to various functions organized by interested local businessmen, or to festivities laid on at other places of entertainment—her sense of diplomacy having directed that she asked her business rivals to participate and receive an equal share in the benefits which would accrue from such activities—so wished to make sure they had everything they would require.

Having gone to various establishments, arranging for things she believed would be needed to help give the visit an opportunity of succeeding, the beautiful and competent young woman had called at the office of the town marshal to learn what, if any, developments of interest might have occurred. She was informed by Mark Counter—who, as first deputy, was in charge during the absence of Dusty Fog—that he had received a telegraph message stating his superior and Deputy

Frank Derringer would be returning with their prisoner from Hays City on the noon train. She already knew this, having received the same message, but the pleasure which she had experienced was not caused by relief that the marshal would soon be available to resume control of the office. The enforcement of law and order had, she was willing to admit, been run quite satisfactorily in his absence by the other three members of Ole Devil Hardin's floating outfit who were serving as his deputies.

However, apart from the news of the impending return, there was nothing positive for the blond giant to report!

Although the bearded *Metis* had regained consciousness, the injury to his mouth had rendered him unable to talk. Because he had behaved in such a violent fashion on his recovery, he was being kept under restraint in one of the cells. Despite the Ysabel Kid and Waco having circulated throughout the town, they had not discovered anything to suggest there might be more of Arnaud *le Loup Garou* Chavallier's adherents lurking in the vicinity with the intention of continuing the attempt to disrupt the activities of the British Railroad Commission.

Returning to the Fair Lady Saloon and coming up to the bedroom of her living accommodation, Freddie had removed her "street" attire preparatory to donning "working" clothes of a more obviously revealing nature. Before she could do so, Babsy—who was already clad in the fashion adopted for wear in the barroom—had brought up the letter. Regardless of the friendly atmosphere which had prevailed throughout the previous evening, bearing the decision she had reached in mind, the black haired beauty was surprised and puzzled by its contents.

Having kept them under surreptitious yet careful observation after the perturbation caused by the attempted assassination and its aftermath had ebbed from her, Freddie had not detected anything to suggest any of the Englishmen were aware of her true identity!

Yet it appeared Ramage had identified her, even though they had never met!

It was, Freddie told herself silently, impossible for the diplomat to have been told who she was since arriving in Mulrooney. With the exception of Babsy, only one other person in the town was party to her secret and neither of them knew the whole of it. Trusting them both implicitly, she was confident neither would have disclosed the information to Ramage, or anybody else. In fact, as Captain Dustine Edward Marsden "Dusty" Fog had not yet returned from Hays City—although expected on the noon train which she had heard was delayed—he would have been unable to betray her even in the inconceivable possibility that he was so inclined.

Nevertheless, faced with the indication that her secret was known, Freddie now considered it advisable to accept the invitation. Because of the extreme delicacy of the situation which drove her from England, only her parents knew of her present location. In the interests of avoiding suggestions of complicity, not even the other members of the Besgrove-Woodstole and Houghton-Rand families had been taken into their confidence. Therefore, she wanted to stress to Ramage —whose letter suggested he was sufficiently cognizant with her affairs to appreciate the need—the importance of continuing to keep everybody else in ignorance of her whereabouts.

"I can't for the life of me decide *what* it is," the black haired beauty admitted, in response to the question posed in a voice redolent of concern and worry by the curvaceous little blonde. "But there's *something* about this letter that just doesn't seem *right* to me."

"I don't suppose's you know whether it's *his* writing, ma'am?" Babsy inquired.

"Unfortunately I've never seen any of it to let me know whether it is or isn't," Freddie admitted. "But, if it *isn't,* who else would have written it?"

"Search me," the little blonde answered, knowing the contents of the message "But, if you're that worried by it, why not send word's how you can't come to meet him?"

"If only it was that *simple,*" Freddie sighed. Then she glanced at the wall clock and followed a gesture indicative of frustration by complaining, "He certainly hasn't given me much time to get there. I'll have the black walking out dress, the mauve blouse and the jockey cap with tassels, please, Babsy."

"Yes'm!" the blonde assented, albeit with less than her usual eagerness to comply with orders.

"What is *that* for?" the black haired beauty asked, after having donned the garments produced by the little maid.

"Nothing, I *hope,*" Babsy replied.

While her employer was dressing, the little blonde—being what a later generation would refer to as "street-wise"—had collected a .442 calibre Webley British Bulldog revolver with a two and a half inch long barrel and a "bird's head" handle from the well stocked firearms' cabinet in the main room of the living quarters. Having checked that it was loaded, despite knowing this was always the case, she had placed it in a specially made reticule and was holding it out with an air of satisfaction over a job well done.

"What's in it?" Freddie inquired, referring to the reticule, the weapon being concealed and undetectable as was the intention.

"The Webley," Babsy replied, with no more emotion than if naming a more conventional item of feminine attire; albeit conveying the impression that she expected to be praised for making the correct selection. A twinkle came into her eye, as being possessed of an irrepressible sense of the ludicrous, she continued, "I didn't think's how that there elephant gun'd go with madam's ensemble."[1]

"What *impeccable* taste you have, my dear," Freddie obliged with a smile, going along with the maid's attempt to lighten her spirits. "But surely the Remington Double Derringer would have gone so *well* with this outfit?"

"Not with madam's "black walking out" and jockey titfer," Babsy corrected, in the fashion she had seen employed by more staid and "proper" female servants in her kind of employment than she had ever aspired to be. "Besides which, I don't trust them *foreign* gadgets. You never know where you are with 'em half the time. Give me something made in good old Blighty any day of the week. Anyway, it only holds *two* bullets."

"I hope I don't need even *two*," Freddie stated and her serious tone was not entirely assumed.

"So do I, ma'am," the little blonde asserted fervently. "But, if you *should*, unless I come with you, you won't have time to send me to fetch you any."

"I'm going *alone*," the black haired beauty affirmed gently but firmly. "And you are starting to think and talk like a *Texan* again."

[1] An occasion when Freddie Woods used her "elephant gun"—actually a .465 calibre Holland & Holland double barrelled hunting rifle regarded by many British sportsmen as being too light for use against such a large and dangerous animal—is recorded in: BUFFALO ARE COMING!

"I'll have to watch out for *that*, it's bleed—*catching*," Babsy claimed, sounding contrite and disturbed by the possibility. Then she glanced at the clock. "Just like a man."

"Who is?" Freddie inquired.

"Cap'n Fog," the little maid replied. "Never around when he's needed!"

CHAPTER EIGHT

Does *This* Feel Like a *Joke?*

Dressed and armed as she felt befitting the occasion, Freddie Woods set out from the Fair Lady Saloon with what she estimated as just sufficient time to keep the appointment which was still a cause of puzzlement. Wanting to arrive at the rendezvous suggested in the letter signed, *"Sir John Uglow Ramage, Bart,"* without the risk of being seen by the other members of the British Railroad Commission who might be at the front of the Railroad House Hotel, she selected a route which would take her along what amounted to a back street.

At first, although the beautiful young Englishwoman had not anticipated meeting many people, there was nobody else to be seen!

However, this satisfactory state of affairs changed as she went around a bend which hid the hotel from sight of the saloon!

Coming into view of a man lounging on the sidewalk at her side of the entrance to an alley separating two buildings, remembering the suggestion she had heard that Arnaud *le Loup Garou* Chavallier could have more adherents in Mulrooney, Freddie studied him carefully yet without allowing her interest to become too apparent.

Around six foot in height, dark haired, with a hard and unshaven face, the man was tall and burly. Although he was dressed in none too clean range clothes, with a hat having the "Montana peak" style and a loose fitting unfastened jacket such as were favoured in the northern cattle country,[1] the gun-belt he wore was more suited to one who earned his living by a willingness to hire out the Colt 1860 Army Model revolver in the fast draw holster tied to his right thigh. There was a noticeable lump under his left armpit which was another suggestion of how he earned his living.

Despite there being no discernible reason for the man to be where he was, leaning a shoulder against the wall of the nearer building, Freddie could detect nothing to make her as-

---

[1]*"Montana peak," a hat with its crown shaped much the same as those once worn by Boy Scouts.*

sume he posed any kind of threat to her. In fact, he appeared
little different from numerous others of his kind who had visited her saloon. His leathery features were less than prepossessing, but were definitely Caucasian in their lines and gave
no suggestion that he might be the product of a mixed marriage. Furthermore, while it had not been cut for some time,
his hair was neither black nor as long as that of the *Metis* who
had carried out the thwarted assassination bid the previous
afternoon. Therefore, even though the street was otherwise
deserted, she felt sure he could not be harbouring any hostile
intentions when he was where a scream for help would bring it
swiftly enough from the other side of the buildings which
flanked the street.

Having drawn the conclusion, the black haired beauty kept
walking at the same brisk pace!

Freddie found nothing out of the ordinary about the scrutiny to which the man was subjecting her. It was something
which she had grown accustomed to receiving even from more
respectable and harmless looking individuals. What was more,
he neither changed his position nor spoke. Albeit remaining
alert in case something should be wrong and keeping the reticule in her left hand where it could be easily reached and
entered by her right, she went by without giving him a second
glance.

Which proved to be a mistake!

As Freddie was passing the entrance to the alley, a movement from it caught the corner of her eye. Because of her
wariness with regards to her still unresolved misgivings over
the letter she had received, she swung her gaze around to
ascertain what had attracted her. She subjected the two men
who were approaching along it to a quick scrutiny.

Both were dressed in much the same fashion as the one on
the sidewalk and neither more cleanly in appearance nor more
prepossessing!

One was tall, lean and blond. Whatever redeeming features
his oak bronzed face might have had, they were removed by a
livid white scar which ran the entire length of his left cheek
from the corner of his eye to the side of his loose lipped
mouth. There was something unusual about the way he was
armed. While there was a sheath of Indian manufacture at the
left side of his gunbelt, which supported an Army Colt in a
fast draw holster on the right, it did not hold a knife.

Freddie found something toad-like and even more repellent about the other occupant of the alley. Short and squat, with little hair if his shoved back hat was any guide, his waxy features suggested he spent little time out of doors. Perhaps because they had no lashes to offer protection, his eyes blinked more than normal. He was wearing two Colt Model of 1851 Navy Belt Pistols—a revolver despite the name—in low cavalry-twist draw holsters. He seemed to move in a progression of hops, much like those of the kind of reptile he resembled. However, regardless of his less than healthy looking skin pigmentation, she gained the impression he was extremely powerful and might prove as dangerous a proposition with his bare hands as when relying upon his guns.

However, while neither man was the kind Freddie could imagine a girl being willing to take home to meet her mother, they too gave no indication of being *Metis* in disguise!

The consolation which the black haired beauty had drawn from the latter consideration ended almost as soon as it was reached!

"Keep right on walking and don't even *think* of yelling out!" commanded a harsh Northern voice from close behind the Englishwoman and she felt something hard and circular being pushed against her spine. "If you make so much as a *squeak,* you'll get a busted head!"

"Whatever you say," Freddie replied, her manner calm despite suspecting the threat would be carried out. What was more, she concluded that she had no reason to anticipate there would be any help forthcoming from the pair leaving the alley. Nor did she believe any of the three were cowhands engaged in some form of harmless mischief. "But, if it's *robbery* you have in mind, you'll get precious poor pickings from me."

"She reckon's how we're figuring to *rob* her, Camb!" scoffed the scar-faced man as he ranged himself swiftly to the Englishwoman's right.

"Why that'd be right *dishonest,* Lecky," claimed the toad-like man who had taken up a similar position on Freddie's left. His somewhat cracking mode of speech added to the impression of being toad-like and gave the same suggestion of origins in the Northern States as those of the other two. "And here we are, working for the law. Ain't we, Camb?"

"Blink 'n' Lecky's got the rights of it, your duchess-ship," the third member of the party declared. "We're making what's knowed as a citizen's arrest."

"If this is some kind of a *joke*—!" Freddie began, although her every instinct warned nothing so innocuous was taking place.

"Her duchess-ship reckon's how we're just funning like a bunch of those beefhead sons-of-bitches in town to spend their pay, boys," Hugo "Camb" Camberwell jeered and ground the muzzle of the modified Army Colt with a shortened barrel— which he had drawn from a shoulder holster causing the lump beneath the left side of his jacket—deeper against the beautiful Englishwoman's back. "Does *this* feel like a *joke?*"

"They reckon's how them rich Limey folk's live in castles ain't over bright, Camb," Russel "Blink" Profitt commented, before Freddie could speak.

"It certainly doesn't strike me as being in the *least* bit *funny,*" the Englishwoman claimed, puzzled by the references to her as "your duchess-ship" and the remark from the man at her left. She had wondered whether the trio might have merely deducted from her attire that she was wealthy, or knew her to be the owner of what was rated as being the most profitable saloon in Mulrooney, so had the idea of kidnapping and holding her for ransom. However, this did not explain the suggestion that they were "working for the law" and making a "citizen's" arrest. For one thing, none of them were wearing a badge and, even if they had elected to keep proof of their official standing concealed until she was surrounded, she felt sure it would have been produced when this was accomplished to lessen the chance of raising a protest. "And I *doubt* whether Captain Fog or any of his deputies will think it is either."

"Be that *so?*" Camberwell replied, sounding unimpressed. Nevertheless, he darted a quick glance around as if wishing to make sure none of the local peace officers were in the vicinity before going on in the same kind of blustering fashion, "We ain't never run across Fog, nor none of his deputies; 'though we've heard you've got him and his lousy beefhead bunch running the law hereabouts for *you.*"

"*I have,*" Freddie said, sensing there might be an advantage in denying the assumption that she had hired the Texans as the owner of a saloon expecting favours from the appointment and not in the capacity of Mulrooney's mayor. "And, as they're running the law for *me,* they aren't going to take *kindly* to what you're doing."

"Time they get to know, it'll be way too late," the burly man asserted. "'Cause we ain't figuring on being seen by none of 'em. Head for Hampton's Livery. Only, on the way there, happen you make a peep to let anybody's we might come across know's how we're not just walking along all friendly-like, *you* won't be the only one's winds up taking lead."

'I won't have to 'make a peep,' as you put it," Freddie pointed out, hoping they would not see anybody—unless it was one or preferably more of the very competent young Texans serving as deputies—who she could rely upon to act in a sensible and effective manner—as she did not wish to endanger the lives of other people. "If they see you with the gun pushed into my back and your friend there carrying my reticule, they'll *know* something's *wrong.*"

"There won't be no gun in your back," Camberwell corrected, withdrawing the weapon and returning it to its shoulder holster. While he was doing so, Profitt reached in front of the Englishwoman and tossed her reticule into an alley they were passing. "It's gone back into leather, same's Blink's got rid of your bag. But don't let either fill you with hope, your duchess-ship. I can fetch it, or its low-tied mate, out again as fast's I've heard it said that beefhead bastard tame law-dog or your'n can. Top of which, Lecky's got his real sharp ole Green River knife shoved up his jacket's sleeve. Even *if* I don't shoot you, he'll be right pleasured to carve you so bad's you'll beg me to make you wolf bait as soon's you see what's left of your pretty face."

"You appear to have thought of. *everything,*" Freddie declared, trying to prevent any trace of alarm showing and allowing herself to be guided in the appropriate direction. "But what I'd like to know is, why are you doing this?"

"For *money,*" Granger "Lecky" Lexington answered, holding forward his right arm so the Englishwoman could see the blade of the J. Russel & Co. "Green River" knife he had slipped hilt first up the sleeve of his jacket before she appeared in front of the entrance to the alley.

"Well, that means you *don't* have robbery pure and simple in mind," Freddie assessed. "And it can't be you're thinking of holding me for ransom, either, because you *say* you're working for the law. But, to the best of my knowledge—and I think I'd be the *first* to know—I haven't broken it in any way."

"That's not what we are told," Profitt croaked. "Is it, Camb?"

"It surely ain't," confirmed the burly man bringing up the rear. "Fact being, going by what I was told, you're wanted *bad*."

"Whoever told you *that* must have been *joking*," Freddie claimed, but she was assailed by an uneasy feeling as she remembered the three members of the British Railroad Commission who had arrived from England and, possibly, at least one of the Canadian contingent, might be cognizant of her reason for coming to the United States. If the letter was genuine, Sir John Ramage certainly did. However, she could not believe he would have set the three men on her trail. Nor did she consider either Lord James Roxton or Colonel George A. French any more likely as suspects. Hoping to learn something to enlighten her, she went on in a well simulated tone of mockery, "Or has he mistaken me for the famous lady outlaw, Belle Starr?"

"He allows there's *no* mistake and he sure as shitting wasn't *joking*," Camberwell denied. "Fact being, I've never seen one of his kind's even knowed how to joke. Top of which, he's already paid us right well to take you over to the marshal in Brownton and, most times, his sort throw their money around like they didn't have no arms."

"Why *Brownton?*" Freddie inquired, concluding she could name one person and probably two who would qualify for the unflattering comments made by the man to her rear. Furthermore, she now realized what it had been about the letter she found disturbing. She could not believe a man like Sir John Uglow Ramage would consider it necessary to attest to his promise of not disclosing her location in such a fashion. On the other hand, adding the reference to her home town, Melton Mowbray, and making such an untypical assertion as the one which ended the letter were the kind of things a person trying to make her believe the baronet was responsible—but lacking any extensive knowledge or members of his class—might do. She felt sure that Sir Michael Dinglepied and the Englishman from the Winstanley Livery Stable came into that category. Wanting to gather all the information she could while remaining alert for the slightest possibility she might be offered to make a bid to escape, she went on, "We have a marshal here in Mulrooney and there's a perfectly good sheriff over at the county seat."

"And they're *both* so deep in *your* pocket their eyes don't barely show over it, big as they allow Dusty Fog to be," Profitt libelled. "We was told to take you to a John Law who'll hold you until you can be extri—something or such fancy. It means they'll take you back to where you come from for trying."

"And, going by what we've heard," Lexington went on, grinning maliciously, "that lard-gutted badge-toter over to Brownton'll be only too pleased to hold you in the pokey."

"Do you trust him to keep me there? Freddie inquired, having no intention of allowing the men to know the summation was accurate. "After all, he's got a real greasy palm and I've got plenty of money to grease it."

"What happens to you after we've got you there ain't none of *our* concern," Profitt asserted. " 'Cause that's *all* we're paid to do."

"Get shut and mind what I told you!" Camberwell put in menacingly, before the black haired beauty could delve deeper into the subject or offer to buy her freedom. Nodding towards the open front entrance of a smaller and not so well kept livery stable than the one in which she accommodated her horses, he continued, "We slipped Hampton's hostler a couple of bucks to stay away until after we've gone. But, happen he's not done it, or anybody else's inside, with what we've got at stake, you can get 'em killed as well as yourself hurt real bad should you give us fuss."

"There's no bounty on you *dead,* more's the pity after what your tame law-dogs done to Tricky Dick Cansole, 'cause that cost us a hell of a lot of money," Lexington added. "But we ain't been told *nothing* about what kind of state you're to be in when we deliver you alive."

"And deliver you we aim to," Profitt affirmed. " 'Cause we don't get the rest of our pay until it's done."

Knowing the lanky man was referring to an outlaw who had died resisting arrest a couple of weeks earlier,[2] Freddie gained the impression that the loss of money rather than any

[2]*Told in:* **THE MAKING OF A LAWMAN.**

genuine remorse for his death was behind the comment. However, although disinclined to take such a course, as she considered it could serve to establish an undesirable precedent, she wondered if she had any hope of purchasing her release. To offer to do so, even without having any intention of keeping to the arrangement, might lull the trio into a sense of false security and offer her a way to escape. They arrived at the stable before she could put the matter to a test.

Glancing around on entering the building, as she noticed her captors were doing, the black haired beauty was more relieved than disappointed at not seeing anybody. Furthermore, it appeared the hostler had done as instructed. At least, a shout from Camberwell did not cause him or anybody else to put in an appearance.

Telling his companions to saddle a horse for their prisoner as well as themselves, the burly man lounged with his shoulder against the wall just too far away from Freddie to be able to reach and tackle him with a single jump. She sensed that, regardless of whether his boast of being faster with a gun that Captain Dustine Edward Marsden "Dusty" Fog was justified, he possessed sufficient ability to be able to stop her before any attack she tried to launch was more than just commenced.

"It's no use saddling a horse for *me*," the black haired beauty claimed, playing for time. "I've *never* ridden anywhere except in a carriage."

"The hell you haven't!" Camberwell contradicted with assurance. "We was told how you sat the bronc those beefhead bastards had down to the other livery."

"That's as *maybe*," Freddie replied and gestured to her long skirt. "But right now I'm not dressed for riding *astride*."

"You'll ride wearing it, or *without!*" the burly man declared. "Which don't make no never-mind at all to *me*. But one way or another, even if it means stripping you buff naked, you're riding with us. Now shut your yapper and stay right where you are until I give you leave to move."

Concluding it would be inadvisable for her to disregard either order, Freddie remained where she had halted. Nevertheless, she continued to watch for any suggestion of a means by which she might turn the tables on her captors. She realized that her chances would grow increasingly more slender once they were mounted and riding away from the town.

However, when she opened her mouth to suggest payment for being set free, as she had contemplated outside the stable, the burly man snarled at her to keep quiet and she considered it wise to do as he told her.

Two of the horses were saddled without even the remotest chance of escape being presented to the beautiful Englishwoman!

While Lexington and Profitt were entering the stalls to commence work on the other two, something happened to divert all their attention!

> *"I saw a big pig Yankee marshal,*
> *A—coming down the street,*
> *He'd got two big pistols in his hands,*
> *And he looked fierce enough to eat."*

Coming closer, the words were being sung in a slurred and less than melodious masculine voice. It had an accent which indicated why that particular ditty was selected even before the second verse was concluded.

> *"Oh big pig Yankee, stay away,*
> *Stay right away from me,*
> *I'm just a lil ole boy from Texas,*
> *And scared's I can b—!*

The last word was halted incomplete as the singer came through the main entrance with an unsteady and slightly weaving gait. It supported the indications given by his voice that he had drunk more hard liquor than was good for him. Halting his forward movement as well as his voice, he stood swaying on widely spread feet. Peering owlishly at the occupants of the stable, as if surprised to find anybody there, he started to toss and catch a piece of wood—which looked like a six inch length from a broom's handle, except it had been rounded at each end and there were half a dozen shallow grooves carved to encircle the middle—he was holding in his right hand.

"Hey!" the newcomer ejaculated after a moment, focusing his eyes with what appeared to be difficulty upon the black haired Englishwoman. "I know *you!*"

"Do you *really?*" Freddie inquired, her manner indicating

she realized no succour would be forthcoming from such an obviously drunken man.

In the way they too were looking at the newcomer, the trio shared the same point of view!

CHAPTER NINE

He Sure as Shitting Knew How to Fight!

"Yes, ma'am," the newcomer slurred rather than drawled, starting to advance across the stable in a similarly unsteady fashion to when he had come through the front entrance. However, in spite of his apparent state of inebriation, he still continued to toss the piece of wood into the air as if he considered it to be a most fascinating toy. "You're that fancy English lady's runs th—!"

Although he had been singing words which would have aroused the ire of many a "Yankee marshal," particularly the Earp brothers about whom they were alleged to have been written, the Texan did not strike any of the hard-cases as being capable of resisting physical objections to his behaviour. For one thing, even aided by his high heeled tan coloured boots, he was no more than five foot six in height. Bareheaded, his neatly trimmed dusty blond hair was rumpled untidily. Seeming to be in his early twenties, while moderately good looking, there was nothing particularly eye-catching about his tanned face. The tightly rolled scarlet silk bandana, dark green shirt and Levi's pants he was wearing had been purchased recently, but he contrived to give them the appearance of being somebody else's cast-offs and they tended to emphasise rather than detract from his small stature. Surprisingly, particularly in view of the way he had announced his arrival, he was not wearing a gunbelt and had no recognizable weapons of any kind visible on his person.

"Get the hell out of here, you god-damned short-growed beefhead son-of-a-bitch!" Russell "Blink" Profitt snarled, before either of his companions could speak.

Having an antipathy towards Texans, the toad-like man liked nothing better than to come into conflict with one. However, despite his strength and ability in a rough-house brawl, he always preferred to have an edge. That he should be offered an opportunity to indulge in his sadistic pleasure with such a diminutive and, especially while so affected by drink, unlikely to be dangerous specimen gave an added filip to his intention. Therefore, he did not even pause to don the hat he had removed before saddling the horse he had just left. In-

76

stead, while speaking, he turned away from the stall he had been on the point of entering and strode across the stable.

"Just who-all the hell do you reckon you talking to, you bald-headed Yankee stink-bug you?" the small Texan demanded with drunken indignation, once again teetering to a halt and clutching the piece of wood so its ends protruded on either side of his right hand. "By cracky, you need teaching some manners and I'm the *man* to stomp so—!"

"The hell you will!" Profitt snarled, aroused to such a state of fury by the reference to his hairless condition—as his companions, if not the small Texan, had known he would be—that he lunged forward instead of offering to draw one or both his Colt Model of 1851 Navy Belt Pistol revolvers.

Watching Profitt reaching out with his powerful hands with the intention of taking hold of what they too considered to be a harmless victim, the other two hard-cases could not conceive any way he could fail. While shorter than either of them, he had an advantage in size and weight which had stood him in good stead against bigger opponents. However, if they had thought to look at her, they would have discovered that Freddie Woods was showing anxiety which was tinged with relief as she kept her eyes on what was taking place.

Regardless of how his companions viewed the situation, while closing in, the squat man began to get an uneasy feeling that something was going wrong. Suddenly and inexplicably, a change seemed to come over the Texan. It went beyond the suggestion of drunkenness disappearing with a speed which suggested this might have been no more than a pose. Somehow, the diminutive figure gave the impression of filling out until Profitt had a sensation of it looming over instead of being smaller than him. Startled by the remarkable and alarming metamorphosis, he tried to bring his impetuous advance to a halt. His hands began to drop and there was nothing he could do to stop them.

Nor was Profitt granted an opportunity to recover his wits!

Generating a much greater speed than he had shown previously, the suddenly and strangely *big* seeming Texan swung his right arm around at a slightly upwards angle. However, he did not deliver a conventional attack. Instead, he propelled the rounded end of the wood—which was *bois d'arc*, acclaimed by Indian bow makers as one of the hardest, finest and most durable of timbers—protruding below the heel of his hand so it impacted against Profitt's temple with savage force. The ridges around the centre of the stick allowed it to be grasped so firmly it as good as formed part of his fist and gave extra impetus to the attack.

Looking as if his limbs had suddenly turned to jelly, the recipient of the unconventional blow plunged sideways in a helpless sprawl!

Going by the flaccid way Profitt measured his length on the floor, he would not be taking any further interest in what went on around him for some considerable time!

Having followed his squat companion more with the intention of helping to deliver a brutal beating to the small Texan than because he believed his assistance might be needed, Granger "Lecky" Lexington hurriedly revised his opinion as he saw what was happening. Instead of relying upon his bare hands, taking warning from the fate which had befallen Profitt, he started to reach for the Colt 1860 Army Model revolver in the fast draw holster on his right thigh. Regardless of how "Blink" had been felled, he felt sure he could protect himself against a man who was not wearing a gun.

Standing by the wall, wanting to keep the captive under observation and convinced his help could not possibly be needed, Hugo "Camb" Camberwell also was afflicted by a change of mind. Spitting out a profanity, he jerked away the startled gaze he had directed at the toad-like man's limply sprawled body. Despite seeing what his second companion was doing, he was unwilling to rely upon it alone to regain control of the situation. Also taking into account the unarmed condition of the intruder, he commenced his draw convinced that he could deal with the matter even if Lexington should fail.

Once again, the small Texan went into action with devastating speed!

However, on this occasion, the intruder did not place his reliance upon the surprisingly effective—albeit primitive seeming—device he was still clutching in his right hand. Instead, he took two rapid steps forward and bounded from the floor. Twisting in mid-air, while amazement at his latest tactic caused Lexington to be numbed momentarily, he flexed and thrust forward with his left leg. The sole and high heel of his boot, the latter feeling exceptionally painful, smashed against the centre of the lanky man's chest.

In one respect, Lexington might have counted himself fortunate. Because of the urgency, his assailant had commenced the leaping attack from further away than the distance required to achieve its maximum effect and it landed with less than its full power. Nevertheless, the impact was hard enough to send him blundering backwards with the revolver which had just cleared leather falling from his grasp.

Amazed as the lanky hard-case had been by the latest example of the small Texan's unorthodox methods and fighting capability, Camberwell instinctively completed his draw. Engrossed by the activities of the man he had thought to be no more than a drunken no-account to be speedily quelled and lulled into a sense of false security as a result of the passive manner in which Freddie had behaved since being captured, he gave not a thought to her being so near.

This proved to be an error!

Starting to swing his Army Colt into the firing position with commendable speed, Camberwell had no doubt that he had regained command over the so suddenly and drastically changed state of affairs. However, before he could satisfy himself that the eight inch long barrel was pointing at the small Texan, he discovered in no uncertain fashion that he had overlooked a vital element which was able to threaten the success of his scheme.

Waiting until the weapon was being lifted into alignment and its owner was absorbed in watching the intruder dropping from delivering the kick with an agility calculated to remove any suggestion of drunkenness which might have lingered, the black haired Englishwoman stepped forward. Powered with muscles which had been strengthened by regular exercise, her clenched left fist whipped down to strike the burly hard-case's extended right wrist. Augmented by its arrival being completely unexpected, the force of the blow was sufficient to do more than just deflect the weapon downwards. Numbed by the impact, he could not retain his grip on the butt and the Colt slipped from his fingers.

Nor were the misfortunes of Camberwell at an end!

While some women would have been content to have disarmed the burly hard-case, Freddie did not restrict her activities in such a fashion. Instead, catching hold of him by the front of his grubby tartan shirt with both hands, she gave a swinging heave while propelled him across the stable. Nor, caught unprepared by the strength she exerted, was he able to resist what was being done to him. However, having completed the throw, his assailant found there was something else demanding her immediate attention.

Although driven backwards some distance by the leaping kick, Lexington retained sufficient of his equilibrium to remain on his feet, Resuming control over his movements, he came to a halt and, despite his chest throbbing where the high heel had ground in, he proved able to continue the fray. Flashing across, his right hand slid the J. Russell & Co. "Green River" knife from the sheath to which he had returned it before starting to saddle the horses. However, having taken warning from the most effective manner in which the small Texan had dealt with Profitt and himself, he had no intention of approaching to the close quarters required to thrust it home by hand. Instead, he swept it back for the kind of throw at which he had become adept.

Confident though she was in the ability of her rescuer, which she had known the small Texan to be from the moment she had heard him singing, Freddie realized that he might not be able to cope with the latest threat to his continued existence. Having seen an acknowledged expert at throwing a knife perform, she did not discount such tactics as being archaic or unlikely to be used in serious combat.[1a] Instead,

---

[1] *We have occasionally received mail claiming that the throwing of knives was never carried out in serious combat. To those who consider this to be correct, we would point out that James Bowie was credited with doing so and killing an assailant fleeing from an abortive attempt to ambush and murder him; see: THE IRON MISTRESS by William Wellman.*

[1a] *There was at least one occasion recorded in World War II. This happened during the close quarters fighting which occurred after the U.S.N. Navy's destroyer, Borie, rammed and was locked against the German submarine, U-405, during the Battle Of The Atlantic. In addition to more conventional ways of fighting, an American sailor threw his sheath knife from the deck of the ship and killed a German on the casing of the submarine to prevent a gun being manned; see: Chapter 7, "Scratch One Pig Boat . . . Am Searching For More," THE SEA HUNTERS, by Kenneth Poolman and, Chapter Twelve, "An Epic Duel," AUTUMN OF THE U-BOAT, by Geoffrey Jones.*

without waiting to discover the outcome, she bent and scooped up the revolver she had knocked from Camberwell's grasp.

Thumb cocking the action while bringing the weapon up to shoulder height with both hands, the black haired beauty proved herself to be as competent in its use as she had the day before in a different fashion when riding Blotchy!

Taking aim in the only way she considered suitable for the circumstances, Freddie touched off a shot. Controlling the rising effect on the barrel caused by the not inconsiderable recoil from the detonated powder charge, she continued to prove her capability at handling the long barrelled Army Colt—a weapon considerably heavier than the Webley British Bulldog revolver which had been taken from her and discarded along with the reticule in which it was concealed—by utilizing the movement to help draw back the hammer with her thumbs ready to fire again if necessary.

The need did not arise!

Flying as it was intended, the .44 calibre bullet ploughed into the side of Lexington's head an instant before he released the knife. However, although it arrived just too late to prevent the weapon from being thrown, it produced the desired effect. Instead of the eight inch long blade going into the chest of the small Texan and sinking "up to the Green River," as its owner had possessed the skill and was meaning to send it, the knife went at a tangent and buried harmlessly in the wall.

Like his lanky companion, Camberwell had contrived to remain on his feet while rushing headlong across the stable. Glancing over his shoulder as he was recovering from the powerful heave, he realized that the situation which had started so well had now passed beyond all hope of immediate redemption. The only thought he had for the fate of the two men he had persuaded to help him was to hope that both were dead and, therefore, unable to supply information about him. Making no attempt to find out whether this was the case, he turned all his attention to effecting his own escape.

Instead of halting as he was regaining control over his movements, the burly hard-case used the still unended momentum to continue running across the room of his own accord. Instead of taking the extra time which doing so would have required to reach and open the side door, hurtling himself through the air, he covered his head with both arms and plunged through the window in the wall. Taking the shattered glass and splintered wooden sash with him, he left the stable in a rolling dive which brought him to his feet when he alighted outside. Without so much as another brief look to his rear, expecting to feel lead either strike him or whistle by at any moment, he started to run as fast as his legs would carry him.

As he fled, without being fired upon, Camberwell realized there was only one way by which he might evade the retribution he did not doubt would be his lot should he be captured by the local peace officers. They were certain to make every effort to capture him, particularly as the intended victim of the thwarted abduction would be determined to extract vengeance and would ensure her "tame law-dogs" did everything within their power to see it was obtained. Despite his pretended disdain for Texans in general and the group running the law in Mulrooney in particular, he was aware that they had performed their duties most competently since taking office. Therefore, he wanted to put as much distance as possible between him and them before they were set on his trail. He also needed money to assist him in what might prove a lengthy chase and, although there would be a considerable element of risk involved, he felt sure he knew where it could be obtained.

Having decided upon what he would do, a thought occurred to the surviving would-be kidnapper!

"Who the hell was that Texan bastard?" Camberwell mused, reducing his pace to a fast walk as less liable to attract unwanted attention, when a glance to his rear informed him he was out of sight of the stable and nobody was following him. "The son-of-a-bitch wasn't *drunk* like he made out to be and, short-growed's he was, he sure as shitting knew how to *fight!*"

"Are you all right, honey?" the small Texan inquired solicitously, swinging his gaze from Profitt to Lexington to satisfy himself that neither posed any further threat.

"Yes, thanks to *you!*" Freddie Woods replied, showing no surprise nor objection over the last word of the question. Instead, taking the Army Colt by the chamber in her left hand, she offered it butt first to her rescuer and, glancing at his unadorned mid-section, went on, "Here. You look as if you need *this!*"

"*Gracias querida,*" thanked the small Texan, again adding a term of endearment without rebuke and, returning the most effective wooden device to the hip pocket from which it had come, accepting the Colt. Then, followed by its donor, he crossed quickly to the window through which Camberwell had left the stable so precipitously. Halting with his back to the wall alongside the now unglazed frame, he held the weapon in both hands with the barrel pointing upwards while peering cautiously outside. As had been the case when he was dealing with his two would-be assailants, his actions were those of one thoroughly conversant with what he was doing. Scanning the area and failing to find what he was looking for, so swiftly had the burly hard-case reached the shelter offered by the nearest buildings, he went on, "He's lit a shuck like his butt was on fire."

"You hardly expected him to wait around, did you?" Freddie inquired, the remark sponsored by relief at her rescue rather than being a criticism.

"I'll collect my own guns and go after him," the small Texan stated, lowering the Colt and setting the hammer to a safe position between two of the percussion caps on the chamber.

"Leave him to Mark and the others, *please!*" the black haired beauty answered, giving vent to her pent up emotions, Advancing and being taken into the arms of her rescuer, she continued, "Oh Dusty, thank heavens Babsy was *wrong!*"

"You'd best run that by again, honey," the small Texan requested, realizing why he had been asked to refrain from going after the departed hard-case and willing to comply. "Babsy didn't know the kind of trouble you were in to tell me."

"I never thought she did," the black haired beauty replied. "But she said that, like all men, you were *never* around when you're needed."

Although Freddie had been through a second traumatic situation in two days, with the latest posing an even more direct personal threat to her well-being than had the attempted assassination at the Mulrooney passenger depot, she did not behave in the manner which was generally attributed to the heroines in the books and melodramatic plays of the day and, with only a few exceptions, would continue to be the case in the future.[2] During the hectic moments following the arrival of her rescuer, instead of standing back with a hand clasped in her mouth or breast regardless of how desperately he might require assistance, she had not hesitated before supplying it as soon as it was needed. What was more, despite being a little paler than usual, her hand was steady as she spoke and prepared to hand over the revolver with which she had just taken another human being's life. She derived neither pleasure nor satisfaction from having shot the lanky hard-case, but accepted she had had no other choice. Nor, having formed an accurate assessment of his unscrupulous and vicious nature, did she feel any remorse over having been responsible for his death.

Nevertheless, Freddie had never been more pleased to see Captain Dustine Edward Marsden "Dusty" Fog!

What was more, the black haired beauty and her rescuer had come to be on sufficiently close terms for her to have no compunctions over allowing him to see her when she was far from feeling her usual calm and collected self!

"I wouldn't've been, but for *luck*," Dusty admitted. "When the train finally hauled in, figuring you'd want to know the how-all of what happened in Hays City in your capacity as mayor, of course—!"

"Of *course*," Freddie assented and, having regained much of her composure, went on, "By the way, dear, do you think it would be considered *proper* if anybody came in and found the marshall hugging the mayor?"

"There's *some* might even reckon's how the mayor shouldn't call the marshal 'dear,'" Dusty pointed out. "And, was I asked, I'd say's how it was the mayor who's hugging the marshal."

"Mr. Bruce Millan most certainly *wouldn't* approve, bless his tiny little heart," the black haired beauty admitted, referring to a man who had consistently opposed her in everything she had done while helping to organize the building of

---

[2] *We have expressed our point of view on the passive role assigned to the majority of heroines and even villainesses of action-escapism-adventure literature, movies and television series, in our Introduction for J.T.'S LADIES and MORE J.T.'S LADIES.*

Mulrooney and since she had been appointed as its mayor. Moving away from the small Texan, she continued in a mock official tone, "But, be that as it may, *marshal*, please tell me how you came on the scene just when you were needed."

"Whatever you want, *mayor*," Dusty assented and gestured towards his sides. "Only let me go fetch my gear from outside. I feel sort of undressed without it."

Returning the Army Colt to Freddie, as a precaution in case the squat hard-case should recover sufficiently from the blow to pose a threat, the small Texan strode swiftly from the stable. He returned wearing a low crowned, wide brimmed black J.B. Stetson hat and buckling on a gunbelt with two bone handled Colt "Civilian Pattern" 1860 revolvers in its well designed cross drawn holsters.[3] However, neither the rig nor the badge of town marshal which was now affixed to the left breast pocket of his green shirt served to make him in any way more noticeable; except that a casual observer might have wondered how one so insignificant in appearance could have received such an appointment as senior municipal law enforcement officer in a Kansas trail end-railroad town and, despite it being only the second time he had held such a position,[4] fulfilled his obligations with considerable competence. Anybody who looked closer would have discovered there was a strength of will, intelligence and an aura of genuine self confidence to the lines of his face. Furthermore, although his clothes served to lessen its effect, he had the physique of a Hercules in miniature.

While he was completing his "dressing," the small Texan began to explain how he had arrived so fortuitously!

Having instructed Waco—who had been on duty at the passenger depot—to help Deputy Town Marshal Frank Derringer to deliver the prisoner they had brought from Hays City to the jailhouse, Dusty had gone to the Fair Lady Saloon. He had been told by Babsy that Freddie had just left. Learning of

[3] *Being primarily intended for sale to the United States Army as a weapon for the cavalry, the first Colt 1860 Army Model revolvers had barrels eight inches in length. However, those produced with the civilian market in mind were half an inch shorter.*

[4] *The first occasion Captain Dustine Edward Marsden "Dusty" Fog served as a peace officer is recorded in:* QUIET TOWN.

the misgivings both had had over the possible motive for the request for a meeting behind the Railroad House Hotel, he had set out after her and was just too late to prevent the interception taking place. However, seeing her accompanying the three hard-cases, he had immediately realized she was not doing so of her own accord.

Being considerably more experienced in such matters than was suggested by his external appearance, Dusty had appreciated the risks involved in going to assist Freddie immediately!

Instead, taking great care to remain out of their sight and being inadvertently helped in this by Freddie having kept the three hard-cases occupied in conversation, Dusty had followed with such skill he had reached the front of the livery barn without being caught in the act. Peering through a gap in the weather-warped planks of the wall, despite knowing he had avoided detection so far, he had seen enough to warn him against bursting in. Even with his Colts drawn and cocked ready for use, his completely ambidextrous ability notwithstanding,he would be unable to deal with all three of the men swiftly enough to serve his purpose. They were too far apart for him to be able to shoot the first and turn his guns on the others before at least one would be able to kill their captive.

Aware of how little he resembled the popular conception of how he should look, the small Texan had seen how he could turn this to his advantage as he had occasionally in the past!

Because he presented an appearance so vastly different from what one might have expected from a man of his reputation, the trio at Hampton's Livery Stable were not the first— nor would they be the last—to fall into error about the potential of Captain Dustine Edward Marsden "Dusty" Fog![5]

What was more, because of the duties which Dusty had to carry out where one section of the town's transient population was concerned, he had the means upon his person to implement the scheme he formulated. As was the case with the cowhands delivering trail herds to the shipping pens, the construction workers on the railroad frequently visited Mulrooney to spend their hard-earned pay in celebrations which mostly entailed excessive drinking. However, unlike the Texans, they tended to rely upon bare hands and steel toed boots to settle

[5] *See:* APPENDIX ONE.

disagreements or resist arrest for legal infractions. Declining to use the methods of such peace officers as the Earp brothers, who never hesitated before using firearms even against un-armed men, he sought to quell such aggression without employing guns. To this end, he carried a most effective—yet seemingly innocuous—device in his right hip pocket.

Removing his hat, Dusty had placed his badge of office and gunbelt in its upturned crown. Then ruffling his hair and conveying the impression of being drunk, he had alerted Freddie to his presence and sought to lull her captors into a sense of false security by singing loudly before going inside the building. The ploy had proved successful. In addition to be-lieving he was as drunk as he appeared, thinking in terms of guns and knives, the three men had paid no attention to a device which could prove equally effective in competent hands. Therefore, he was helped achieve his purpose by the unexpected potency of the seemingly innocuous *yawara* stick he had wielded with such devastating effect.[6][6a] He had been taught how to use this primitive weapon, along with certain unarmed fighting techniques—including the leaping kick he delivered to Profitt—little known outside the country of their origin, by Tommy Okasi, a Japanese *samurai* who acted as valet to his uncle, General Jackson Baines "Ole Devil" Hardin.

"Mind you, honey," Dusty drawled at the conclusion of his story. "I could've got by without *your* help."

"You know what they say," Freddie replied, now completely recovered from her tension. "Behind every successful man, there's a *woman*."

"*You* can be behind me *any* time you're so minded," the small Texan declared, then glanced at the two sprawled out figures on the floor. "Only, before you do, I want to find out the how-come of all this."

---

[6] *A grandson of Captain Dustine Edward Marsden "Dusty" Fog, Alvin Dustine "Cap," received a similar educa-tion in the Japanese martial arts from Danny, a nephew of Tommy Okasi and also a* samurai.

[6a] *Two occasions when Alvin Dustine "Cap" Fog put to use his skill with the yawara stick are recorded in:* RAPIDO CLINT *and* THE RETURN OF RAPIDO CLINT AND MR. J. G. REEDER.

"They'd been hired to kidnap me and take me to the marshal in Brownton," the beautiful Englishwoman replied and glanced towards the main entrance from beyond which the sound of hurrying footsteps indicated somebody was approaching. "I can't tell you what it's all about right now, but I will later."

"*Bueno*," Dusty assented."And I'll be *real* interested to find out who-all hired them to do it."

CHAPTER TEN

Somebody Knows the Answer

"No matter we *walked* this town from end to end—!" the Ysabel Kid commenced.

"Which I'd tell anybody's *asked* is one fair piece to *walk*," interrupted Waco, sharing the antipathy his companion—and practically every other cowhand—had towards travelling from place to place on foot. Despite being aware of the situation's gravity, he could not resist injecting the comment. "Not that I figure *I'll* get asked."

"I know *somebody* who'll get asked to ride the blister end of a shovel unless he closes his feeding-hole," Mark Counter threatened. "You'll have to *forgive* him, Freddie. Like Cousin Solly says, he knoweth not what danged fool thing he does."

"Let's confine ourselves to the *local* barbarians, shall we?" the beautiful young Englishwoman requested, despite knowing the man named as being responsible for the extemporized biblical quotation was building a reputation as a competent and incorruptible peace officer.[1][1a] She showed no objection to or annoyance at the youngest of the Texans' apparently frivolous behaviour, nor the familiarity with which the tallest had employed her first name. Instead, patting the subject of the request gently on the cheek with what was obviously genuine affection, she continued, "And I'm *always* willing to forgive this *dear* boy. He's so *cute.*"

"Anyways," the first speaker went on, his tone redolent of resignation over such flippancy when he had news of importance to impart. "'Spite of all this *walking* and looking, we couldn't find hide nor hair of him!"

Almost two hours had elapsed since the attempted abduc

[1] *At the period of this narrative, Solomon Wisdom "Solly" Cole was serving as a United States' deputy marshal. Some information regarding his career can be learned by inference in:* IS-A-MAN.

[1a] *After attaining promotion to United States' marshal, Solomon Cole makes "guest" appearances in:* CALAMITY SPELLS TROUBLE: Part Seven, "Deadwood, August 2nd, 1876," J.T.'S HUNDREDTH *and Part Six, "Mrs. Wild Bill,"* J.T.'S LADIES.

tion of Freddie Woods!

Showing no signs of distress over her narrow escape, the black haired beauty was sitting with her rescuer in the dinning-room of her living quarters at the Fair Lady Saloon and listening to reports from three of the local peace officers. Acting in a way which suggested he was not paying his first visit, on entering, Captain Dustine Edward Marsden "Dusty" Fog had removed his well designed gunbelt and placed it with his low crowned, wide brimmed black Stetson hat on the table alongside the door through which he had come in. His three companions were almost as completely at home there. However, having only just arrived, they had only taken off their headdress before starting to deliver the news they had gathered. Regardless of being aware that the situation was serious, neither they nor Freddie could restrain the banter which almost always passed between them.

Attracted from where they were patrolling the town by the shot, the Kid and Waco were told what had happened. Leaving them to start searching for the man who had fled and asking them to send a doctor while doing so, Dusty had remained at the livery stable with Freddie until the second instruction was fulfilled. As he had suspected would be the case, having of necessity been compelled to strike the toad-like man with a much greater vigour than he normally applied when using the potentially dangerous *yawara* stick, the medical practitioner had said his victim was in a state of deep concussion which nothing but time and more than a little good fortune would end.

Asking the doctor to obtain assistance from the small group of spectators who had gathered to remove the unconscious man and the corpse to the appropriate destinations, Dusty had escorted Freddie back to the Fair Lady Saloon. Finding Mark there, she had invited him to join them in her dining-room and told all she had learned about the reason for her abduction. Then he was sent to check whether Sir John Uglow Ramage had written to suggest the rendezvous. He had returned with an answer in the negative, which Freddie had claimed she anticipated would prove the case, but said he had dissuaded the accused Englishman from coming to the saloon to find out what had prompted the enquiry. They were discussing the possibilities suggested by some of the comments made to her as she was being taken to the livery stable when the other two deputies arrived from what had proved an abortive mission.

"It'd make things *easier* happen *some* folks didn't whomp a feller so hard on his lil ole pumpkin head he hasn't woken up yet to answer questions," the Kid commented, eyeing Dusty in an accusatory fashion. "And, 'cording to the doc, likely won't be able to when he does wake up, neither."

"I've heard tell's a feller talks some *better* when he hasn't had a blue window put in his hat-rack," Waco went on, ostentatiously refraining from looking at Freddie.

"*Cute* or not," the beautiful young Englishwoman warned. "The blister end of that shovel's getting *closer* by the *second!*"

"It's a pity we haven't got one of them able to talk," the small Texan drawled; knowing the levity was intended to help Freddie over any trauma which might have been created by the dangerous events she had passed through. "I'd surely admire to find out who-all's behind what happened."

"*Somebody* must know the answers," the Ysabel Kid asserted.

"All's needs doing is finding said *somebody*," Mark declared, his manner implying he believed such a contingency would never occur to his black clad *amigo*. "And *somebody* should do *something* about that."

"Well dog my cats, I'd *never* have come up with anything so smart's *that!*" the Kid answered, his manner redolent of spurious admiration. "But, seeing's you and Dusty outrank Waco 'n' lil ole me, top of Derry not being on hand for you to pick on,[2] [2a] I know who-all the *somebody's* gets sent to do said *something* is going to be."

"Seeing that you know *that* much," the blond giant replied, so officiously it might have been his true nature. "Speaking as *first* deputy in the office, I'd reckon's how you pair should oughta go and get to doing it."

"Am I *pleased* to see you pair?" declared the pretty little red haired woman who had emerged from the Longhorn Saloon. "I was just coming to find some of you!"

---

[2] "Derry"; sobriquet for professional gambler Frank Derringer, who was serving as a deputy town marshal under Captain Dustine Edward Marsden "Dusty" Fog.

[2a] "Guest" appearances by Derringer are recorded in: QUIET TOWN *and* THE GENTLE GIANT. He "stars" in his own right in: COLD DECK, HOT LEAD.

Although she had long since almost forgotten her christian name, looking as she had been described by Waco—including having the fiery red hair which had created her sobriquet—Phyllis "Ginger" Winchell could have passed as a sister—probably a twin—of Barbara "Babsy" Smith. Wearing the kind of just barely decorous clothing which Freddie Woods and Buffalo Kate Kilgore ruled was permissible when walking around outside her place of employment, there was an expression of concern on her face all too obvious to anybody who knew her as well as did the men she was addressing.

"What's up, Ginger-gal?" the Ysabel Kid inquired, recognizing the symptoms and halting with Waco at his side.

While speaking, the black dressed Texan was hoping the answer to his question would not interfere with the duty he and his young companion were trying to carry out!

Before setting off upon their mission to try to discover who and what exactly had been behind the attempt to abduct Freddie Woods, showing the flair for deductive reasoning which had already served him well since becoming a peace officer, Waco had suggested the signs pointed to a member of the British Railroad Commission from Canada being implicated. He had supported his supposition by reminding the others that whoever was responsible must have known there was a connection between Sir John Uglow Ramage and Freddie's family which would be calculated to make her respond to a request for a meeting with him. Admitting the logic behind the conclusion, she had pointed out they were all men of importance and the result of their findings could prove beneficial to both countries. Therefore, she had asserted, it would be impolitic to do anything which might embarrass and antagonize even one of them. Then she had asked for the deputies to seek out confirmation and bring it to her before taking any action, even if no more than asking questions, in that direction.

Taking to the streets, the Kid and Waco were visiting all the places from which they hoped to learn something to help in their quest!

Failing to achieve their purpose elsewhere so far, the young Texan had started to look for a source of information which had proved most reliable in the past!

"It's Jimmy," Ginger replied, pointing towards the batwing doors through which she had emerged. "He's in there, playing poker with Joel Collins and his crew."

"Shucks, there's *nothing* to worry about in that," the Kid

claimed, aware that the little red head was taking Lord James Roxton on a tour of the town. "Bob Shafto'll make sure the game stays honest and I reckon His Lordship can afford to lose more than he's likely to against them."

"That's just *it!*" the little red head answered, showing no sign of being relieved by the assessment. "He's not *losing*. He's the only one who's doing any *winning!*"

"I'm not surprised at that," Waco asserted, having watched the men mentioned by Ginger in the company of Deputy Town Marshal Frank Derringer—a successful professional gambler —a few days earlier as they were playing poker in another saloon from which he had formed an accurate opinion regarding their ability. "Good enough jaspers though they might be in other ways, the way Joel Collins and Sam Bass will keep trying to fill inside or bobtail straights and holding a kicker,[3] [3a] [3b] they're more like' to lose than win."

"It's not Joel and Sam's I'm worried about," the little red head answered, despite having reached the same conclusion about the play she had watched. "That lard-gutted Jim Murphy and that cousin of his—!"

"Alec Hogg?" the Kid suggested, knowing the pair and having formed a low opinion of them.

"If that's his name, he sure looks like it should be," Ginger answered. "Anyways, they're starting to look meaner'n hell."

"We'd best sort of drift on in and take a look, *amigo*," Waco suggested, having duplicated his companion's antipathy towards Murphy and Hogg.

"I was just coming 'round to think along them self-same lines, boy," the Kid admitted, moving the Winchester Model of 1866 rifle a trifle across the crook of his left arm. "Anyways, even if there's nothing to it, maybe we'll find Mousey in there."

Entering the saloon, with Ginger following closely upon

[3] An "inside straight" is a hand with four cards which lack a fifth somewhere in the middle of the required sequence to complete the five; i.e. six, seven, nine, ten.

[3a] A "bob-tailed straight" has a card missing at one end or the other.

[3b] "Holding a kicker", retaining an ace or a king in conjunction with a pair at draw poker. This is considered ill-advised as it reduces the chances of "improving" the pair by restricting the number of supporting cards to be drawn to two.

their heels, the deputies concluded from what they saw and heard that they had arrived at what would be a crucial point in any game of poker played west of the Mississippi River!

"My pot again, I believe, gentlemen," Lord Roxton was saying cheerfully, drawing the money which lay in the centre of the table towards him with both hands. Having accepted Dusty Fog's advice upon his attire for the evening, he was wearing the suit and Homburg hat which was no different from those the Americans in the barroom had on. "Gad, this poker is a *fascinating* game and *most* gratifying when your luck is in as well as mine appears to be."

"If *luck's* all it be!" growled the burly, heavily moustached man whose sullen features and voice suggested he had drunk more than was wise, having bet unjudiciously on what had proved to be a losing hand.

"That remark calls for some amplification, *sir!*" the English aristocrat said, his clipped tone taking on a cold timbre.

"Maybe you'd like it put *different?*" Jim Murphy asked, thrusting back his chair and starting to stand up, in spite of having noticed he was being given looks of disapproval by at least two of the other players.

"Like we have to come right on out 'n' say you're too god-damned lucky for it just to be *luck*," supported Alec Hogg, who was just as big and porcine looking as his cousin and his voice also indicated sufficient of an excess of hard liquor to make him truculent. He too was dressed in a town dweller's three-piece suit, shirt and necktie, albeit retaining a gunbelt with an Army Colt in its holster. Rising from his seat, he continued in a challenging fashion, "So what do you aim to do about i—?"

"Let's all stay nice and still!" Waco barked, striding forward faster than his companion.

"Who says s—?" Murphy commenced, but the words died away as he turned his head and saw the Kid following closely to the right side of the blond youngster. Putting what he hoped was a timbre of righteous indignation into his voice, he amended his original comment. "This Limey's a tinhorn or I've never seen one, *Cabrito*. Ain't that right, Cousin Alec?"

"He just never *stops* winning!" supposed Hogg, feeling certain that the two young newcomers would accept the word of other Texans despite being peace officers. "Which I reckon's how you'll agree that *don't* sound natural on luck alone?"

"Damn it, Kid, Waco!" Roxton snapped, dull red patches having come to his lean and tanned cheeks. He too came to his feet, going on just as indignantly, "They're as good as calling me a *cheat!*"

"And you're saying just as much's how you're *not?*" the black dressed Texan drawled, hoping the Englishman would show enough good sense to let him handle the matter in his own way. "So we'll have to find out who-all's got the rights of it."

"So *that's* the way of it, huh?" Hogg growled, his manner redolent of suspicion.

"The way of what, *mister?*" the Kid inquired, his tone mild although there was nothing mild about his red-hazel eyes and expression.

"This Lime-juicer's one of them bunch from back East's that high-toned saloon gal of Dusty Fog's is sucking up to," Hogg explained, glancing at the men still seated around the table as if expecting them to substantiate his comment.

"How'd you like my boot stuck down your throat?" Waco snapped, always ready to leap to Freddie and Dusty's defence if considering either was being subjected to a slight.

"Easy there, *amigo!*" the Kid snapped, catching the youngster by the right arm as he was on the point of lunging forward. "You're always *way* too quick to temper. This *hombre* didn't mean no disrespecting to Miss Freddie."

"The hell I didn—Augh!"

The denial ended in a strangled croak!

Before Hogg was able to complete the heated words, he was given cause to regret having started them!

All the leisurely seeming posture left the Kid. His Indian-dark features lost their innocence and acquired a chillingly savage aspect. Brought from his left arm and being gripped with both hands, the metal shod butt of the Winchester was rammed with sickening force into the pit of Hogg's stomach. No man who ever over indulged in food and drink as he invariably did could accept such treatment in that region without showing its effect. Letting out the croak and starting to fold at the middle, he stumbled backwards with his hands clasping at the point of impact.

Snarling a profanity as he saw what happened, Murphy started to reach for the Army Colt in the holster of his gunbelt. He too quickly discovered that antagonizing the Kid was not the wisest or safest thing to do. Pivoting more swiftly than he was capable of moving, the black dressed Texan slammed the wooden foregrip of the rifle against the front of his face. Although the blow was deliberately held so it did not render him unconscious, he reeled backwards with a livid red mark across the bridge of his nose and forehead.

Spluttering incoherently and breathlessly, straightening up with his face diffused by rage, Hogg attempted to draw his holstered gun. Before he could do more than close his right hand around the butt, he too was prevented from completing the hostile action.

Not by either of the peace officers, however!

Leaving his place at the table with a rapid bound which sent his chair skidding away, the ruggedly good looking, stocky and medium sized cowhand who was closest wrapped his arms around and gave Hogg a swinging shove which sent him sprawling to the floor. Nor did Murphy fare any better when attempting to renew the movement which had caused him to be hit by the Kid. The oldest of the players, tall, well built and dressed in a more prosperous fashion than the others, rose with an equal alacrity and jerked his descending hand away.

"God damn it, Jim Murphy!" Joel Collins snapped, his tone angry. "I don't mind you getting *killed*, but I'd sooner not have it happen when it could spoil our fun."

"Hell, yes," supported Sam Bass, swinging a disdainful gaze from the man he had thrown to the floor to the other protestor. "The English gent there's been *lucky*, sure enough. but there ain't no call to go saying's how it's anything else 'cept luck."

"We can right easy prove whether it is or *isn't*," Waco declared and looked at where the bulky owner of the saloon was aproaching. "Would you check over the cards and this gent for us, Mr. Shafto?"

"There's no call for either," the owner asserted. "They're a house deck and I've been by a couple times watching how they was used."

"Just the same," the blond youngster drawled, glancing at Roxton. "What's been said about this gent and Miz Freddie, I reckon's how it's better proved so *nobody's* got any doubts."

Wise beyond his years, the youngster was aware that what he had said would be repeated around the town. He knew there some of the population who did not approve of Freddie's competent administration as mayor and resented the possibility of the British Government being involved in the making of the spur-line to Canada. They would be eager to use anything which might show her, or a member of the British Railroad Commission, in a bad light. In fact, he had noticed one of her most frequent critics on both counts was watching and listening with great interest. Medium sized and undistinguished looking, albeit well dressed, Bruce Millan could be counted upon to shed doubts unless these were refuted completely before they were uttered.

"I agree, sir," the English aristocrat asserted. "And I'm willing to let myself be subjected to any tests you feel are necessary."

"*You* can do it, Waco," Joel Collins suggested, making the offer in his capacity as the trail boss who had brought the other Texans in the game to Mulrooney. "We've been hearing tell how well Frank Derringer's been teaching you and'd like to see what you've learned."

"Go to it, deputy," Shafto agreed. "Whatever you say'll be good enough for me."

"And me," Sam Bass seconded.

"I've not the *slightest* objection to whoever is satisfactory to the rest of you gentlemen making the examination," Roxton declared, giving Waco a smile and nod which indicated he understood why the suggestion of a check was made. "Carry on, old boy."

"You and Mr. Millan's *amigo* over there'd best watch to make sure I do it right," Waco suggested, nodding to the gambler seated at the table with the man he had named.

Waiting until the gambler came over, the youngster conducted a thorough examination. First he subjected the deck of cards to the tests he had been taught by Derringer to ensure they were not marked, then handed them to Millan's crony for verification. This was given and he turned his attention to Roxton. Although he felt certain he would find nothing, he checked as he had been instructed for hidden cards identical to those in play, or devices to help make them. Neither were forthcoming, so he looked at the aristocrat's hands. These proved to be devoid of the stains which always showed when "daubing" was carried out and neither the signet ring nor the fingernails were suitable for making secret signs of identification.[4]

"*Nothing,*" the youngster declared, after concluding an examination which none of the professional gamblers in the room could have faulted. "Do you gents *agree?*"

"He's *clean,*" Shafto supported and Millan's crony gave reluctant concurrence.

"*We* never thought it'd be otherwise," Collins stated, then glanced pointedly at the cousins. "You pair look a mite peeked, so you'd best head to bed and get some sleep. We're pulling out in the morning."

"Do you fancy some more poker, friend?" Bass inquired and, remembering how he and Collins had used their acquaintance with Ginger to get the Englishman into the game, he went on ruefully. "Although, way you play, I'm not sure's how that's a good idea."

"No thank you, much as I enjoyed the game," Roxton replied, but his manner was polite. Wanting to indicate the refusal was not caused by the incident, he gestured to the red haired girl and continued, "I've kept Ginger waiting *far* too long. However, I never like to leave the table a winner. So take what's there and buy drinks as far as it will go."

"Everybody looks satisfied, 'cepting maybe Mr. Millan and his tinhorn," the Kid commented as he and his companion were going towards the main entrance. They had received an assurance from Collins that Murphy and Hogg would not try to take the matter further and watched the Englishman leave with Ginger while the others players—including the cousins —went to the bar to partake of his largesse. "You handled things real good, boy."

"When *don't* I?" Waco replied, but he was clearly pleased by the praise. "Tell you what though, Lon. Happen Joel Collins and Sam Bass don't learn to play poker, they're going to lose a heap more than they can afford one of these days."

If either had remembered the comment some time later, when hearing that Joel Collins and Sam Bass were wanted for trying to recoup gambling losses by committing an armed robbery, the Kid would have decided his companion was a pretty fair prophet.

---

[4] *Fuller details of the checks used to detect marked cards and other crooked gambling ploys can be found in various volumes of the* Floating Outfit, Waco, Calamity Jane *and* Waxahachie Smith *series.*

As it was, the two deputies had kept the peace and prevented an incident which might have had an adverse effect upon the negotiations between the British Railroad Commission and Todhunter. Now they were going to carry on with the task they had been given in the assurance that there was nothing further to worry about at the Longhorn Saloon.

CHAPTER ELEVEN

Talk To Me, Amigo

"Well just take a look at who-all we have here, boy," the Ysabel Kid requested, sounding delighted, as he and the blond youngster stepped from an alley to confront a man approaching in the light thrown by the window of a general store about half an hour after they had left the Longhorn Saloon.

"I'm *looking*," Waco replied, his voice holding a similar timbre of well simulated pleasure, although he would not have accepted the appellation given by his black clad companion from anybody else except the other members of the Mulrooney town marshal's office. They all treated him like a favourite younger brother and he often wondered when, if ever, he would cease to be "boy" to them. "Isn't he just the sight for sore eyes, Lon?"

"You don't have no right to keep a-hounding me!" asserted the man about whom the comments were made, ensuring he kept both hands in plain sight and away from his sides. His voice had a whining Chicago accent and, glancing around as if contemplating flight or seeking assistance, he continued, "I ain't *never* done *nothing* wrong!"

If David "Mousey" Nellist had had the slightest inkling that he might meet any of the local peace officers and that pair in particular, he would have taken very rapid steps to avoid doing so. Not that, as he claimed, he had any reason to fear apprehension for some criminal act. His disinclination to make contact with them stemmed from knowing they, as had lawmen in every other place he had been, frequently sought him out for information regarding illicit activities in their bailiwick. He did not have the slightest moral objections to supplying such news when it came his way. In fact, he spent much of his time seeking it. However, he preferred to pick his own time and place for imparting what he had discovered. By doing so, he could often obtain a better price for his wares.

Small, skinny, his thin and vicious looking face having protruding teeth which in part accounted for his sobriquet, Nellist gave the impression of being some kind of less likeable rodent. For once his attire gave a suggestion of modest affluence. However, his selection would not have struck many peo-

ple as being the epitome of sartorial elegance. A pearl grey
derby intended for a larger man perched at the back of a head
with black hair going thin on top. He had on a lime-green shirt
with an attachable white celluloid collar marred by a couple of
fingermarks, a black and white three-piece check suit which
"fit where it touched" and ox-blood red Hersome gaiter boots.
Being so diminutive, a noticeable bulge could be detected
under the left side of his jacket where a revolver of some kind
rode in a shoulder holster. There was a thick chain, which
might have passed for gold if bits had not flaked away to
expose a baser metal underneath the gilt, extending slackly
between the pockets of his vest. He reeked of the cheapest
brand of bay rum and a somewhat wilted red flower sprouted
from his buttonhole, but neither did anything to improve an
aspect more garish than tasteful.

"And wasn't neither of us said's how you *had*," the Kid
pointed out, in a voice so mild and caressing the tiny man
knew it boded no good for him. "Talk to me, *amigo*. That's all
I ask."

"T—*Talk?*" Nellist asked, sounding as if he had never
heard the word. His right arm was grasped in a way which
would have prevented him from drawing the newly acquired
four shot Colt Model of 1871 "Cloverleaf Cylinder" House
Pistol revolver from its open-fronted spring retention shoulder
holster, even if he had contemplated such a piece of folly
while in his present company. Reluctantly starting to walk
between the Texans into the dark shadows of the alley, he
went on, "What do you want me to talk about?"

"Any old thing's comes to mind," the Kid answered, his
manner obliging. It had taken some time to find the tiny man,
but he suspected having done so would prove worthwhile.
"Not the birds, the bees 'n' the flowers, though. Waco's still a
mite young for *that*. Which being, tell us about how the
weather looks to you. The price of beef. Which gal's doing
the best business down to Mrs. Gouch's fancy-house. Where
you get them real high-toned clothes, seeing's how I bet's
Mark'd surely like some just the same. Or, happen you're so
minded—who-all's behind those jaspers who tried to grab off
Miss Freddie Woods?"

"How would I know *that?*" Nellist almost wailed, having
noticed how the bantering tone had taken on an edge like steel
as the final sentence was uttered.

"Mousey, *Mousey,*" the black clad Texan purred, the response he had elicited convincing him that he and his companion had come to the right source to satisfy their curiosity. "How do I know my old Nigger-hoss's white?"

"Don't tell me's how you reckon Lon's a liar, what he told me about you," the blond youngster put in, but there was no gentleness in his tone. "He allows there isn't an owlhoot 'tween here and Honesty John's in Brownton 'n' back the long way's you don't only know how many times a day he goes for a shit, but which page of the dreambook he uses to wipe his butt when he's through."[1]

"I wouldn't've put it's coarse as *that,* being raised right, proper 'n' respectful," the Kid asserted, with what would have been taken for prim superiority by anybody who did not know him. However, neither of his audience fell into that naive category. "But such's *allus* been my belief." He paused for a moment before going on in the manner of one paying a compliment, "'Cepting Waco's selling you *short* by all accounts. Why I do believe you know *every* crooked doings's goes on 'tween here and Kansas City and from the Canadian line down's far as the Indian Nations at the very least."

"Which being," the youngster went on. "It doesn't seem right, natural, nor possible, that you can't help us on something as's happened slap spang in your own front garden so to speak."

"I don't know *noth*—!" Nellist commenced, but the protest died away into uneasy silence. The Kid had released his arm as he started to speak. However, he found no comfort in his liberation. Steel rasped on leather and he stared at the massive blade of the James Black bowie knife which was slid from its sheath and glinted just a little in the light filtering between the buildings from the rising moon. The time had come, he concluded, to be frank. "Well, I don't know *much.*"

"Feed us crumbs," the black clad Texan requested, but the words were clearly an order as the tiny man was well aware. Flipping his knife in a spinning arc and catching its ivory hilt once more in the palm of his right hand—no mean feat as he had the Winchester Model of 1866 rifle in his left—he went on, "We're so hunger-parched for news, we'll take *anything* no matter how small."

---

[1] *Information about "Honesty John's in Brownton" is given in:* DIAMONDS, EMERALDS, CARDS AND COLTS.

"Only just you make sure they be for-real crumbs," the blond youngster advised, having produced and started to twirl his left side Army Colt rapidly on his triggerfinger. "We get *real* quick to temper should we be given *mouse*-droppings."

"Would I *lie?*" Nellist squawked, exuding what sounded like genuinely righteous indignation.

"Only should you reckon you could get away with it," the Kid declared dryly. "Which I allow you're smart enough to *know* you can't with *us*."

"Lon's part-Comanch," happen you didn't know it," Waco drawled, his tone seemingly solicitous and he returned the Colt as swiftly as it had been drawn. "Which means he can smell a lie from a mile back, even over that fancy nose-scent you're wearing."

"What I heard was those three jaspers came here to take on for somebody, only he didn't show." Nellist supplied hurriedly. "So they hired out to one of those Limey high mucky-mucks down to the Railroad House."

"Which one?" the blond demanded.

"I dunno," the tiny man replied and his voice took on a note of urgency as he reiterated, "I *don't* know and may God strike me dead if I'm lying!"

"Either He's not listening, or you're telling the truthful true," Waco assessed, having glanced at the sky in obvious anticipation. "Which, Him likely being so all fired eager to get a fine catch like you in his net afore the Devil can, I reckon you're speaking true."

"'Cepting you know *more* than you've let on," the Kid growled, sheathing the knife. "Which I'm getting quick sick of playing this game so's you can make out to all your owl-hoot *amigos* how us mean old John Laws tried to make you talk, but you slickered us by not telling *anything* we was wanting to know. Give us what you have and make it *muy pronto!*"

"Which means, happen you don't *habla* Mex', more *pronto* than just *pronto*," the blond offered, not too succinctly, being aware that they had been indulging in the kind of routine described by his *amigo*. "Give it afore I gets to five and I'm starting the count at *three*."

"Where at's the son-of-a-bitch's got away from Hampton's?" the Kid demanded, with the air of getting down to serious, no more frills, business.

"I dunno," Nellist claimed.

"Are you sure of that?" Waco challenged.

"It's like the ground's swallowed him up," Nellist countered, but apologetically, knowing he had gone as far as he dare with the two young peace officers and the suggestion in his voice that he was aggrieved by the paucity of information he had acquired was not simulated. " 'Bout all I've picked up is the message-passing was done by that young Limey softshell's Miz Freddie stopped being hoorawed by three fellers from the drive's come in yesterday. Which, knowing how co—*friendly* Cap'n Fog is with her, you can bet your life I tried for *more*."

"Had you said, '*cozy*' like you started," Waco growled, angered by what he considered to have been a near insult to two people who he greatly respected and admired. "I'd have stomped those buck teeth of your'n until they was sticking out of your butt."

"D-Don't get riled, I wasn't meaning *nothing!*" the tiny man yelped and decided there was cause to make amends. "I didn't get nothing out of him, but maybe you'll have better luck."

"You mean we should bust into the Railroad House and ask him?" the Kid suggested sardonically.

"He ain't *there,*" Nellist replied. "Fact being, where he was headed when I saw him last, you ought to be able to talk to him without *nobody* seeing you!"

"Where'd *that* be?" the black clad Texan inquired.

"Not knowing the town," Nellist answered. "He asked me where he could get some—*company.*"

"And you sent him to Mrs. Gouch's fancy-house, for shame," Waco guessed.

"Nope," the tiny man denied. "She don't have the kind of *company* he wanted. You know what them soft-shells're like. It's '*hims*' they fancy, not gals."

"You couldn't have sent him anywhere 'round Mulrooney for *that!*" Waco declared, having any normal man's revulsion for the kind of sexual deviation implied by the informer.

"I told him where I'd heard tell there *used* to be one of 'em," Nellist asserted. "Fact being, it's where *you'll* know how to find i—!"

"Those god-damned buck teeth are getting closer to your butt by the second!" the blond growled, the words having been directed specifically at him.

"Take it *easy*, I didn't mean it *that* way!" the tiny man yelped hurriedly, alarmed by the anger with which he was addressed. "It's where you took down Tricky Dick Cansole and everybody knows he was a no-bullfighter, even though he ain't there no more."[2]

"You mean you took that jasper's money and sent him *there?*" the Kid demanded, feeling sure the information had not been given without payment. "I'll say one thing for you, Mousey, you're one of a kind. There just *couldn't* be another."

"That's for sure," Waco agreed, his good humour restored by learning of the destination supplied by the little man. "When the Good Lord made you, he threw the *mouldy* away."

Striding through the moonlight, Shaun Ushermale was in far from a pleasant frame of mind!

Left to his own devices, the young Englishman had gone in search of the kind of company he always selected when finding time hanging heavily on his hands. Being unfamiliar with the town, he had had no idea where to start looking. Bruce Millan had stated a disinclination to receive further visits, even of a social nature, which ruled him out as a source of information. However, calling at a small saloon, he had found what appeared to be the solution to his problem.

To have been made appear foolish in such a fashion would have been bad enough by itself, but for it to happen at the hands of a terribly dressed and miserable smelling little wretch, all too clearly one of the "little people" Ushermale disdained while pretending to admire, to whom he had given money made the feeling far worse. On his arrival at the big house where he had been assured he would find the kind of sexual relationship he sought, the door had been opened by a large and formidable looking *nun*.

It had taken Ushermale a few seconds to realize he had been sent to a convent and not a home of an obliging homosexual!

Such was the young Englishman's sense of fury and humiliation, he did not notice the two tall figures approaching along the alley he had entered until he was addressed by the one in all black clothing.

---

[2] *The incident, an early example of Waco's flair for deductive reasoning, is recorded in:* THE MAKING OF A LAWMAN.

"Where at's that son-of-a-bitch's you sent to grab off Miss Woods?"

"I—I don't know what you mean!" Ushermale stated, but with more alarm than conviction.

"Then we'll likely have to sort of jog your remembering," the slightly taller of the pair warned.

"D—Don't you dare *touch* me!" the Englishman wailed, trying to turn and run, but finding his legs would not obey the dictates of his mind. However, regardless of the disparagement he generally expressed for officers of the law, he gained a little heart from seeing both of the men wore badges on what he would have called their waistcoats, "If you do, *Sir Michael Dinglepied* will take up the matter with your superiors."

"Would you be the boot-cleaner for this Sir Michael what-the-hell-you-said," the Ysabel Kid inquired.

"I'm Sir Michael's confidential secretary," Ushermale corrected, annoyed at it having been implied he held a menial position.

"Then we'd best go ask *him*," Waco suggested.

"*No!*" the Englishman close to shrieked, aware of just how inadvisable such a visit might prove.

"*Yes!*" the blond corrected, realizing the objection was made with a greater vehemence than the situation appeared to warrant on the surface and passing his supposition to the Kid in the kind of Spanish spoken along the Rio Grande.

"Could be," the black clad Texan admitted, employing the same dialect with an even greater fluency. "He's too riled for it just to be over what he's been out looking to do. Way he talks about his boss, I'd say they're the same kind and it wouldn't make no never-mind to his "sir-ship" that his hired man goes for boys not girls. Like's not, he's so inclined his-self."

"Let's rile this feller up a mite and see what he does," Waco suggested and, reaching out with his right hand, reverted to English, "All right, *hombre*, we'll just head on down to the Railroad Hou—!"

"Don't *touch* me!" Ushermale screeched, pushing at the young blond and starting to turn.

The attempt at flight did not achieve its desired effect!

Caught by the shoulder with a strong set of fingers, the Englishman was pulled by a force he could not resist until he had reversed his direction. Almost immediately, a rock hard fist crashed against the side of his jaw and he went sprawling helplessly on his back. Through the whirling mists and eruptions of brilliant lights which seemed to be filling his head, he heard the hateful voice of the black clad "detective"; as the absence of uniforms caused him to assume the pair must be.

"Striking a duly swored and 'pointed officer of the law 'n' trying to escape arrest. Them's crimes against this here fine town of Mulrooney, *Deputy Marshal* Waco."

"You're forgetting being like to bust one of the said duly swored 'n' appointed officer's fist with his jaw, *Deputy Marshal* Lon," the second went on. "Feller like that's a menace to decent folks. I reckon it's our duty to haul him down to the hoosegow, afore he does any more damage."

"You do it, boy," the Kid instructed. "I'll go 'n' tell his boss what's happened to him."

"Trust *you* to hog the best chore, *amigo*," Waco complained through force of habit. "I'm sure his 'sir-ship' would want to know."

CHAPTER TWELVE

They'd Never Believe You

"What the devil are *you* doing in here?" Sir Michael Dinglepied demanded, albeit in a quavering tone, having turned and looked in alarm from one to the other of the hard-faced men he had found in the sitting-room of his suite at the Railroad House Hotel. Even when he was not quivering with fear, he was far from being a particularly distinguished or impressive figure. Nor did wearing a formal evening dress improve his usual slovenly appearance. Sucking in a nervous gulp of breath, he went on with no greater spirit, "G—Get out, or I'll call the ma—!"

The baronet had just returned from a lengthy and expensive dinner paid for by a group of local businessmen. Although receiving a free meal of such quality always put him in as near an amiable frame of mind as he ever attained, especially when it was paid for by what he often referred to in speeches as "bloated capitalists," this had all ebbed away quickly. He was silently cursing himself for having entered backwards, so he could keep watch on the other members of the British Railroad—having a full measure of the paranoid hatred his kind were already developing towards the United States, he insisted upon saying "Railway"—Commission who had come upstairs with him and closed the door when one glanced his way. Now he was wishing that he had left it open.

"You *won't* do no such thing," corrected Hugo "Camb" Camberwell with complete assurance, crossing the room quickly. Taking the key from Dinglepied's unresisting fingers, he turned it in the lock and dropped it into the side pocket of his wolfskin jacket he was now wearing. "'Cause, even happen we didn't stop you real mean sudden afore you could get out, we're the fellers's *you* had hired to grab that Limey gal from the Fair Lady."

"I—I don't know what you're talking about!" Dinglepied bluffed. Then he remembered something he had heard over dinner. "Oh no you *aren't*. I was told only *one* of you got away."

"So I lied a smidgin," Camberwell replied, showing no sign of being abashed over the deception. He waved a hand towards the thickset and medium tall bearded man in dirty range clothes who was sitting at the table. "But Jasp here needs to light a shuck like I do and, seeing's how him 'n' me's been good friends from way back, I reckoned you'd be right pleasured to help him on his way along of me."

"You want *me* to help *you?*" the baronet queried, being extremely parsimonious by nature and never offering to donate any of the considerable fortune he had inherited to help finance the various schemes he put forward for "improving the lot" of what he always referred to as the "down-trodden masses" of the working class. Furthermore, despite his usual willingness to give vocal support to any criminal with a complaint against the police, he had never done anything positive to assist one personally and saw no reason why he should start in a foreign country. "Why tha—!"

"I conclude you don't have no other choice but help us," Camberwell claimed, returning to the table and pouring a drink from the decanter of brandy the baronet had had concealed in the cupboard of the sidepiece to avoid having to share it with visitors. "Happen we get caught, 'specially by them beefhead bastard's're running the law hereabouts, we're just natural' going to have to tell 'em's how it was *you* paid us to grab the Woods gal."

"Th—They'd *never* believe you!" Dinglepied croaked, watching the bearded man take and further deplete the contents of the decanter and resenting the visible evidence that at least part of his quarters had been searched and pillaged in such a fashion.

"Are you willing to *bet* on it?" Camberwell challenged in a mocking tone.

"They won't take *your* word against *mine!*" the baronet asserted, but his voice lacked conviction as he realized he would pretend to believe any story, no matter how blatantly untrue, if doing so served his own ends.

"All you have to do is go over to that talking tube there, whistle up the jasper at the desk and tell him to fetch the John Laws a-running," the burly hard-case pointed out, indicating the voice pipe attached to the wall and serving as a means of communication with the receptionist of the hotel. "You'll right soon find out whether you're right, or I am."

"Being in the pokey here ain't over bad, what I've heard," Jasp commented jovially, wiping a dirty hand across his lips.

Having given a massive belch, he elaborated, "Least-wise they feed you well and regular."

"I—I *think* I may be able to help you," Dinglepied began, realizing—although he had never indulged in games of chance, because he was afraid of losing even a portion of his money—his bluff had been called.

"I *know* you're sure as shitting going to help us," Camberwell corrected. "Because, mister, my mother didn't raise no son to go to jail; 'specially for as long as the British gal's tame judge'd send me."

"I—I'm not a *rich* man—!" the baronet commenced, as he invariably did when a call was made upon his purse.

"If you ain't, you'll do until one's is rich comes along," the burly hard-case interrupted dryly. "So you can have some of the cash you've got stashed away in the safe downstairs fetched up."

"And some grub while you're at it," Jasp added. "We ain't been able to go out for a meal and I'm hungry."

"H—How long have you been here?" Dinglepied asked, throwing a nervous look at the drapes covering the window. Then, although he realized such could not have been the case, he went on. "Did *anybody* see you coming in here?"

"Now is that *likely?*" Camberwell scoffed, studying the cringing figure before him in a less than flattering fashion. "We'd followed that boy of your'n here, knowing he didn't have sense nor sand enough to be the boss and found out he's working for you 'n' which room you was in. After I got away, I hid up out of town where Jasp was waiting with our spare hosses. Then, soon's it got dark enough, we snuck in again 'n' come up the back stairs when wasn't *nobody* around to see us."

"B—B—But I locked the door when I went down to dinner," Dinglepied objected.

"And we opened it again," Camberwell answered, having acquired sufficient skill at picking locks to have found little difficulty in gaining admission.

"Ain't no call for you to stand wetting your pants, *mister,*" the bearded man declared derisively, studying with amusement the consternation being displayed by the unprepossessing baronet. "*Nobody,* 'cepting us three, knows we're here and we won't get bothered none afore you've done the right thing by us and we can light a shuck away from you."

"I'm getting quick sick of *talking!*" Camberwell growled

and started to stalk forward in a menacing fashion, causing Dinglepied to retreat at an angle and, being in a state of near panic, unwittingly edge along the wall away from the door."Either you get on that tube there, or I'm going to make you wish you had!"

If the three men had been able to see the front lobby of the building, they would have discovered the assessment made by Jasp was not as valid as he assumed!

"Do you have a key's'll open all the doors, Walt?" the Ysabel Kid inquired of the tall, wide shouldered, smartly dressed, albeit rugged looking, young clerk on duty at the reception desk.

"A pass-key, you mean?" Walter Braithwaite suggested in his Bostonian accent, but amiably and not in the manner of displaying superior wisdom to one he considered a social inferior. "Certainly, Kid. Who do you want to—*visit*—unannounced?"

"Well now," the black clad Texan drawled. "I sort of thought I might drop by and take a cup of Limey tea with one of them British Railroad Commission gents."

"Which one?"

"Sir Michael Ding—or some such."

"Sir Michael Dinglepied?"

"You've slapped the brand on him as neat's you won that fancy 'Boston game' you've been teaching fellers hereabouts last Saturday," the Kid declared. "Air that his for *real* name?"

"I had to have to win," Braithwaite corrected, grinning at the memory of the game of football which he had organized had hoped would become a regular feature of the town's sporting activities.[1] "And 'Sir Michael *Dinglepied*' has to be for *real*. Nobody would pick it for a summer name."

"Which room's he in?" the Texan asked.

"One-Eleven, on the second floor to the left along the pas-

---

[1] Being based upon a variant of soccer first played in the British Isles at Rugby public school during 1823, the "Boston game" and other regional varieties in the United States would evolve into the highly organized professional and amateur game of "American," or "gridiron" football. Becoming popular at various Eastern colleges and universities, with the main emphasis being on kicking although carrying the ball was becoming an accepted tactic, it was played on occasion with up to twenty-five men in each team.

sage," the clerk supplied. "There's one thing, though."

"What'd that be?" the Kid inquired.

"If you're expecting to get a cup of tea from him, Limey or otherwise," the clerk answered dryly, having formed a very accurate assessment of the man they were discussing's character. "you'd best make sure you've got enough money on hand to *pay* for it."

"He's that tight with his money, huh?"

"He's so tight, if he was a diving duck no water would get up his butt while he was under."

"I'll bear it in mind," the Kid promised, so soberly he might have received information of great importance.

"Here's the pass key," Braithwaite said, reaching to take the required object from its place on a hook inside the desk without inquiring why it was needed.

"Can I have that drinking glass of your'n as well?" the Texan requested. "I'll leave my Ole Yellowboy here in trade."

"I'm getting the *worst* of the bargain," the clerk claimed, but he accepted the Winchester Model of 1866 rifle and handed over the tumbler, once more refraining from showing curiosity.

"Gracias, amigo," the Texan thanked.

"Es nada," the clerk replied, having learned the correct response in Spanish. "Hey though, seeing as I've given you the key and glass, how about joining my team in next week's Boston game?"

"Not *me,* thank you 'most to death!" the Kid refused emphatically. "It's *way* too dangerous for a delicate lil old boy from Texas like me."

"What a *pity,"* Braithwaite smiled.

"Is his sir-ship up to his room?" the Texan asked, tossing the key he had received up and down in his left hand.

"Yes," the clerk confirmed. "I saw him going up about five minutes ago."

"Then I'll drift on up and say, 'Howdy, you-all, your sir-ship.'"

"There is just one *small* thing about using the key—!"

"Tell it and it's your'n," the Texan asserted, knowing he did not need to issue a warning against having his impending arrival announced over the speaking tube after he had left the lobby.

"I know it's not likely to happen, dealing with the likes of him," Braithwaite explained. "But I hope you don't have to start shooting off that *cannon* you persist in carrying instead of a *revolver*."

"You've been listening to that blasted Mark 'n' Waco," the Kid accused. His insistence upon retaining the massive old Colt Model of 1848 Dragoon revolver, despite there being lighter—albeit not quite so potent in the matter of the acceptable powder charge—handguns manufactured by the same Company available, was a frequent cause of friendly criticism from his *amigos*. Slapping the worn walnut grips with his right palm, he went on in the manner of one conferring a favour, "But I'll do my damnedest not to cut loose at his sir-ship with Granny here, less'n he shoots me *twice* in the leg first."

"Which nobody could ask for *more*," the clerk replied and turned his attention to where the member of the British Railroad Commission who had lingered after the others went upstairs was coming from the barroom with some of the local businessmen. "Do you want to go up now, or wait until after Sir John Ramage has gone to his rooms?"

"I'll go now," the Texan decided, turning his gaze to give the tall, bronzed, hawk-faced and immaculately attired middle-aged Englishman a quick scrutiny. Although he liked what he saw, he went on, "It'll take 'em a spell to say their goodnights I reckon and Dusty don't like his hired help spending time in what he calls loafin 'n' idleness."

"There's *some* might say Captain Fog has right good sense," Braithwaite claimed, but his words were directed at the back of the Kid's shirt.

Going upstairs with swift strides, the Texan went to the room for which he had been supplied with the number. Glancing in each direction to make sure he was not being observed, although the passage was deserted, he placed the top of the tumbler against the door and rested his ear against the base.

"Well I'll be switched," the Kid breathed after a moment. "Belle was *right*, not's I thought she wouldn't be. You *can* hear through one of these things.[2]

Even while the thought was passing through his head, the Texan decided the conclusion reached by Waco was correct!

Although he arrived as Camberwell was making the threat,

---

[2] *The lady in question was Belle "the Rebel Spy" Boyd. For her connection with the Ysabel Kid, see:* APPENDIX THREE.

but had missed the comment from Jasp which preceded it, the Kid did not wait to hear any more!

On the point of drawing his Colt, the Texan remembered the promise he had made to Braithwaite. Grinning slightly, which caused all the misleading suggestion of innocence to leave his Indian dark features and transform them into the mask of the *Pehnane* Comanche dog soldier—to which war lodge of exceptionally competent fighting men he had won admittance as a boy—preparing to make war, he slid free the James Black bowie knife. Holding the concave hand-fitting ivory hilt in his right fist, with which he also contrived to grasp the doorknob, he put the pass-key to use. Feeling sure the click made by the lock would not go unnoticed, he made no attempt to effect a surreptitious entry. Instead, the instant he felt the action of the lock being manipulated, he twisted at the knob.

Nothing happened!

At least, there was no movement to suggest the knob was performing its function!

However, even as the Kid was about to let loose and deliver a kick which he hoped would serve his purpose, the lock clicked. Instantly, he felt the door begin to move inwards. There was no time for him to realize the hotel had had the catch portion of the knob removed so that guests could gain access with greater ease when inebriated or incapacitated in some other way. Giving a vigorous shove, the moment there was sufficient space, he thrust himself into the room.

At the sight of the door being thrown open in such a fashion and the black dressed figure coming through, Camberwell did not need to notice the badge of office on the vest or the big knife to realize what was portended by the unannounced visit. He had seen such entrances performed by peace officers in the past and, under less exacting conditions, might have conceded few had been done better. Giving no thought to such distinctions, he forgot his intention to compel the cringing baronet to supply the money needed for his escape from Mulrooney. Instead, he reacted by sending his right hand towards the butt of his low hanging Colt Army Model of 1866 revolver.

The move was made with considerable speed and would have succeeded against many an opponent!

Unfortunately for Camberwell, he was up against an exception!

Much as he would have preferred to take a living prisoner,

the Kid realized this would not be possible under the circumstances. To have attempted to do so would almost certainly have cost him his own life. Therefore, moving with the deadly rapidity and precision indicative of long practise in wielding the big knife, he responded in a manner which would have gladdened the hearts of his *Pehnane* Comanche warrior ancestors on his mother's side.

Around lashed the eleven and a half inch long, two and a half wide, clip point blade, sparkling in the light of the large lamp suspended from the ceiling. Having an edge many a barber would have admired for a razor to be used while shaving an influential customer, the cutting surface passed beneath Camberwell's chin and sank into his throat an instant before his Colt came clear of leather. It was a mortal wound, delivered with a force which slashed through his windpipe as well as the veins and arteries of the neck.

The impact also caused its recipient to stagger sideways involuntarily, giving a strangled incoherent bellow of anguish which caused blood to gush from his mouth as well as out of the terrible gash in his flesh. What was more, his instinctive adherence to the sensible habit of refraining from starting to cock the hammer and keeping his forefinger out of the trigger-guard while the weapon had remained in leather was not as beneficial as previously.[3] Although he had raised the gun above the lip of the holster, even if he could have elevated the barrel towards his assailant, he would not have been able to shoot.

"*A:he!*" the Kid grunted, as he often did involuntarily when handling a knife in combat brought back memories of the training he had received from his maternal grandfather during his childhood amongst the *Pehnane* Comanche.[4][4a]

Despite having disposed of the more immediate menace,

[3] *For an example of how dangerous a failure to take such a precaution could be, see:* THE FAST GUN.

[4] *"A:he," "I claim it;" the coup cry given by a Comanche warrior when striking down an enemy, or—preferably—laying a hand upon one while he was still alive. For a description of the ritual being carried out in the latter fashion, see:* IS-A-MAN.

[4a] *Details of the education received by the Ysabel Kid from his maternal grandfather, Chief Long Walker of the Peh-nane Comanche see:* APPENDIX THREE *and, in greater detail,* COMANCHE.

the Texan realized he was far from being out of danger!

Knowing only one of the three hard-cases involved had escaped after the thwarted abduction of Freddie Woods and having arrived too late to hear Jasp speaking, the Kid had thought only two men would be present, and he discounted the baronet as posing an additional potentially dangerous factor needing to be overcome. Unfortunately, having just missed hearing something while eavesdropping which would have given an indication of the true state of affairs, he had been unaware of exactly what he would be facing when he made his entrance. However, he needed only a single glance to warn him of what he would be up against.

As soon as he saw the door being opened so precipitously, the bearded hard-case had started to thrust himself from the chair in which he had been lounging. However, not only did he lack his companion's speed in normal conditions, he was feeling the effects of the brandy he had found and been drinking in a greater quantity than was wise with such a potent liquor. While he was not sufficiently drunk to be incapable, he was under the influence to an extent which rendered him less speedy than usual. When dealing with a man like the Ysabel Kid, that was far from being a condition to ensure success!

Knowing he could not hope to cross the room and reach his intended assailant quickly enough for his needs, the Kid did not try. Instead, whipping back his right hand, he hurled the knife. It flashed through the air with awesome speed. Even as Jasp realized the danger, it was too late for him to do anything to avert it in his slightly befuddled condition. Like Camberwell, he had removed his hat on entering the room. If he had followed his more usual habit of keeping it on even when indoors, he might have saved himself.

Driven with the full impetus the wiry, steel-muscled body of the Kid was capable of producing, the knife made contact at the centre of the bearded man's forehead. Such was the excellent quality of the steel and the superb balance James Black had imparted during its manufacture, it was able to cope with the thin bone at the front of the skull. Forcing its way onwards, it buried into his brain and killed him as instantaneously as would a bullet to the same area. The path was to some extent opened by the needle-sharp point, then expanded with the aid received from the last few inches of the otherwise unsharpened "back" of the blade joining and forming an extension of the main cutting surface in a concave arc. Jerking backwards in a purely automotive reaction, his hands rising involuntarily as if trying to pluck out the knife, he struck the chair from which he had risen. Disintegrating under his weight, it precipitated his already lifeless body to the floor.

Despite having hoped to produce such an effect, the Texan had not waited long enough to ascertain the success of his throw. Instead, the moment the knife left his grasp, his right hand dipped down. Turning palm outwards, it wrapped about the walnut handle and twisted the old Dragon Colt from the well designed black holster. However, by the time he had thumb-cocked the action, he concluded the weapon would not be needed except to induce the already frightened Englishman to supply self-incriminating evidence with regards to the attempted abduction.

Hearing voices raised in the passage and the sound of hurrying footsteps, the Texan realized with a sense of annoyance that the opportunity to deal with Dinglepied as he wished would not be granted!

"God damn the luck!" the Kid breathed. "Well, at least I didn't have to shoot off ole Granny here!"

CHAPTER THIRTEEN

He Saved My Life

"What the blazes is going on here?" demanded a masculine voice with a British upper class accent far more authoritative then the somewhat nasal whine of Sir Michael Dinglepied.

Having come upstairs to show the local businessmen some documents to do with the proposed railroad, instead of lingering over saying goodnight in the lobby as the Ysabel Kid had evisaged, Sir John Uglow Ramage had reached the passage in time to hear the gruesome cry given by Hugo "Camb" Camberwell. His career in the diplomatic service had been far from desk-bound and sedentary. Experiences during native uprisings in India and South Africa had taught him the meaning of the sound which came to his ears. Therefore, even though he disliked the other baronet intensely, he had not hesitated before coming to investigate.

Striding through the still wide open door, having moved more swiftly than the man accompanying him, Ramage swept his keen gaze around. First, he glanced briefly to where Dinglepied was huddled against the wall facing a corner and vomiting unrestrainedly. Next, he gave as quick a scrutiny to the body lying just inside the room. There was no need for a close or longer examination to know death had been caused by the throat being cut almost to the depth of the neck bones. Finally, he took in the sight of the tall, black dressed young figure retrieving an enormous blood-smeared knife from the skull of a second corpse lying supine beyond the table. His stomach felt decidedly queasy, despite this not being his first contact with sudden and violent death, but he was made of far sterner stuff than the other baronet.

"What's happened, deputy?" yelled the businessmen who had suggested employing torture to Mark Counter during the meeting in the Fair Lady Saloon on the day of his arrival in Mulrooney, looking over Ramage's shoulder and anticipating the question he was on the point of asking.

"Trouble!" replied the Kid bluntly, but did not elaborate. Instead, his voice took on a polite timbre which nevertheless indicated he expected to be obeyed. "I'd be *obliged* happen you gents'd wait outside while I talk with Sir John and his sir—the feller's rooming here."

"That will be best, gentlemen," the taller baronet supported, grateful the suggestion had come from the very young and innocent looking—albeit somehow dangerous-seeming—peace officer. He did not know what had happened, but had no wish for anything untoward in which Dinglepied had become involved to be discussed in the presence of their hosts for dinner. "Perhaps you would like to wait in the bar and have a drink or so on me until I can join you?"

"We'll do that, John," a local businessman promised, having learned the taller baronet preferred the prefix, "Sir" to be deleted when being addressed informally. Living in Mulrooney, he was better acquainted than the previous speaker with the Kid and willing to oblige on that account. "Come on, Sid, fellers, let's leave the deputy 'tend to his duty."

"Well, young man," Ramage said, after his hosts-cum-guests had retired and the door was closed. "I'd say this requires an *explanation.*"

"In more ways than one," the Kid agreed, but was not allowed to continue.

"H—He saved my *life,* Ramage!" Dinglepied asserted, turning around and walking forward on unsteady legs. His face was still ashy grey and, if possible, more unpleasant than usual as he quelled the desire of his stomach to continue the vomiting and went on, "I found those two here when I came back from dinner. They said they'd come to rob and kill me. I was afraid they would do, but this fine young man came to my rescue."

Although nauseated by what he had seen, such violent happenings having been something he had not previously encountered, the shorter baronet had had time to think while huddled in the corner and retching the contents of his stomach over the floor. He could not imagine how it happened, but he suspected that the black clad "detective" had learned of his connection with the first of the men to die. However, he hoped to be able to dispel the suggestion when it was levelled and had set about paving the way.

"You're to be *commended,*" Ramage informed the Kid, his tone unemotional although a cynical smile had twisted briefly at his lips as he had listened to the shorter baronet say, "a fine young man" and compared it with the less flattering references he had frequently heard made about law enforcement officers from the same source. *"Deputy,* isn't it?"

"Deputy town marshal, *sir,"* the Texan confirmed, deciding his original summations with regards to the tall Englishman showed no sigh of being incorrect.

"How did you come to be here so fortuitously, deputy?" Ramage inquired.

"Just *fortunate,* I reckon," the Kid replied, realizing the explanation given by Dinglepied might seem acceptable to anybody who was not conversant with the true facts and wanting to discuss these with Freddie Woods and Dusty Fog before telling even the tall baronet.

"Very *fortunate* for you, Dinglepied," Ramage commented dryly. "You're not looking any too good, old thing."

"I d—don't *feel* any too good!" the shorter baronet admitted, which was true enough as far as it went. Despite suspecting the remark had only been made in a sense of malicious mischief, he saw how it might offer a way of avoiding further embarrassing and perhaps even incriminating questions. "Th —Those m—men—The way they di—!"

"Most *distressing,* I'm sure," Ramage consoled, although his voice held little sympathy. Aware that Dinglepied was one of those most vocal in favour of abolishing corporal and capital punishment, he went on sardonically, "Of course, it's probably saved the expense of trying and *hanging* them."

A shrill whistle came from the speaking tube before any more could be said. Giving the smaller baronet no time to speak or move, the Kid crossed over and picked it up.

"It's Wal—the desk clerk, for me," the Texan reported, having removed the plug made of cork from the brass tip of the tube and listening to the voice at the other end. Then he spoke into the mouthpiece, *"Gracias, amigo.* I'll stay put until he gets here and you'd best have a couple of swampers standing by, there's a mite of cleaning up needs doing in here." He transferred the device to his ear for a moment, then resumed talking down it. "No, you wouldn't've heard no *shooting.* Didn't I promise you *faithful* I wouldn't start using ole Granny?"

"I thought somebody would talk when they got downstairs," Ramage remarked, restraining his curiosity over the last part of the conversation.

"They did," the Kid confirmed, returning the speaking tube to its holder on the wall. "Wa—the desk clerk allows he's sent for Cap'n Fog."

"I'm pleased to hear it," the taller baronet claimed. "Not that I'm belittling *you,* deputy, of course."

"I—I've got to get out of here!" the shorter baronet gasped and, although having a desire to avoid being subjected to further interrogation, his distress was far from being simulated.

"Why don't you go down to the bar and see if a drink or two will put you to rights before Captain Fog gets here?" Ramage suggested. "You can charge them to *me.*"

"I—I *never* let intoxicating liquor, or tobacco, sully my lips!" Dinglepied claimed, contriving to sound pompously righteous.

"Then you'd better go—!" the taller baronet offered, darting a pointed glance at the almost empty decanter on the table and deciding it confirmed his suspicions that the other was a secret drinker in spite of repeatedly denouncing the "evils" of alcohol and smoking.

"Into the bedroom?" the shorter asked, starting to turn in the appropriate direction.

"I was going to say the bathroom along the passage," Ramage corrected and swung his gaze deliberately to the patch of nausea by the wall. "I'm *sure* you wouldn't want to put the hotel's *workers* to the unpleasant task of cleaning up any more of *that.*"

"N—No!" Dinglepied conceded, although the thought had not crossed his mind and, even having had it brought to his attention, being entirely uncaring about how unpleasant a task of cleaning he had made for the staff of the hotel. "Of course *not!*"

"Then toddle off to the bathroom, old thing," the taller baronet ordered rather than merely suggested. "Stay there until we let you know those chaps have been moved and things tidied up. Shall I call Ushermale to give you a hand?"

"He's gone out for the evening." Dinglepied answered, scowling at the reminder of his confidential secretary's absence. Then a stronger sensation assailed his stomach and, clutching at it, he gasped, "I—I'd bet—go!"

"*Poor* little man," Ramage remarked, still without giving any discernible suggestion of whether he was expressing genuine or false sympathy. Having watched the shorter baronet scuttle from the room, he turned his attention inwards. "Just how *fortunate* was it that you happened to be here, deputy?"

"We go 'round all the hotels on occasion," the Kid lied. "Just to make sure everything's kept nice and quiet."

"And you're always given the pass-key?" the baronet said sardonically, gesturing towards the still open door.

"We couldn't get into a room, was we needed, without one," the Texan countered.

"That's *logical*," Ramage conceded, his hawk-like tanned face showing no expression. "But what made you decide to come into *this* particular room?"

"I just sort of reckoned it *could* be worth looking into."

"Ah! you mean like when one of your skunk things ran through the lounge of the White Lion Hotel in Melton Mowbray one night?"

"Huh?"

"Instinct!" Ramage said, still without a change of expression. Then a frosty smile creased and made his features more amiable. "Sorry, old chap. Shouldn't make jokes after poor *Dingers* was almost robbed and foully done to death in his bed."

"*That was a joke?*" the Kid challenged, deciding he must remember the story to try on Waco.

"You should hear some of them," the baronet answered and, waving a hand which encompassed the room with its gesture, he became serious. "Would this have anything to do with the other deputy who came this afternoon to find out whether I'd written to ask Freddie Besgr—*Miss Woods* to meet me here?"

"It *could* have," the Kid replied evasively.

"Good man!" Ramage praised, nodding with what was clearly approval at the reticence shown by the black dressed young Texan. "I'll wait until Captain Fog gets here and then we can talk *freely*."

"W—What do you *want?*" Sir Michael Dinglepied asked, looking nervously at the three Texans who converged upon him as he emerged from the men's rest-room at the passenger depot.

"We heard tell's how you're leaving Mulrooney, your sirship" the Ysabel Kid explained. "And come to see was it true."

"Y—Yes," the baronet confirmed. "I—I'm not a *well* man and after last night—!"

However, despite the solicitous way in which the question had apparently been couched, Dinglepied was still uneasy. Then he noticed something which added to his instinctive belief that all was far from being as it seemed on the surface. Although they had done so at all times when he had seen them previously, not one of the "detectives"—his paranoiac dislike for the United States would not allow him to even think of them in the American fashion as "deputy town marshals"— was wearing his badge of office in plain view.

The words came to a quavering halt!

To give Dinglepied credit, the events in his room at the Railroad House Hotel the previous evening had shaken him deeply. It was not until after he was left to himself, in new accommodation as he had declared he would be unable to sleep in the bedroom of the suite even though its walls and access door would shield him from looking at where the two men had been killed, that a full appreciation of his situation had come to him. It went beyond the realization that he might really have been murdered after he was robbed by the pair.

Although nothing had been proven, the baronet had felt certain the *big* blond haired senior "detective" was far from being convinced that he was innocent of trying to arrange the abduction of Lady Winifred Amelia Besgrove-Woodstole. What was more, he was just as sure that the matter would not be allowed to end if he remained in Mulrooney. Knowing Shaun Ushermale, Dinglepied was disinclined to rely upon his continued discretion if he should be subjected to questioning of the kind which the black dressed "detective" in particular looked capable of conducting. In fact, he had stated frankly that he wanted to leave the vicinity as quickly as possible on returning after being released from arrest—with instructions to, "Go back and take care of your boss"—when the peace officers returned to the jail.

Having no faith in the loyalty of his confidential secretary, but filled with a grudging respect for the ability of the *big* blond Texan, the baronet had decided the time had come for departure even before the visit he had received that morning.

Speaking with a bluntness which startled Dinglepied, Sir John Uglow Ramage had demanded rather than suggested he retired from the British *Railway* Commission and left Mulrooney without delay. He had been aware that the other baronet belonged to a family which could exert considerably more influence in the "corridors of power" than he had ever achieved and, supplemented by the far from niggardly sums in prize money earned by Captain Lord Ramage, R.N., during the previous Century's wars against France,[1] were vastly more wealthy. Therefore, he had had no desire to antagonize such a powerful potential enemy. Stating that he intended to do so, because of "ill health," he had made immediate arrangements to go. However, he had no intention of forgetting his desire to seek revenge for the deaths of two *very* good friends and ruination of a third's career.

Arriving at the "railway station" to catch the midafternoon east-bound train, which was the earliest he could reach, the baronet had left Ushermale to organize the tickets while he went to attend to the call of nature.

Now Dinglepied was wishing he had controlled, or ignored, his bodily functions and remained with his secretary!

"You going back to England, huh, you sir-ship?" the Ysabel Kid inquired.

"Only to *Washington,*" the baronet replied, but refrained from correcting the repetition of the incorrect honorific he had been granted.

"They do say's how Washington's mighty unhealthy this time of the year," the black dressed Texan drawled and there was something in his demeanor which frightened the recipient of the information. "And could be 'specially so for *you!*"

"Are you *threatening* me?" Dinglepied queried, noticing with growing alarm that the youngest of the trio had intercepted and was preventing Ushermale from joining him and the blond giant was standing a short distance away in the other direction, stopping anybody else from coming close. "If you are, being detectives—!"

---

[1] *Details of how Captain Lord Nichols Ramage, R.N. earned two very large sums in prize money are recorded in: RAMAGE'S DIAMOND and RAMAGE'S MUTINY, by Dudley Pope.*

"We're not detectives, nor ever have been," the Kid corrected. "And, seeing's how we're not wearing our badges, we're not even peace officers right now. Which means this's just between us personal' and you. So, like I said, Washington could be 'specially unhealthy for *you.*"

"W—Why *me?*"

"Those three yahoos allowed they'd been hired by *somebody* to grab Miz Freddie and take her to Brownton to be held until she could be extradited to England and stand trial for something she's *supposed* to have done."

"I—I know *nothing* about that!" the baronet asserted, his sense of perturbation growing as he realized the three "Yankees" considered they were no longer bound by the rules which were applied to all peace officers and he did not care to contemplate what the absence of such restrictions might mean to him.

"*Somebody* does," the Kid replied. "Which me, Mark and Waco there, we're tolerable certain it was *you.*"

"How could it be?" Dinglepied asked, feeling relieved that the three men hired by Ushermale at his instigation were dead and unable to give evidence against him. "The only time I left the hotel was in company with the other members of the *Railway* Commission."

"That tame lap-dog of your'n was out and about, though," the black-clad Texan reminded. "But it doesn't make no never-mind whether you paid those yahoos or not. 'Cause they're dead and, even if we could, we wouldn't haul you to jail to stand trial's doing it would make fuss for Miss Freddie."

"Then why are you here?"

"To get something cleared up in your head."

"And what might that be?"

"You won't chance hiring no more knobheads to come after Freddie like the last time," the Kid claimed. "Which we both *know* is what you who put up that *hombre* I throat-slit 'n' coup-counted and his two *maigos* to do, no matter who-all did your talking. But you still might be hankering, you being such an upstanding believer in law 'n' justice and all, to see as how Freddie gets hauled back to Merrie Old England and put on trial for whatever it is she's done."

"I—I wouldn't do *that!*"

"But you might know somebody's *would,*" the Kid pointed

out, with justification as this had been Dinglepied's intention. "Or have some other notion."

"What kind of *notion?*" the baronet was unable to resist inquiring.

"You missed out on trying it your own way," the black dressed Texan explained and, suddenly—although Dinglepied had never seen one—his Indian dark features once again acquired the savage aspect of an angry *Pehnane* Comanche dog soldier. "So you could be figuring on having it done legal-like through your stinking soft-shell buddy, Senator Foulkes—"

"I—I—!" Dinglepied croaked, terrified by the change which had come and wondering why he could ever have thought the young looking "detective" seemed innocent. He also could not imagine how the other had learned the identity of the man with whom he was meaning to make arrangements for the extradition. "How did you kn—?"

"So listen good to me, *your sir-ship*," the Kid commanded, as if the interruption had not been made and without mentioning that Dusty had guessed who would be involved if any more legal attempts were made to bring about the purpose for which the abduction was employed. "Let just *one* more thing be even *tried* against Freddie and this whole goddamned wide world of our'n won't be big enough for you to hide in. 'Cause, *hombre,* soon's it does, *we'll* be coming after you. Which, even without calling on Dusty or Freddie, Mark's got more'n enough money of his own to let us do it." Pausing as if wishing to let what he had said so far to be absorbed, he continued with an even more chilling tone, "Then, *when* we find you, what I'll do to you, you'll wish I'd let those two sons-of-bitches in your room done *their* worst afore finishing you off. And you've got my *word*, which I've *never* yet broke', nor *ever* mean to, on *that. Sabe?*, which means, 'Do you understand?'"

"I—I *understand!*" Dinglepied confirmed, his face ashy white and he was feeling more terrified than ever before in his life, so decided that—intimate as their relationship had been —he would forget trying to take revenge in behalf of his three friends. "And you can res—!"

The assurance which the baronet had intended to give was not complete!

There was a thud, followed an instant later by the crack of a rifle shot from across the railroad line and the bullet shattered its way through Dinglepied's skull!

Almost at the same instant, there was another rifle shot from the same area!

Jerked backwards as if struck by a powerful yet invisible hand, Ushermale went sprawling on to the wooden boards of the platform with the lead in his chest!

CHAPTER FOURTEEN

You're A Mite Late

"The big jasper's still acting mean, Dusty," announced the deputy town marshal who had come from the rear section of the building which was given over to a line of cells for prisoners. "What're you going to do about the telegraph message you had from good ole Senator George Foulkes, 'friend of the under-privileged masses,' asking was it true what he'd heard about you keeping a 'fellow human being chained like an animal to the wall'?"

In spite of the badge of office he was wearing, even though his black cutaway jacket was hanging with his low crowned, wide brimmed white "planter's" hat on the rack alongside the main entrance, everything about the speaker indicated he was a successful professional gambler.

About six foot in height, with a reasonably good build suggesting hard flesh rather than the effects of dissipation, Frank "Derry" Derringer had dark hair and a neatly trimmed moustache. However, because of the manner in which he normally earned his living, his pleasant face—schooled to show only such emotions as he considered warranted by any given situation—lacked the tan of the man he was addressing. He wore a white silk shirt, with a black string bow-tie, an unfastened vest which was multihued at the front and had a glossy dark green back, slim legged grey trousers having a black stripe down the seams of the legs and black Hersome gaiter boots. Designed for a fast withdrawal of the ivory handled Colt 1860 Army Model revolver in the holster tied to his right thigh, his gunbelt was black and well cared for.

"Like I sent word back, I'll 'give the matter my *full* attention'—soon's I can find the time," Captain Dustine Edward Marsden "Dusty" Fog drawled, from where he was seated at the desk in the centre of the well equipped office.[1] He was quoting from the reply he had dispatched in response to the message to which the gambler had referred. "But, until that

---

[1] *A detailed description of the Mulrooney town marshal's office and its furnishings can be found in: THE TROUBLE BUSTERS.*

hombre settles down more peaceable, no matter how the good senator feels we're not respecting his 'rights,' or Mr. Bruce Millan comes to that, he's stopping just as he is."

"You should've said he *isn't* chained to the wall," Derringer pointed out. It was he who had learned from the telegraph operator that Millan had sent a false report to Foulkes regarding the incarceration of the man they were discussing. "And, no matter how that soft-shell son-of-a-bitch told it, he never has been."

"You don't reckon the good senator would want to believe *that,* now do you?" Dusty challenged dryly. "His kind *always* want to think the worst about *anybody* who wears a badge and to persuade everybody else to do the same."

"Huh huh!" Derringer grunted, although he agreed with what his superior had said about Foulkes.

"God damn it, Frank!" the small Texan barked, the accusation from the "liberal" politician having annoyed him far more than he cared to let anybody other than a trusted friend see. "I don't like having to keep him hawg-tied like that. It goes against *everything* my pappy taught me."

"You're treating him the only way it can be done," the gambler claimed. He knew that Dusty's father, Sheriff Hondo Fog of Rio Hondo County, was respected as a competent peace officer with a reputation for fair play and never mishandling or physically abusing prisoners without good cause. "He may be uncomfortable and not able to get around any too easy, but I figure he'd be like' to hurt himself far worse, way he throws himself at the bars, was he free."

Even though he had not been subjected to the treatment falsely ascribed by Millan, there had been no change in the hostile behaviour of the enormous bearded *Metis*. Still unable to communicate with any coherence, as a result of the damage his mouth had sustained, he had continued the attempted aggression which had caused him to have his wrists and ankles manacled. To further restrict his violent actions, there was a chain with a heavy iron ball attached to the links connecting the leg-irons. Despite this, without waiting for them to enter, he had repeatedly attempted to attack everybody who went near the cell.

"Anyway," Derringer continued, deciding a change of subject would not come amiss. "What do you reckon the Judge'll tell that mealy-mouthed law-wrangler who's been sent to represent the big jasper when he asks for a bail bond to be set?"

"What do *you* think he'll say?" the small Texan countered.

"Was I a *betting* man, which everybody nows I'm *not,*" the gambler replied, "I'd be willing to give odds's how the answer's going to be a real big and *definite,* 'Not on your cotton-picking, chicken-plucking life!'"

"No takers," Dusty refused with a smile, feeling confident the local judge would not even consider granting a bail bond where such a serious crime was involved. "And, speaking of *takers,* I've never seen Mark, Lon or Waco so all fired eager to take on the train watch."

"Could be my *good* influence has caused them to see the light, brother," Derringer suggested, in the manner of a circuit riding preacher of the worst kind extolling nonexistent virtues. "Or, more like', knowing them, they'd heard a few mighty pretty lil gals were coming in."

"Was *I* a betting man, which I've got *better* sense than be," the small Texan said dryly, suspecting the gambler was aware of the real reason and, as he had not been informed himself when the trio had announced their intention of going on the passenger depot, knowing better than to ask what it might be. In accordance with the procedure he had established, at least one of the deputies attended the arrival of every train to dissuade undesirable travellers from alighting. Nevertheless, knowing them all very well, he had felt there was something more than this involved. "I'd be willing to lay odd's high as Lon says every *Pahuraix* Comanch' bets, that it's a whole heap more like' to be the last than the first."[2]

"Tell you what, though," Derringer said, sitting at the desk and becoming more serious; although only somebody who knew him as well as did the small Texan would have noticed the change in his tone and demeanour. "I reckon I know why the big jasper's been taking on the way he has."

"Why?" Dusty inquired, having considerable faith in the

[2] *According to Comanche folklore, being inveterate gamblers, members of the Pahuraix band—their name, "Water Horse," having originated as a result of their preference for making camp alongside a stream or lake—had acquired their uncharacteristic tall and lean physical conformation as a result of having to stand and reach high to pile up the large amount of property they invariably used as stakes for bets.*

judgement developed by the gambler as an aid to the assessment of an opponent's character which was part of his stock in trade.

"He's never been locked up like he is now any place afore and it's—well—unlikely as it seems, the way he looks, it's scaring the hell out of him."

"He doesn't look so all fired *scared* to me."

"That's what it is, though." Derringer claimed with conviction. "Mark busting his mouth that way, he can't talk any too clear—!"

"He sounds more like a grizzly roaring than a feller talking," Dusty estimated. "And, going by what Mark said, it was the same even *before* he had his mouth busted."

"I'm not gainsaying it. Only I've been listening pretty care-ful' and, from late yesterday, started to catch some of what he was saying."

"I thought he was cussing us out."

"So did I, first off. Then I got to listening more careful. He was yelling in French, which didn't make it any easier to follow, being some different from the *patois* I picked up around New Orleans. But I've come 'round to figuring he's been bellowing all along for us to let him out."

"I've heard tell there're some folks who can't abide being shut in, no matter what the cause," Dusty admitted. "And, from what I've heard about the *Metis*, could be he's been raised so wild, woolly and full of fleas way out in the piney woods back home, he's likely never been locked in any place before he woke up in our pokey."

"Man like that wouldn't take kind' to it," Derringer pointed out. "Fact being, I reckon he'd be willing to do *plenty* of talking, was he told it'd help him get out."

"You reckon so, huh?"

"I *do!*"

"Do you want to put it to him, or shall I?"

"It might come better from me," Derringer assessed. "I've been going easy on him—!"

"None of us have been over hard, considering the way he's been taking on," Dusty put in. "Hell, had Mark been one of the Earps, it'd've been lead that stopped him and—!" Realizing he had spoken too quickly and with excessive heat, he sought to make amends. "Sorry, Derry, it's just tha—!"

"Hell," the gambler answered, waving a hand in dismissal of the apology. "What're underlings for if it's not so's the boss man has somebody to bawl out when he's so minded?"

"I allus knew you bunch of underlings were good for *something*," the small Texan declared, grinning in a somewhat self conscious fashion and knowing his deputy understood why he had reacted in such a fashion. "But, dog-my-cats, this's the *first* time I ever found out just what it was."

"We learn something new every day," Derringer declared, pleased he had lessened the tension.

"I almost hope you can't persuade him to talk, though," Dusty remarked, once again looking his usual composed self.

"How come?" the gambler inquired, being genuinely surprised even though it did not show.

"It'll start Mark to crowing's how *he* brings in prisoners who can still tell us things," the small Texan explained, the man he had felled with the *yawara* stick at Hampton's Livery Stable having died without regaining consciousness. "Anyways, *amigo,* you go talk to him and see if he's ready to tell us anything worthwhile in return for being let loose."

"You'll be willing to let him go?" Derringer asked.

"Can you think of any reason why I shouldn't?"

"He might not've thrown the bomb, but he came at the boys like he was meaning to do *something*."

"Why sure. But a smart-assed dude law-wrangler could make out he figured his *amigos* was being attacked and aimed to protect them."

"Talking of smart-assed dude law-wranglers," Derringer said quietly. "That jasper's was here earlier is headed back right now."

"Maybe he's come to tell us's how the Judge's said there doesn't need to be no bail bond fixed," Dusty suggested sardonically. "So his client's free as a jay-bird to take flight."

"We'll soon know, anyways," the gambler estimated, watching the front door starting to open.

"I can *hardly* wait," the small Texan declared.

The man who entered the office was tall and scrawny. Despite being the junior partner of a lawyer known for less than scrupulous tactics and having no moral sense when it came to helping such clients as could meet the high prices charged for legal assistance to evade the consequences of their misdeeds, his dress and demeanour seemed more suitable for a poorly paid assistant of a not too prosperous undertaker. His sombre black attire looked in need of cleaning and his face was so sallow, he might have been raised in a deep and dank cellar far away from light and air. Nevertheless, while he was clearly trying to comport himself like one who considered he was dealing with unimportant nobodies, his expression struck Dusty and Derringer as being strained.

"Well howdy, Counsellor *Spit*," the gambler greeted, strongly emphasising the error he had made when saying the surname. If the scowl he received was any guide, he suspected the visitor knew it was made deliberately. Nevertheless, he continued in a similar tone of mock pleasure, "This *is* an *honour!*"

"It surely is," the small Texan confirmed, with an equally spurious sincerity. "How much did the Judge set that jasper in the back's bail bond at?"

"I'd like to see my *client,* marshal," Counsellor James S. Pitt demanded, rather than asked, instead of supplying the information. Having no desire to admit that his attempt to arrange the bail bond was unsuccessful, even though he felt sure the small Texan and the gambler knew it would be, he had adopted a manner he had found effective when dealing with older peace officers other than the pair before him. "I trust you have no objections?"

"None at all, Counsellor," Dusty authorized, sounding so unctuous he might have considered he was being granted a favour by having the request made. "My deputy will show you through."

"That won't be nec—!" Pitt began, his thin and pallid face working angrily as if wishing to register his disapproval of such blatantly false treatment.

The words were cut off abruptly!

Although there was no sound to account for it, a thudding crash—such as might be made by something heavy being precipitated violently to the floor—came from the cell block!

"Cap'n Dusty!" bellowed a voice from the same general direction. "Derry!"

Even before the second name was uttered, the small Texan and the gambler were on their feet and running towards the door giving access to the rear of the building!

However, despite the interest he had expressed in seeing his client, Pitt did not follow them!

"Hot damn!" Dusty ejaculated as he crossed the threshold, staring at the body of the enormous bearded *Metis* sprawling

on the floor of the cell. Why this should be was established by
the blood mingling with the greyish ooze of dislodged brains
flowing from where the top of his head had been burst open.
"What happened, Pickles?"

"Somebody gunned him from up on the roof across the
street!" barked the tall and lanky man who had been hired by
the small Texan to act as jailer. Holding the shotgun which he
kept readily available to quell violent disturbances, or prevent
attempts at escaping, he had entered an empty cell and stepped
on its wooden framed bed so he was able to see out of the
barred, but unglazed, window. "That's where it must've come
from, but I don't see nobody!"

"I'll take a look outside, Dusty!" Derringer barked, drawing his Colt with the speed of long practice.

"Get yourself a rifle and my carbine first!" the small Texan
commanded, realizing that such a weapon would have been
necessary to make the hit upon the *Metis* from where Pickle-
Barrel had claimed the shot was fired and wanting to ensure
they would not be at a disadvantage in the matter of arms
when they went to investigate.

"What's happened?" Pitt gasped, as the gambler returned
to the office.

"Looks like you're a mite too *late* to see your client, Counsellor," Derringer answered coldly, wondering why the lawyer
had not come into the cell block. "And he won't be able to go
out on a bail bond, even happen the Judge'd been fool enough
to let you take one out for him."

Having left his Winchester Model of 1866 rifle leaning
against a stack of boxes which were to be put in the caboose
of the east-bound train, the Ysabel Kid wasted no time in
leaping to collect it. Scooping it up, he drew back the exposed
hammer from the half cocked position which was the only
means of attaining a state of safety supplied in the mechanism.
While doing so, he swung around ready to take whatever action might prove necessary. Failing to locate whoever had shot
the two Englishmen, he sprang from the wooden boarding
platform and started to run across the railroad tracks towards
where he estimated the assailants had been.

Reacting as swiftly as their companion, Mark Counter and
Waco each brought his right side Army Colt from its holster!

However, the blond giant did not go with the youngster as
he set out to accompany the Kid!

Instead, Mark strode swiftly along the platform to ascertain the extent of the injuries suffered by Sir Michael Dinglepied and Shaun Ushermale. Only one glance was needed to inform him there was nothing anybody except an undertaker could do for the baronet. Nor, despite the twitching movements he saw as he went towards the younger Englishman, did he believe the wound was any less fatal even though death had not yet quite come. In fact, even as he arrived and started to kneel down to make a closer examination, Ushermale's body gave a violent convulsion and flopped limply to lie still.

Racing side by side towards the alley between two buildings from where they suspected the attackers had fired, the Kid and Waco were alert for the slightest hint of danger. Without having discussed the matter, each assumed they had been the intended targets. However, despite the suggestion provided by the results that the still unseen assailants were less than skillful shots, they were ready to take whatever kind of evasive action might prove necessary should a second attempt be made on their lives.

The threat did not materialize!

Fanning out so that each arrived behind the shelter of a different building, the Texans waited for a moment. Then, working in smooth conjunction on a nod from the Kid, they thrust themselves around the respective corners and into the alley. Their weapons were held ready for instant use. The precaution proved unnecessary, although neither regretted having taken it. Not only was the open space deserted, but the sound of leather creaking and horses' hooves departing rapidly from beyond their range of vision at the other end explained why this should be.

Sprinting between the buildings, the Kid and Waco did not take the same precautions on reaching the other end. Instead, they kept going until able to see along the street they had reached. There were several people on the sidewalks, all staring and some shouting to inform them that the two riders who were galloping away had done the shooting. However, while grateful for it, neither deputy needed to be given the information. The sight of the Winchester rifles carried by the pair, and their obvious haste was sufficient evidence to suggest this was the case.

However, what the Kid and Waco found disconcerting and puzzling was the attire of the fleeing pair!

Like the garb worn by the deputies, the style of each rider's clothing was that of a cowhand from Texas.

Wasting no time wondering which of the enemies made by the floating outfit—either prior to reaching Mulrooney, or during their time in office as its lawmen—had tried to take revenge, the Kid whipped his Winchester upwards. Cradling the butt against his right shoulder, he squinted along its barrel. The situation was too urgent for him to seek additional assistance by elevating the "Sporting Leaf" rear sight which bore graduations for aiming at ranges from one hundred to nine hundred yards. Nor, as the distance separating him from his quarry had not quite reached the lowest graduation, did he consider such an aid was necessary. Instead, he made use of the U-shaped notch of the "fixed" sight fitted at right angles to the "leaf" so as to meet the needs of similar situations.

Although he began to raise his Army Colt in a double handed grip, Waco quickly appreciated there was no advantage to be gained by his trying to use it. Good shot though he knew himself to be, he was equally cognizant with his limitations. The men were already beyond any distance at which he could cope to be certain of making a hit. What was more, he would not have any control over exactly how far the bullet went. It would fly onwards and might hit somebody beyond the pair who was still within the range at which its arrival could prove lethal. Bearing the possibility in mind, he lowered his weapon and watched how his companion fared.

Even as the Kid squeezed off a shot, almost as if anticipating the need, the riders started to swerve their fast moving mounts towards a gap between two buildings. By doing so, one of them saved his life. Although the variation was not great, the bullet aimed to strike his head flew a little high and ripped the low crowned, wide brimmed Texas style hat from it.

However, the effort was not entirely wasted!

The forcible removal of the Stetson caused shoulder long black hair which had been concealed inside its crown to drop down!

Then, before the Kid could try again, the two men had gone from his view!

"Did any of you good folks see who they were?" Waco inquired, duplicating his *amigo's* unspoken summation that it would be pointless to continue the chase on foot and returning the Colt to its holster after having set its hammer to a safe position.

"I don't *know* them," Bruce Millan answered, being one of the people who were coming forward. "But they were some of you *Texans* who come here rampag—!"

"The hell they was!" denied a leathery faced old timer, whose accent was Northern and reduced the possibility that he was trying to prevent such a stigma from attaching itself to Texans. His buckskin attire and battered black Burnside campaign hat suggested he was employed as a civilian scout for the United States' Cavalry, or had been, so gave added credence to what he said next. "Look of their faces and the way they got on the Injun side of the hoss, which the rigs for sure *warn't* Texan, I'd say they was half breeds with likely more'n half of it red blood."

"Hot damn!" the youngster ejaculated, too engrossed by what he had heard to resent the attempt by Millan to lay the blame upon his fellow Texans. "We've got to get to the Railroad House *muy pronto*, Lon!"

"How come?" the Kid inquired.

"Those two son-of-bitches wasn't after *us!*" Waco explained. "They're more of them *Metis* and they hit who they was aiming for. The rest of the Railroad Commission could be next!"

CHAPTER FIFTEEN

You Haven't Seen The Last Of 'Em

"So it's your opinion that those *Metis* chaps are still trying to stop the negotiations," Sir John Uglow Ramage said. "Do you mind telling us why you think it?"

"Way I see it, there's some sign's points that way," Waco replied, looking a trifle embarrassed at finding himself the focus of attention for so many older and more worldly wise-men than himself. "First off, Lon and me thought's how those jaspers were somebody we'd riled come after us and got the wrong fellers by mistake. But a few things, 'specially that hat I found, made me reckon's how it wasn't so."

The tone in which the baronet had asked the question held no suggestion of doubt over what he and the other men in the room at the Railroad House Hotel had just been told. Rather it implied satisfaction for work well done and a desire to learn further details of why the conclusion he referred to had been reached. However, while he had a genuine interest, he also considered receiving the information might help improve what had been degenerating into a less than satisfactory meeting between the various parties investigating the possibility of building the spur-line from Mulrooney to join the inter-conti-nental railway under construction in Canada.

Almost an hour had elapsed since the two shooting inci-dents, which had happened less than five minutes of one an-other had taken place!

However, while the intervening time had been well spent, the results were more negative than positive!

After having delayed their departure only long enough to collect armament offering a greater range of fire power than their basically defensive handguns,[1] ignoring the attempt to question them made by Counsellor Peter Pitt while they were taking the appropriate weapons from the well supplied rack on the wall in the office, Captain Dustine Edward Marsden

---

[1] see: Item 3a, APPENDIX FIVE.

"Dusty" Fog and Frank "Derry" Derringer had left the jail-house by the back door.

It had very soon become apparent to the small Texan and the gambler that they had not moved quickly enough!

First Dusty and Derringer had carried out a quick check which satisfied them that Albert "Pickles" Barrel had been correct in his summation. Because of the window of the cell's height above ground level, there was no other point in the vicinity which would have allowed whoever fired to aim and make such a hit as had killed the enormous bearded *Metis*. However, despite there being traces of very recent occupancy —including a spent cartridge case from a Winchester Model of 1866 rifle lying near the appropriate edge—the roof of the building immediately opposite the rear of the jailhouse was deserted by the time they had reached it. Nor had their at-tempts to find a witness to the affair, or even someone who had seen anybody hurrying away carrying a weapon capable of firing such a bullet, achieved any success. Whoever had carried out the murder, and the second person they felt sure was also involved, had disappeared without leaving any sug-gestion of where to continue searching.

Nor had the efforts of Mark Counter, the Ysabel Kid and Waco proved much more productive!

Going along the street, the youngster had retrieved the hat shot from the head of the fleeing rider. Discovering it was brand new, albeit only a cheap "woolsey" such as any cow-hand worthy of his salt would feel ashamed to own and was most unlikely to purchase when flush with wages received at the end of a successful trail drive, he had suggested it might supply a clue to the identity of the owner. Told by his com-panion to prove his point, he set off to make the rounds of the general stores in search of the one from which it had been obtained.

Just after the blond youngster had departed, having left the supervisor of the passenger depot to make arrangements for the bodies of Sir Michael Dinglepied and Shaun Ushermale to be taken to the undertaker's, Mark had joined the Kid. Learn-ing what had taken place, he had given his concurrence with the conclusion drawn by his two companions and suggested the black dressed Texan borrowed one of the horses tethered at a nearby hitching rail and went after the fleeing killers.

As soon as the Kid had set off, letting it be known he was

acting in his capacity as first deputy and senior peace officer of the scene, the blond giant had set about dispelling the misconception created by Bruce Millan, who he suspected was motivated by a malicious desire to cause bad feelings towards everybody and everything to do with Texas. He was assisted in this by the continued assertions from the old timer that the fleeing men most certainly had not been Texans. Corroboration was supplied by comments from others sharing the conclusion that the pair were of mixed blood and did not use the low horned, double girthed saddles practically *de rigueur* for cowhands hailing from the Lone Star State. However, nobody could suggest who the killers might be. Therefore, having faith in Waco's judgement, he had gone to the Railroad House Hotel to act as guard for the surviving members of the British Railroad Commission and their associates.

The youngster's quest had been somewhat more productive in that the owner of the establishment responsible said the hat was part of several items sold to a pair of men in town dweller's style clothing the previous day. They had been described as "about average in height and build" and having just "ordinary" faces apart from being suggestive of mixed blood. However, although their hair had been concealed beneath derby hats, the colour of their eyebrows and one's moustache had indicated it was almost certainly black. An additional piece of information was that, despite having insisted upon the headgear being of the fashion favoured by Texans, the accents of the purchasers had sounded "sort of funny and foreign," being closer to that of the French Creoles with whom the owner had been acquainted in Louisiana than Anglo-Saxon denizens of the Lone Star State. Nevertheless, having been helpful up to that point, the proprietor had been unable to say any more except that the pair had been headed west in a buggy when last seen.

Despite having asked questions of various people he came across, the Kid had been unable to obtain more than general directions to guide his search. He had discovered the point at which the fleeing killers had taken their departure, but they were nowhere to be seen when he arrived at the edge of the town. The trail they were travelling along was too well used for even a tracker of his superlative ability to be able to pick out the signs left by their horses as an aid to discovering where they turned off—if they had done so within a reasonable distance—and then continue following until he could catch them up. Conceding he would be wasting his time if he should go further and might also be playing into the hands of other conspirators intent on carrying out more assassinations, he had adopted the example set by Mark without knowing it had been made.

Leaving Derringer to continue what they both considered might prove an unproductive attempt to locate the murderer of the bearded *Metis*, Dusty, having matched the summation of the blond youngster regarding the possible reason for the killing, had also gone to deliver a warning and offer protection to Ramage's party. He had arrived as Mark was approaching and, having exchanged news, they had gone to see the men for whose safety they were now concerned.

The arrival of the two Texans had come at an auspicious moment as far as the baronet was concerned!

Ramage had taken advantage of the information brought by Dusty and Mark to gain a pause which he hoped would ease what he considered to be a deteriorating situation!

The ploy had succeeded and the baronet was desirous of making as extensive as possible the delay which was allowing tempers to cool down. Having heard what the small Texan and the blond giant had to say, he had suggested all further negotiations were postponed until after the results of the investigations being carried out by the Kid and Waco had been heard. The arrival of the other two Texans, who had reached the hotel at about the same time, had been so soon after he made the proposal that he was unable to fend off pointed hints to carry on with the interrupted talks. After the black dressed Texan and the blond youngster had delivered their reports, noticing even the most dissident of the men was showing signs of being as impressed as he was by the thoroughness and summations of the two Texans, he had asked his question.

"So having got that far along," Waco continued, more delighted by the obvious approval of his three *amigos*—who were closer than brothers to him and whose opinions he valued more than practically everybody else in the world—than the interest displayed by the other men present. "When I got told about that jasper being made wolf bait down to the jailhouse, I reckoned's how it was all done by some of those *Metis hombres* on the rampage."

"That's how I see it, too," Dusty declared and the other

two Texans muttered concurrence.

"And so do I," Ramage supported.

"There's one good thing about it," commented the man who had aroused Mark's animosity during the earlier meeting in the Fair Lady Saloon by suggesting the use of torture. "With them having run out that way, we've seen the last of them."

"I wouldn't say *that,* mister," Waco put in before any of his *amigos* could express the same point of view.

"Why not?" Ramage inquired, although the American businessman was clearly far from enamoured at having his theory rejected by one so young and far below his social standing.

"While those two were gunning down his sir-shi—Sir Michael and his boot-clean—*secretary* at the depot," Waco replied, making such last minute amendments as he felt were called for by the situation. "Another two of 'em killed that *amigo* of their'n as we was holding in the pokey."

"Why do you say there were *two* men involved?" Ramage asked, wanting to continue the discussion as long as possible, although the point had already been cleared when Dusty told his version of the incident.

"Somebody had to call for him to haul his-self up to the window and let the *hombre* with the rifle lay a bead on him," the youngster explained. "Which it'd have to be done in a bellow fit to wake the dead from the top of that roof's he got shot from."

"No matter how many were involved," the dissident businessman injected, with the air of stating the obvious, "they did it to stop him talking."

"Why sure," Waco agreed, but proved he had thought out the matter far more than the man who made the suggestion. "Only, was they going to light a shuck after downing those two fellers at the depot, why'd they figure it was worth going to so much trouble and risk to put a blue window in one of their own?"

"To stop him *talking,* as I just said," the dissident claimed, again with the attitude of considering he had covered the entire issue beyond any need for further clarification.

"What Dusty told me about it," the youngster admitted, his manner becoming less embarrassed and colder in the face of being treated in such a fashion. "They sure as shit comes down the back way did just *that.*"

"Earthily put, but accurate," the baronet said, eyeing the dissident in a less than amiable fashion. "And there's *more* to it, isn't there, young man?"

"I'd say there *has* to be," Waco confirmed. "Way I see it, all they stopped him talking about was something's wouldn't matter any which ways to 'em happen all they was doing was lighting a shuck back to home."

"He could have told which way they'd be going 'back to home,'" Colonel George A. French pointed out, despite seeing what the explanation had struck the dissident, so wanted to prevent it being uttered in a way likely to arouse the ire of the blond youngster still further. "Where 'home' is and who they are, none of which they'd like known as they're members of Chavellier's gang and probably already being hunted by the authorities in Canada."

"Yes, sir," Waco conceded, but there was a subtle difference in the way he did so. It made clear he did not resent the line taken by the officer. "I'll go along with you in reckoning's how they're already on the dodge in Canada. Way they've been handling things hereabouts, they for sure aren't yearling stock new' brought on to the trail. Which means, even after we was give' their names, they likely don't have no regular home's they could be found in. Top of which, that big jasper couldn't give but a general way they'd be headed, 'cepting it's 'most certain to be towards Canada and they'd reckon we'd likely've figured that one out for ourselves."

"He could say what they're going to do when they get back to Canada," the dissident offered and, once again, his demeanour implied he was saying something overlooked by everybody else.

"From the way he behaved when we were attacked, I wouldn't say he's intelligent enough to have been let into many of their secrets," French assessed. "Nobody with good sense would have tried to tackle an enemy with a knife from the distance he did when he had a gun on him."

"He *could've* known something, though, Colonel," Waco contradicted, but politely and with a timbre of respect in his voice which had been noticeably absent when he was addressing the dissident. "And it was said *something's* got him gunned down."

"What would that be?" Lord James Roxton inquired, making his first active participation in the debate he had been following with great interest. "From what I've been told, he wasn't showing any signs of betraying them."

"That *was* for true, so far's we knew," Waco conceded. "Only they maybe reckoned as how he could change his mind after being kept cooped up in the pokey for a spell."

"Which Frank Derringer reckoned we could talk him 'round to doing," Dusty supplemented. "Seems he was trying to bust his way out, not get at us for putting him there."

"And, what they're figuring on doing *next* hereabouts, they didn't dare take the chance of him talking about it," the blond youngster asserted. "Because, gents, unless I'm sore' wrong, you *haven't* seen the last of 'em yet."

"You mean they're going to try to stop the railway being built?" Ramage suggested.

"That could come later," Waco replied and subsequent events were to prove him as accurate a prophet as he had been when suggesting the possible future for Joel Collins and Sam Bass. "Right now, I'll be willing to bet's how they're hiding up somewhere and figuring to keep on trying to make wolf bait of at least enough of you gents to get the others to say the spur-line won't be built into Canada."

"I'll go along with Waco on *everything* he's said," Dusty announced, coming to his feet and gesturing with his right hand towards his three *amigos*. Such was the strength of his personality, it created an impression—much the same as the one formed by Russell "Blink" Profitt at Hampton's Livery Stable—that he was the largest man in the room. "Which being the case, gentlemen, we're going to stop them in their tracks!"

"What can *we* do to help?" Ramage asked, deducing he and his associates were not included in the designation.

"Stay put in the hotel," the small Texan replied, his tone definite. "I've got some good friends deputized, along with the house detective and Walter Braithwaite, the boss desk clerk, to keep guard."

"How long do you expect us to stay here?" the dissident inquired, showing he was not enamoured of the restriction to his movements. "I've other business besides this needing to be attended to."

"You'll be able to get on with it a whole heap better while you stay *alive,* Mr. King," Dusty pointed out. "Which, unless you do as I say, I can't promise you'll stay that way."

"What if I decide I don't *need* your promise?" the business-man challenged, having no liking for receiving what were orders undoubtedly made with his welfare in mind.

"That's up to *you,*" the small Texan answered, in such a way the dissident felt as if an icy hand was touching his spine, "But keep one thing in mind, *gentlemen.* I've given *orders* to the deputies who'll be around and about that, should any one of you insist on leaving, he's to be hauled to the jailhouse for conduct likely to disturb the peace and held there until this business is through."

"And *that,* gentlemen, puts us firmly in our place," Ramage declared, watching the four young Texans leaving the room.

"It *does,*" Harland Todhunter agreed. There was a note of admiration in his voice as he went on, "Tell me something, John. How the hell did I *ever* think of Captain Fog as being *small?*"

Although he had taken no part in the discussion, one member of the party in particular had been fascinated by the way in which Dusty had commanded the proceedings. Listening to the response from the millionaire, he saw a way he might be able to solve a very serious problem with which he was faced. All he had to do, he told himself silently, was find some way of enlisting the assistance of the *big* and very competent Texan who was leading the other three out of the door.[2]

Scuttling along a darkened street with all the furtive aspect of a rodent expecting to be hunted, David "Mousey" Nellist did not believe this was the case. In fact, he was completely at ease and, as a result of something he had just learned, very content with his lot. Nevertheless, living as he did, he was still employing his normal mode of progression through a world containing numerous people who might take reprisals of a serious nature should they learn of how he had been respon-

[2] *What happened at the meeting prior to the arrival of Captain Dustine Edward Marsden "Dusty" Fog and as a result of the conclusion reached about him by one of the men attending it is recorded in detail in: THE CODE OF DUSTY FOG.*

sible for whatever misfortunes had befallen them as a result of
his activities.

Despite an awareness of his so far unsuspected *status quo*
amongst the outlaw fraternity, the little man was less wary
than usual that evening. By sheer persistence and not a small
measure of good fortune, he had acquired some information
which he had instantly realized was of considerable value. The
problem facing him was where he could obtain the best market. It might command a higher price if he was to take it to the
man who stood to lose most by its disclosure to official
sources, but there was a far too high element of risk involved
for him to consider it for more than a moment. While it would
be advantageous for Bruce Millan to recompense him hand-
somely for his silence, the payment was more likely to be in
hot lead.

Nellist was aware that his information would be received
with financial gratitude by various officers of the law, but he
was unable to decide which of them would be most generous.
He discounted the Pinkerton National Detective Agency as
unlikely to be sufficiently interested to suit his needs. On the
other hand, the affair was of sufficient importance to make the
United States' marshal regard it as being worthwhile.

Although the same would be even more applicable in the
case of the municipal lawmen, Nellist doubted whether the
benefits which would accrue from them would match those of
"Big D," who had the advantage of being backed by considerable sums of Federal money and a far more potent protection
to reward those deserving of his largesse. This was particularly the case as, if rumour was correct, Captain Fog was to
hand over as town marshal to Daniel Troop in the near future
and would be returning to Texas with the other members of the
Ole Devil Hardin's floating outfit.

The little man had the decision taken from him in no uncertain fashion!

Emerging swiftly from the entrance to the alley Nellist was
passing, a hand which gave him the impression he could have
sat in it took hold of him by the throat!

With no more apparent difficulty than if the little man was
a newborn baby, he found himself being raised in a painful
fashion and lifted into the shadows!

"I've no time for the usual fol-de-rols right now, Mousey!"
growled a voice which Nellist would have recognized even

without the added evidence of how he was being treated. "Where are they?"

"Who, Mister Count—?" the little man began instinctively.

The words ended in a strangled gurgle as the already less than gentle fingers, holding the little man suspended with his feet waving futilely some inches above the ground, began to tighten!

"Those *Metis* of *le Loup Garou*," Mark Counter supplied, unnecessarily he believed, employing the sobriquet as being indicative of possessing considerable knowledge about the man he named.

"Of *them!*" Nellist gasped, as the fingers loosened just sufficiently to make speech possible.

"*Them,*" the blond giant confirmed. "And talk up *muy pronto,* which mean's—!"

"I *know!*" the little man interrupted. "It means faster even than fast."

"*Somebody's* been talking," Mark drawled, setting the captive down on his feet with a jolt which jarred his buck teeth.

"It was that butto—*amigo* of your'n," Nellist supplied. "Waco, ain't it?"

"Ain't it *always,*" the blond giant answered, without releasing the little man. His voice took on a harsher timbre as he continued, "So where're Chavellier's sons-of-bitches at?"

"They're laid up in that small place Bruce Millan keeps about a couple of miles north of town," Nellist advised. In the brief contact with his captor, he had decided that to dispense with the information he had acquired about the three killings to his present interrogator—rather than waiting to decide which market would be most advantageous—was the only safe way left to him. "Do you know Millan—?"

"That I do," Mark confirmed, moving his hand. "And I reckon we can right easy find that place of his. So come around tomorrow about noon and, happen I'm still able after we've dropped by to say, "Howdy, you-all" to whoever's out there, I'll see's how, like Cousin Solly says, 'the labourer is worthy of his wad.'"

Watching the blond giant striding rapidly away, Nellis was filled with mixed emotions. Of all the Texans in the office of the town marshal, being a member of a very wealthy family in the Lone Star State, Mark Counter was certain to prove more generous than the others. However, fingering his throbbing throat and thinking malevolently of how roughly he had been handled, the little informer wondered whether he would not be just as pleased if circumstances prevented the blond giant from meeting him at the appointed time and place.

CHAPTER SIXTEEN

I Don't Think They Mean To Surrender

"Give the blighters *credit*," Lord James Roxton remarked *sotto voce*, sounding no more than mildly aggrieved despite the gravity of the situation which had provoked the comment. He was wearing a "deerstalker" hat, a dark suit of the kind worn for that specific kind of trophy hunting in the Highlands of Scotland, a black turtleneck pullover, tartan woollen socks and untanned *veldtschoons*. A bandoleer holding massive bullets was suspended around his shoulders and he was carrying a magnificent Holland & Holland double barrelled rifle. Unlike the one owned by Freddie Woods, it had a calibre of .600 Nitro Express and, therefore, qualified as an "elephant gun." "They haven't made things too *easy* for us. In fact, if I was inclined to pessimism, I'd even go so far as to say they've made it *hard*. Oh well, to quote the family motto, '*Nil illegitium carborundum.*'"

"That's strange, Jimmy," Sir John Uglow Ramage commented just as quietly, being dressed and armed in a similar fashion. "I always thought your family's motto was, '*Semper im excretum?*'"

"We traded it with Dingers Dinglepied after Her Majesty had him 'round to Buck House and 'sirred' him, as his people had never had one of their own," the younger aristocrat replied.[1] Although I don't suppose it's good form to speak ill of the dead."

"I'd reckon's how it'd be hard to find anything *good* to say about him," Waco commented dryly, also holding down his voice. "Anyways, seeing's how I'm just a half smart lil ole boy from Texas, what does them fancy motto things mean?"

"I'm afraid you're too young to be told, dear boy,"[2] [2a] Roxton answered. Then he turned his attention to where Captain Dustine Edward Marsden "Dusty" Fog stood cradling a Win-

---

[1] "Buck House;" Buckingham Palace.

[2] *Nil illegitium carborundum*; put politely, "Don't let the 'illegitmates' grind you down."

[2a] "Semper im exeretum;" put politely, "Always in the excreta." We deny most strongly allegations that this is the Edson family motto.

149

chester Model of 1866 carbine. "A bit of a sticky wicket, what?"

"If it's *not*," the small Texan replied, deciding he had no need to worry over having the two aristocrats along on what he knew was almost certain to be a dangerous mission. "It'll do 'til one comes along."

"We've had *easier* chores," the blond youngster supported. In addition to his twin staghorn Colt 1860 Army Model revolvers in their holsters, he was armed with a Winchester Model of 1866 rifle and had a small buckskin pouch suspended over his left shoulder. "Here comes Lon."

Although locating David "Mousey" Nellist had not been accomplished until eight o'clock in the evening, Dusty had claimed the time was well spent when Mark Counter brought him to the town marshal's office!

On being questioned further, the little informer had asserted that from six to ten *Metis* were at the cabin owned by Bruce Millan outside Mulrooney. However, he had claimed he did not know whether Arnaud *le Loup Garou* was with them. Nor was he able to say exactly how they were armed, except that he suspected they were not short of repeating rifles and other weapons. His knowledge of the property in which they were located was restricted to its general direction outside Mulrooney, but that had not created any particular problems. Satisfied that he could not help further, Dusty had ordered that he be kept in a cell for being "drunk and disorderly." After he had been removed, at first protesting at being subjected to such an indignity—but putting on a convincing performance to substantiate the charge for the benefit of the other occupants when passing into the cell block—instructions for his activities in the not too distant future had been given to Albert "Pickles" Barrel.

Telling the Ysabel Kid and Waco to locate and scout the property, Dusty had set about dealing with the situation. While he had complete faith in the ability of his three *amigos,* he had known the four of them were not sufficient to tackle the kind of men they would be up against with any positive hope of success. Nor, with the murderer brought back from Hays City in a cell, could he spare Frank Derringer and Barrel to support them. Instead, he had gone to the Railroad House Hotel and sought assistance from the men deputized to guard the delegation.

As he had anticipated, Dusty had acquired all the reinforce-

ments he would need. However, three had not been anticipated. Having been playing poker with some of their guards,
Colonel George A. French had offered his services and
pointed out he knew much about the *Metis,* so might prove
useful as an interpreter conversant with their dialect. Also in
the game, although they had admitted they did not possess
such qualifications, the two aristocrats had insisted upon being
included. Each had brought a battery of rifles and shotguns
from England for sporting purposes and they had selected
those which they considered most suitable as well as appropriate attire from their fairly extensive wardrobes.

Waco was back when Dusty had returned to the jailhouse.
Having located the property and ensured their quarry were in
occupation, the youngster had come back to act as a guide for
the main body while the black dressed Texan had remained to
scout the premises more thoroughly. Before setting off again,
Waco had made an unconventional addition to his armament.
Saying it should go back to where it belonged, he had put the
improved version of the Haynes "Excelsior" hand grenade in a
shoulder bag along with a small box of percussion caps to
prime it should it be required.

Leading the posse to the vicinity of their destination, the
youngster had called a halt when still far enough away to
avoid the danger of their horses being overheard by the *Metis.*
Completing the remainder of the journey on foot and with a
greater silence than would have been possible if mounted,
they had halted in a clump of trees which offered the only
available cover for so many of them in a group.

Being experienced in such matters, Dusty had refrained
from trying to establish a line of action until he was sure of
what would be entailed. Nothing he had seen led him to assume the raid would be sinecure. There was sufficient light
from the moon for him to be able to study the buildings and
ascertain that going closer would require great care. While
there was a reasonable amount of concealment available up to
within about twenty yards of the small frame house, which
was illuminated in a way indicating there were still occupants
awake and active, the immediate surroundings were completely bare ground.

To add to the problem, two men armed with a Winchester
and a double barrelled shotgun were seated on the front porch.
However, they were repeatedly imbibing from a shared bottle.
Judging from the fact there were several more around them,

some lying in the manner of having been emptied and discarded, the experienced watchers concluded they might be somewhat less vigilant than French had warned could prove the case. Nevertheless, all were in agreement that the possibility of the guards failing to maintain a careful watch should not induce a sense of false security and, as a result, a reduction of caution while moving in.

The *sotto voce* conversation between the two young Texans and the Englishmen was brought to an end by the return of the Kid.

"There's at least ten inside, Dusty," the black dressed Texan reported. "All still awake and taking liquor."

"It's going to make them even less likely to surrender," French put in. "The kind of *Metis le loup Garou* recruits from have all the worst traits of both sides of their family, including a tendency to get drunk. When that happens, they'll fight at the drop of a hat."

"And likely drop it themselves, should your Injuns in the Land of the Grandmother be like our'n," the Kid suggested, employing a colloquial term for Canada, based upon it being under the sovereignty of Queen Victoria. "Which being, what I saw through a gap in the curtains, they're loaded for bear. Unless I'm mistook, it's not all just for wiping out you railroad gents neither. Least-wise, I don't conclude they'd reckon on needing a couple of cases of dynamite for *that.*"

"Dynamite, huh?" Dusty said, showing no surprise that his *amigo* had been able to approach so close as to acquire the information.

"Dynamite," the Kid confirmed. "They *had* a feller on guard out back, same's those two on the front porch. But, even though he's not there no more and they're guzzling liquor copious-like, I can't see *any* way of us getting 'em to give up peaceably by shouting, no matter we've got the whole place surrounded."

"They *won't* surrender," the Colonel confirmed grimly. "Even if they've not got a noose waiting for them for crimes they've committed on behalf of *le Loup Garou*, I'll be willing to wager they're almost all wanted for offenses elsewhere."

"Then we'll have to get them out un-peaceable and this's how we'll set about doing it," the small Texan answered, being willing to accept French's assessment as stemming from a far greater experience of the *Metis* than either he or the Kid possessed. He spoke with a cold and deadly seriousness which warned he had accepted the inevitable and was willing to follow it through to the bitter end. Giving his instructions to the assembled well armed men, he concluded, "Just keep one thing in mind. Happen they're so minded, they'll be given the chance to come out with their hands raised."

"As you say, Captain Fog," Ramage assented and there was a low rumble of agreement from the rest of the party.

"There is one thing, though," Roxton put in.

"What'd that be?" Dusty inquired, feeling sure the matter was of some consequence.

"A point of pure *legality*, old boy," the younger aristocrat explained. "I've learned a little about your amazingly *complicated* judicial system over here in the colonies while we were playing poker earlier. I'm not *complaining* about it and all that. You *seem* to be muddling along all right with it. But, as we aren't within the bounds of Mulrooney, have you *legal* jurisdiction *here*."

"That *is* the point," the baronet agreed. "If they *should* surrender, with the kind of legal representation I'm *sure* will be provided by their—soft shell, as I believe you put in— friends, I'd hate to see them having to be released when on trial because of a legal technicality."

"There won't be any," Dusty claimed with assurance. "When we took office, Freddie arranged for the county sheriff to make us all *his* deputies and that gives us jurisdiction all through his bailiwick as well as our own."

"Deuced *clever* these Chinese," Roxton praised in a manner he felt sure would prove even more satisfying to its recipient than a more formal expression of the sentiment.

"*Deuced!*" Ramage seconded, having been equally impressed by the forethought which had been displayed by the beautiful Englishwoman and the small Texan, who he suspected correctly, had suggested the precaution. "And, with *that* settled, old boy, we're yours to command."

"Then let's get her done!" Dusty ordered, satisfied his orders had been understood and would be carried out. Noticing some activity not too far away, he went on, "What are *you* doing, boy?"

"I'm just priming this lil ol sucker," Waco replied, looking up from where he was attaching the fourteenth percussion cap to the inner portion of the grenade with the assistance of a small "bull's eye" lantern held by Roxton so the *Metis* on the porch would not see its light. "'Cause, happen she's needed, I don't figure there'll be time to do it *after* then."

"You could be right at that," the small Texan conceded, gratified by the change he had helped to bring about in the youngster which was proven by this commendable behaviour. "Only don't tell Cousin Betty as I said so. She's *never* forgive me for giving you notions above your station, as Freddie would call it."

"Now there's another *lady* with a real mean tongue," Waco claimed, having set the inner component into position and starting to screw the outer shell into place. "Fact being, Betty and her're like two peas in a pod for that and a man'd have to be either *loco,* or *real* brave, to tangle with either of 'em *permanent.*"

"Are you *ready?*" Dusty inquired, without responding to what he knew had been a hint—albeit made with the best of intentions and permissible amongst such good friends—about the increasingly closer relationship which had developed between the beautiful Englishwoman and himself. Receiving an answer in the affirmative, he continued after the fashion of a trail boss giving the order to start a herd on its one-way journey, "Head 'em up. Move 'em out!"

Acting upon the instructions they had received, the members of the posse divided into two sections and started to move off. The intention was to form a circle at a reasonably safe distance, with the small Texan at its connecting point, around the building. When word was passed that Mark and the trail boss who had led the other section had come together, Dusty issued the order most frequently given to set a herd of cattle moving on the trail.

It said much for the ability of the whole party that the encirclement had been achieved so quickly and effectively, without the men on the porch detecting it. What was more, such was their skill that even those moving in from the front were able to keep their presence unsuspected. Although the liquor which the pair had been imbibing helped to some extent, this was achieved by employing extreme caution while advancing from cover to cover. Each man in turn remained still and covered his neighbours as they went to their next position. With this attained, the roles were reversed in what amounted to a living noose being drawn even tighter.

Nor did the two Englishmen and French—who, although British born and educated, was considered a Canadian in view of his part in the negotiations—prove any less adept than the

Americans. All had done considerable hunting and had
learned the value of such tactics when on *shikar* in India, or
seeking out big game elsewhere in the world.[3] Not that Dusty
had expected any of them to prove a liability. If he had, he
would have accepted the chance of rousing animosity and refused to allow them to accompany him. As he had put his
point of view to them at the hotel, he had ended it in a fashion
typical of a cowhand from Texas, "Should you-all get made
wolf bait, I'll bet *none* of you'll come and help me tell Freddie
the why of it."

Just as the men at the front were approaching the last of the
cover before the open ground, a clamour arose from the rear
of the building!

A shot was fired, followed by more shouting!

Lurching to their feet with speed, but in a fashion indicative of having drunk rather more than was advisable when on
what was obviously guard duty—albeit not sufficient to produce a state of befuddled incapability—the *Metis* ran towards
the end of the porch!

"It's not our chaps who've been seen!" French announced,
having understood what had been said behind the building
from where more shooting was taking place. Noticing the rest
of the posse were following orders not to open fire unless in
self defence, he glanced towards the Kid and went on, "Somebody's found the body of the chap you dealt with!"

"*Seemed* like the thing to do at the time," the black clad
Texan replied, having been compelled to use his big bowie
knife to silence the *Metis* who had confronted him unexpec-
tedly as he was passing around the end of the backhouse on
his way to scout the main building.

"What now, Captain?" Ramage inquired.

"Hold your fire at the back!" Dusty thundered and the
words were repeated by the men to either side. Waiting until
he was obeyed, at least by his own men, he continued, "Tell
them who we are and that, should they be so minded, nothing
'cept being hauled off to the pokey'll be done to them if they
toss out their guns and follow with hands raised high."

"Certainly," French obliged, but did not state his belief that
the offer would be rejected summarily and with violence.

[3] *The term, "Going on safari"—the Swahili word meaning
a journey of any kind and not just a hunting expedition—had
not come into usage at the period of this narrative.*

On hearing the Colonel begin to shout in their native tongue, the guards swung around. With their attention attracted, they proved sufficiently in control of their faculties to locate his position. Snarling profanities, they started to bring up their weapons. Seeing the speed with which they reacted and the skill being displayed, aware that the shotgun in particular would prove most effective at such close quarters, neither Dusty nor the Kid hesitated before responding.

Brought into alignment, the Winchester carbine held by the small Texan and the "Old Yellowboy" rifle in the hands of his black dressed companion crashed almost simultaneously. Each having drawn the appropriate conclusions on how the other would act, due to their having been in action together a great many times, they selected different targets regardless of appreciating which one would pose the greater threat. Struck between the eyes by the Kid's bullet, the man with the shotgun spun from the porch before he could squeeze its forward trigger. Nor, while more fortunate in that he received a wound in the chest unlikely to prove lethal, was the other *Metis* allowed to fire his rifle. Slammed backwards against the wall of the building, he rebounded from it and, smashing the rail on the porch, sprawled on the ground.

"Somehow, old thing," Roxton commented, with his usual suggestion of ennui, watching the front windows being smashed and the barrels of weapons thrust through to open fire. "I don't think they mean to *surrender*."

"You know something?" Waco answered, the words having been directed his way. "I was sort of starting to think along them self-same lines."

"Do you know how to throw that?" Ramage inquired, seeing the youngster laying down his Winchester rifle and taking the grenade from the bag which he had had slung on his back to ensure it did not get jolted.

"I figured you just hauled back and let go," Waco admitted. "Would there be some other way in Merrie Ole England?"

"Well, there's 'letting go' and there's '*letting go*,'" Roxton advised, after sending two bullets from his elephant gun which ripped sizeable chunks from the framework of a window on their way into the building. Breaking open the breech and ejecting the empty cases, ensuring he did not expose himself from behind the bush he was using as concealment, he replaced them with two of the bullets from his bandoleer. While doing so, he went on, "Now *if* it could be put *through* there, it ought to have quite an *effect* upon the blighters inside."

"That's be *some* throw," the blond youngster assessed dubiously, wondering whether he possessed the skill to make it.

"About the length of a cricket pitch, wouldn't you say, Jimmy?" Ramage inquired, watching along the twin barrels of his Holland & Holland rifle for a suitable target to be presented.

"Perhaps even a fraction less," Roxton estimated. "But that window is *wider* than the stumps were when you bowled your hat-trick against the M.C.C. at Lords's."

"And there's *nobody* standing in front of it," the baronet said, in what might have passed as a casual fashion to an unknowing observer.

"I don't know whether you've noticed or not, old boy," Roxton replied. "But there *could* be a chap or two *behind* it."

"Quite!" Ramage admitted and turned his gaze to where Dusty was kneeling in similar concealment. "Can you keep those blighters inside *occupied* for a few moments, Captain Fog?"

"I reckon so," the small Texan replied. "Would there be any particular' special call for it?"

"I think popping that grenade thing in amongst them might produce *results*," the baronet replied. "But I don't *believe* they'd *approve*."

"They might even react in a *hostile* fashion," Roxton supplemented, his manner implying he considered he was the only one to have thought of the contingency.

"I'd say you could get your bottom dollar on *that*," Waco asserted.

"In which case," Ramage said, his manner showing no more emotion than if he was requesting his hat ready to go for a stroll around Picadilly Circus in London. "If you'll have *our* chaps do *something*, I'll pop it through and see what happens."

"*You?*" Dusty and Waco said in the same breath.

"I'm a *far* better bowler than James, or George if it comes to that," the baronet pointed out. "And, as I doubt whether any of you colonials have *ever* played cricket, I feel I'm the most suitable to do it."

The conversation had been carried out to the accompaniment of gun shots at and from the building!

Glancing around, Dusty assessed the situation rapidly and with an experienced gaze!

As yet, no casualties had been reported from the members of the posse!

However, the small Texan realized it was only a matter of time before some of the men who had volunteered to accompany him were hit!

Accepting there was no chance of persuading the *Metis* to surrender without some strong inducement being applied and —having the instincts indispensible to any good leader— wanting to avoid injuries to the posse if possible, Dusty could see the wisdom of the suggestion made by Ramage. However, he was less enamoured of allowing the baronet—who was of considerable importance to the outcome of the negotiations which Freddie, whose wishes were of considerable importance to him, wanted to succeed—making the throw.

"It *isn't* really a matter for debate, old boy," Roxton stated, guessing correctly what was causing the small Texan to hesitate. "I assure you that John is the *best* man for the job!"

"And so do I," Ramage confirmed. "So, if you'll pass that thing to me, Waco, I'll do it."

"Go to it, boy," Dusty authorized. "Only, *when* Sir John gets shot, I'm going to tell Freddie it was *you* who said he could try it."

"I think I would have preferred you to say, '*if*' rather than '*when*,' old boy," the baronet commented dryly. Laying aside his elephant gun, he removed first the bandoleer and then his jacket. "But no matter."

"Anyways, Freddie'll forgive lil ole me, 'cause I'm so *cute*," Waco declared and continued without losing the suggestion of light-hearted detachment, "Ready or not, here I *come!*"

Saying the last word, extending his right arm above his head to keep the grenade clear of the ground, the youngster rolled from where he was lying. Two bullets threw up spurts of dirt very close to his body, the man who fired one being shot in the head by the Kid just after the trigger was squeezed, but he reached and handed the device to Ramage. With the delivery completed, he returned to his position and picked up his Winchester.

"Pass the word for everybody to load up and leave one in the chamber!" Dusty ordered, wanting to avoid giving the *Metis* a suggestion that something was going to happen by shouting and added a supplement which he felt sure would indicate just how serious a situation he was envisaging.

"Then, when I shout, 'Now,' cut loose as fast as you can."

"You'd better toss across your gun, old boy!" Roxton requested of the baronet. When this was done, without either of them being hit by bullets sent their way, he glanced from one big double barrelled rifle to the other in a critical fashion and breathed, "Damn it. I wish I had that Hottentot, '*Ventvögel*,' of Quatermain's. I've never seen *anybody* who could reload faster."[4]

"You *ready*, Sir John?" Dusty inquired.

"Yes!" the baronet replied, having compared the difference between the grenade and a cricket ball, then adopted a crouching posture much like a sprinter waiting to commence a race.

"On *three* then," the small Texan instructed. "One! Two! Three! *Now!*"

Hurling himself out of his place of concealment as the last word was let out in a stentorian bellow, Ramage started towards the building. As he did so, he drew back his right arm and extended the left ahead as a counterbalance in the way which had helped him to acquire a well deserved reputation as a most efficient "round arm" bowler. Although somewhat heavier than the permissible five and a half to five and three quarter ounce weight of a regulation cricket ball, the grenade did not have a circumference much greater than the mandatory eight and thirteen-sixteenth to nine inches.

As the baronet commenced his movements, a veritable hail of lead poured from every rifle held by the members of the posse!

Wanting to attain greater speed in handling their Winchesters than was possible in a prone position, or even when kneeling, Dusty, the Kid and Waco lunged erect regardless of the danger to themselves. Between them and the other men, they contrived to put down such a barrage of flying lead that it quickly made the front of the building untenable. However, before this happened, the blond youngster's Winchester pre-

---

[4] *We do not have any information about when or where Lord James Roxton made the acquaintance of the famous white hunter, Allan Quatermain and his Hottentot gun bearer, Ventvögel—"Windbird"—but assume it was during a hunting expedition in Southern Africa. Some details of the careers of "Hunter" Quatermain and Ventvöogel are given in: KING SOLOMON'S MINES and ALLAN QUATERMAIN by H. Rider Haggard.*

vented a *Metis* from firing at Ramage. An instant later, letting out a boom far deeper than the bark of the repeaters, Roxton's elephant gun propelled one of its massive charges through the wall alongside the window frame he had smashed. In spite of this, the bullet retained sufficient power to literally pick up and fling backwards another of the defenders, who had been too well hidden to be hid otherwise while attempting to draw a bead on the baronet.

For his part, paying no attention to the fusilade going on all round, Ramage concentrated upon what he was doing. Like every good bowler, he was able to pitch the ball to within a foot of a selected point. However, regardless of considerations of personal safety, he was aware there were two *very* important differences for him to take into account on this occasion. Firstly, the grenade was slightly heavier than a cricket ball. Secondly and even more essential, he must send it through the window without allowing it to land on the ground before doing so.

Estimating the time had come, the baronet commenced his swing!

The grenade was released at what Ramage assumed was the correct instant!

Curving through the air, as the baronet threw himself face down on the ground, the black sphere went where it was intended to go!

Descending to the floor with little diminished velocity, one of the thin supporting wires holding apart the outer and inner segments collapsed!

In turn, a percussion cap was crushed and sent a spurt of flame into the central component's charge of black powder!

An instant later, to the accompaniment of an ear-splitting roar, the whole building was shattered by a vastly greater explosion than seemed possible from such a small object!

"Hot damn!" Waco ejaculated, as he and his companions picked themselves up from where, despite being some distance away, they had been thrown off their feet by the blast. Turning an accusatory gaze to the Kid, he went on with well simulated wrath, "You let *me* go fooling around with a thing's could do *that!*"

"*You* wouldn't take 'no' for an answer, like always," the black dressed Texan countered, justifiably displaying not the slightest suggestion of contrition. Running his gaze over the remains, he continued, "Anyways, it was helped just a *lil* mite by the dynamite they'd got in there."

"That's all right then," the blond youngster claimed and his voice took on a timbre of persecution as he continued, "But now *I'll* be the one's gets blamed 'cause there won't be none of 'em going to *surrender!*"

CHAPTER SEVENTEEN

I've Come to Arrest *Freddie*

"Well howdy, you-all, Solly," Captain Dustine Edward Marsden "Dusty" Fog greeted, looking up as he heard somebody approaching his desk in the town marshal's office shortly before noon on the second day after the removal of the threat posed by the *Metis*. "You here on *business,* or to swap some more bible quoting with Mark?"

Even as he was speaking, the small Texan realized something of considerable gravity had brought his visitor to see him!

What was more, Dusty wondered whether it had anything to do with the successful raid upon the *Metis* he had led!

Due to the force of the detonated dynamite, there had been no survivors from the explosion caused by the improved version of the Haynes "Excelsior" hand grenade!

Even the *Metis* guard on the porch who was wounded by the small Texan had been killed, so there was nobody to say whether Arnaud *le Loup Garou* Chavallier was amongst those who had died inside the building. With everything which might have provided evidence of complicity destroyed, there was no hope of proving Bruce Millan had known the men were occupying his cabin. Nor, if it came to a point, had Dusty hoped there would be. He was aware of the complications and possible animosity which would arise if the owner of the property was arrested and put on trial for involvement in the activities of the men from Canada and he felt, under the prevailing conditions, to do so would not be advantageous to the aims of Freddie Woods.

With the latter consideration in mind, the small Texan had given instructions to Albert "Pickles" Barrel before setting out with the posse. Waiting until certain there would not be sufficient time for David "Mousey" Nellist to get a warning to the *Metis,* in the unlikely event that such should have been his intention, the jailer had set him loose. However, before he was given his liberty, he was told to let Milan know what was happening and warn of the danger of possible incrimination should the raid produce prisoners.

The ploy had been successful!

Acting upon Dusty's recommendation by calling at Mil-

lans' home the following morning, ostensibly to discuss a do-
nation for a charity, Freddie Woods had been told by a servant
that he had gone on "urgent business" to an undisclosed des-
tintion just after daybreak and had left no indication of when
he would return!

Satisfied there was little chance of the man coming back,
the small Texan had not anticipated the latest development!

On medium height and in his late twenties, Solomon Wisdom "Solly" Cole had a black Texas-style Stetson hat tilted
back on his head to show rusty-red hair. Despite a luxuriant
moustache enhancing a solemn expression, his face had a
rugged attraction. His stocky, powerful frame was clothed in a
sombre black three-piece suit, white shirt and black necktie
such as a stringently practising member of one of the more
strict religious denominations might wear. However, his black
boots had a cowhand's sharp toes and high heels and the silver
badge of a United States' deputy marshal glinted on the left
breast pocket of his vest. What was more, about his waist, on
a stiff two and a half inch wide belt, in an open fronted spring
retention holster—of a kind more usually seen in shoulder
rigs—riding somewhat higher than was normal, was a Rogers
& Spencer Army Model revolver with bell-shaped, square
bottomed black walnut grips.

"Business, I'm afraid, Dusty," the newcomer replied, his
Texas drawl as sombre as his appearance. He ran a quick
glance over Mark Counter, the Ysabel Kid and Waco, who
were gathering around to greet him and went on, "You're *none*
of you going to *like* this, but I've come to arrest *Freddie."*

"You'd best run that on by me again, Solly," the small
Texan instructed quietly. Like his *amigos,* he was startled by
what he had heard. What was more, he shared their summation that—although possessed of a far more droll sense of
humour than was suggested by his sombre attire and demeanour—Cole would *never* make such a remark as a joke. "It
passed so fast I couldn't even see, much less, read its brand."

"I don't know much about it myself," the deputy admitted,
removing his hat and accepting the chair indicated to him.
"But, from what I heard, Senator Foulkes came hurrying in to
see the boss like his butt was on fire just afore sundown yesterday. Reckoned's how he'd got word Freddie was wanted for
murdering two men in England and he'd been asked to have
her held for extradition. I'm damned if I've *ever* knowed him
so all-fired eager to help the law."

"He's not known for it," Dusty conceded, aware that the man in question was of a similar political persuasion to Bruce Millan and the late Sir Michael Dinglepied.

"Anyways," Cole went on, wondering why he was getting so little reaction from the small Texan and having the feeling that the most important part of the information he had given was already known. "The boss asked if Foulkes was sure of what he was saying and he hauled out an affidavit signed by some English jasper with a hook to his name saying it was so. Which being, he said for me to drift along on this morning's train 'n' fetch her back."

The deputy marshal was correct in his assumption!

Despite their increasingly closer relationship, Dusty knew only that Freddie had left England for a *very* serious reason which made it unlikely she could return in the foreseeable future, if at all. However, even before being summoned to the Railroad House Hotel by Walter Braithwaite's message on the night the survivor of the men who tried to abduct her was killed by the Kid, he had learned enough for him to suspect Dinglepied wished to bring about her extradition. He had heard from Waco what had taken their *amigo* to see the baronet and the reason for Shaun Ushermale being brought to the jail. Questioning the young Englishman, he had discovered nothing of an incriminating nature. The small Texan had suspected that, having had time to think, Ushermale had concluded the only hope of avoiding the consequences of the negotiations he had conducted with Hugo "Camb" Camberwell was to deny all knowledge of them and rely upon Dinglepied being so afraid of what he could say that his liberation would be procured to prevent him from doing so.

After having arranged for the bodies to be removed to the undertaker's on arriving at the hotel, hoping to obtain confirmation of his suppositions, Dusty had conducted an inquiry into the incident. Once again, he discovered that he was starting too late. Despite still showing he was suffering from the effects caused by having seen the way in which the two hardcases died, Dinglepied had recovered his wits sufficiently to appreciate the danger he was facing. Possessing the courage of a cornered rat and realizing his career as a politician—if nothing worse—hung in the balance, he had stuck to the story he told to the Kid and Sir John Uglow Ramage. Nor had the pretence by the small Texan that Ushermale had supplied a different version shaken him. Knowing his confidential secretary, he had guessed this was not the case.

Concluding there was no chance of obtaining the truth at that time and equally conscious of the wish Freddie had expressed to avoid anything which might endanger the negotiations with the British Railroad Commission, Dusty had not pressed the issue. Instead, conveying the impression that he was satisfied with Dinglepied's explanation, he had stated his intention of returning to the jail.

However, when unobserved by the others, the small Texan had asked Ramage to accompany him to a different destination. Going to the Fair Lady Saloon, they had acquainted Freddie with the events of the evening and he had been given the basic facts concerning her decision to leave England and live under an assumed name in the United States. While he knew that the reason her abductors had used to entice her was correct, he also knew that the town marshal of Brownton would have been only too willing to hold her in order to settle a personal grudge. He had considered that the death of Dinglepied and Ushermale had removed the threat to her, so he had not anticipated the development which had arisen with the arrival of Cole.

"Said jasper wouldn't be called 'Sir Michael Dinglepied,' would he?" Dusty inquired.

"The boss didn't let me see the name," the deputy marshal replied. "I just caught a glimpse of the 'Sir' on it. Look, *amigo*. You know Matt. He isn't no happier than we are bout this."

"That's *bueno!*" Waco put in. "Because you don't reckon as how *we'd* let you take her, do you?"

"I know there's *nobody* in this world could make you fellers do *anything* unless you was so minded; 'cepting maybe General Hardin his-self," Cole replied, meeting the blond youngster's hostile glare without animosity. He was equally aware the Kid and even his cousin were looking at him far from the friendly way in which they had greeted his arrival. "Only trouble being, I've been given orders and, day I took this badge, I *swore* on my oath's I'd do my duty so long as I wore it. Which means, seeing's how I've been sent to arrest Freddie, I'm going to have to do my level best to *try* no matter who aims to stop me."

If the small Texan had needed further information of how badly his visitor felt about the situation, even before the declaration of intent, one thing more any other would have supplied it. Normally, Cole would have sprinkled his conversation with his own variations of real biblical quotations, or been making up some which appeared to be genuine, albeit revised. The omission was convincing proof of his sentiments. What was more, regardless of the timbre of regret in his voice, he was in deadly earnest when he said he would do his duty. Being the kind of men they were, while they were all determined to save Freddie if possible, none of the members of Ole Devil Hardin's floating outfit thought any the worse of him for his attitude.

"I'd sort of figured that already," Dusty drawled, having grown to like the deputy marshal, and the same applied to the gigantic peace officer who was his visitor's immediate superior.[1] "And I reckon that's why Matt picked *you* to send."

"There was at least two more he could've sent," Cole admitted. Then, showing he had devoted considerable thought to the course he was about to propose, he continued, "One of you'd best go tell Freddie to light a shuck while I take off my badge and go get me a real long lasting meal someplace."

"That's *not* the answer, *amigo*," Dusty pointed out gently, showing his gratitude for the suggestion, which he knew had not come easily to a man with such a strong sense of duty as was possessed by the United States' deputy marshal. He also suspected that after such a dereliction Cole would feel honour bound to resign. In spite of that, he continued, "But you going to take that meal sounds like a mighty sensible notion to me."

"Where—and for how long?"

"Buffalo Kate serves up some mighty tasty victuals, but's kind of slow. I'd reckon you'd need an hour to get through there."

"An hour it is then," Cole assented, wondering what the small Texan had in mind. "Will you come and join me, Cousin Mark?"

"I'll take a rain check on it, Cousin Solly," the blond giant

---

[1] *The researches of the world's foremost fictionist geanologist, Phillip José Farmer—author of, in addition to numerous other works,* TARZAN ALIVE, A Definitive Biography Of Lord Greystoke *and* DOC SAVAGE, His Apocalyptic Life—*with whom we have consulted suggest "Matt," or "Big D" as David "Mousey" Nellist called him, was United States' Marshal Matthew Dillion, some of whose career was recorded in the television series,* "GUNSMOKE."

refused, but in a more friendly fashion than he had been showing. "Right now, I'd sooner stay with Dusty."

"There's one *slight* detail wrong with what you've heard," Freddie Woods stated, looking at each Texan in turn as they stood with worried and where Mark Counter, the Ysabel Kid and Waco were concerned—for them—close to sheepish expressions, in the sitting-room of her living accommodation. "I didn't kill those two men, although I can't deny I meant to if necessary."

"They need killing?" the Kid inquired, his manner indicating he believed this must have been the case.

"They *deserved* it," Freddie stated. "And you'd all better sit down."

"Why'd you figure they needed taking out, ma'am?" Waco asked, after he and his companions were seated, with Dusty alongside Freddie on the settee.

The fact that the blond youngster applied the word, "ma'am" instead of the usual, "Freddie" was a clear indication of how strongly he felt about the matter under discussion. What was more, his manner implied his belief that the reason must have been completely justified.

"It all started with me trying to act like Belle Boyd, who I'd met while she was visiting London during the War," the beautiful Englishwoman explained. "In Britain, we have what we call 'Civil Servants.' They're Government employees permanently appointed to handle continuing routine issues which politicians liable to be in and then out of office couldn't cope with satisfactorily. Some are the very finest kind of men, dedicated to their work, loyal to their country and who do their duty conscientiously regardless of whether it is the Tories or the Liberals currently forming the Government. Unfortunately, there have always been—and probably always will be—others who, being completely disloyal and untrustworthy, seek only to feather their own nests, or to use their positions of trust to try to bring discredit to whichever political party they do not support."

"I've heard tell we've got some of that kind who're just as ready to sell their saddles,"[2][2a] the Kid commented.

---

[2] "Sold his saddle"; in this context, one who has betrayed his trust.

"I suppose most countries have," Freddie admitted. "Anyway, I picked up a rumour that three of the kind fairly high up were betraying their trust and country by selling military and other information to Russia and salving their consciences by giving some of the money to various radical groups.[3] As it is practically impossible to have their kind discharged from office for any but the most serious offence, I decided I would try to obtain the proof to have them removed."

"And you got it?" Waco stated rather than asked.

"I *did*," Freddie confirmed. "Unfortunately, when I told daddy, he said it would create too much of a scandal and could do irreparable damage to the Civil Service as a whole if what they had done was made public. But I was determined they wouldn't get away scot free. So I went to pay them a call at the house they shared, meaning to tell them of my proof and pretend I would hand it over to the appropriate authorities unless they resigned and left England."

"Only it didn't work out that way?" Mark guessed.

"It didn't," Freddie agreed. "Knowing their kind wouldn't hesitate to try to silence a lone woman, I had my Webley Bulldog with me. What I didn't know was that somebody else had an even more serious reason that I had for dealing with them."

"*More* serious than selling out their country?" Waco queried.

"*Much* more. It seems that a sergeant in the Rifle Brigade, with whom I was acquainted by the kind of coincidence you'd never believe if you read it in a book, had a son who was working as a page-boy at the home of one of their friends. They—well, I suppose *raped* is the only way to put it—the lad while they were paying a visit. He committed suicide from the shame, but before he died, his father had the truth from him. Having learned of their perversion, although not about the unfortunate lad, I'd arranged for them to believe some boys would be calling, so that there was only the three of them

[2a] *As a cowhand relied so much upon his saddle as an essential means of carrying out his work, only the most desperate of situations would induce him to sell it. No matter how good the cause, he was regarded with suspicion and even disdain by his contemporaries for having done so.*

[3] *At the period of this narrative, Russia was considered an enemy of the British Empire; particularly where the affairs of the Indian subcontinent were concerned.*

on the premises when I arrived. I was standing covering them with my gun when the sergeant burst into the room. Before I could stop him, he'd snatched it from my hand and shot two of them dead. The other escaped by throwing himself through a window and fled the country."

"Then, as it was the sergeant who did it and with damned good cause, I'd say," Waco put in, as Freddie paused for a breath. "How come *you* had to light a shuck?"

"The flight of the third man attracted attention and people were coming to investigate. Although the sergeant and I managed to escape, it was reported to the police that a woman and man were seen running way. The sergeant wanted to give himself up and clear my name, but daddy and I wouldn't let him. With the kind of friends the pair had, especially as he was a soldier who had received awards for valour in the field, they would do all they could to make sure he wouldn't receive a fair trial. So, as his battalion were leaving for India shortly, we suggested he kept quiet and went with it. He refused because he claimed I might be implicated and would only agree to go if I too put myself beyond the reach of the law. He swore he would come back to clear me if I should be arrested. Daddy agreed with the first part and we couldn't sway the sergeant from his determination to do the second, so here I am. I thought I would be safe, but clearly Dinglepied suspected I was implicated and tried to have me taken home to face trial for the killings."

"And, going by what Cousin Solly said," Mark commented. "It looks like he'd fixed things for getting it done before he was made wolf bait."

"Or Millan did it to get evens with us for busting up whatever game he'd got going with the *Metis*," Waco estimated. "We should oughta go see *Mister* Millan wherever he's at and tell him what we told his sir-ship just afore he was cut down."

"You'll do no such thing!" Freddie denied emphatically. "That would only bring the whole business even more into the open."

"As *you* want it, ma'am," the youngster assented without hesitation, albeit displaying obvious reluctance. "Which being. How're we going to get you away from here?"

"Get me away?" the beautiful Englishwoman queried.

"We are sure as shitting aren't going to let *anybody* take you in to be sent back to England," Waco declared vehemently and the fact that he employed such a term in Freddie's presence without making an apology was testimony to the strength of his emotion. "Even if it means going up against Solly Cole, Matt Dillon and the whole god-damned Federal Government to stop it."

"You took on oath with that badge, Waco!" the black haired beauty reminded, but her tone was kindly and indicative of the gratitude she felt for the motives which impelled the youngster.

"Then it's easy tossed in the discards 'long of this tin star!" Waco announced, reaching upwards.

"*You* too, Dusty?" Freddie asked, watching the other Texans duplicating Waco's action by removing their badges of office. "*Damn it!* I'm not having you all breaking the law on my account!"

"I'm not fixing for us to *break* the law, honey," the small Texan replied. "Happen you boys'll wait outside for a few minutes, I'll be fetching Freddie along."

"Have a good meal, Cousin Solly?" Mark Counter asked, when the United States' deputy marshal returned without wearing his badge after an absence of an hour and, as previously, found all the local peace officers were present.

"Tolerable fine," Cole replied, glancing from one to another of the Texans and Frank Derringer in an attempt to discover why they were there. None of them looked as if they were concerned over the possible fate of a woman he knew they respected and greatly admired. "The steak was just a teensy mite overcooked, though."

"I hope you haven't eaten too much," Dusty Fog remarked, gesturing to an apparently blank sheet of thick and somehow official looking paper lying on the desk in front of him. "By the way, about you arresting Freddie and holding her for extradition—!"

"Yeah?" Cole inquired, sensing there was a development of a kind he could not envisage which might save him—and his superior—from having to carry out a duty they both found abhorent.

"Now I'm only a half-smart small town John Law," Dusty claimed. "But I reckon I've heard a person can't be extradited from their own country."

"That's the legal law all through the world," Cole admitted, but he could not see how the information—which he felt sure was already known by Dusty—could affect the situation.

"Only Freddie's English and they're figuring on having her extradited from over here back to her home country."

"Freddie *was* English," Dusty corrected and the grins on the faces of his companions grew even broader.

"Was?" Cole querried.

"Was," the small Texan confirmed, picking up and displaying the hitherto concealed side of the sheet of paper. It was most definitely an official document, although not one Cole would ever have expected to see in such a context. "While you were eating over at Buffalo Kate's, I went to the Fair Lady and proposed on bended knee to Freddie. She said, 'Yes, please' and now she's Mrs. Dusty Fog. This's our wedding certificate, all signed and notarized legal and proper."

"Which makes her an *American* citizen and not eligible for extradition," Cole continued and, as he took out and pinned on his badge, his normally solemn expression changed to one of delight.

"I'll take *your* word for that," Dusty grinned. "Although the Judge agreed same was the case when we asked him to come to the Fair Lady for a wedding feed. After you've telegraphed to tell Matt what's happened and asked him to come up to join us, *Mrs. Fog*, American citizen, and I'll be expecting you along as well."[4]

---

[4] We asked the member of the Besgrove-Woodstole family who supplied the information given in this chapter why it had been decided to end the reticence previously shown over the affair. We were informed that the details had been withheld out of a desire to avoid showing members of the Civil Service in such an unfavourable light. However, as a result of recent happenings, the family consider they are no longer bound by such a consideration.

Following his enrolment in the Army of the Confederate States,[1] by the time he reached the age of seventeen, Dustine Edward Marsden "Dusty" Fog had won promotion in the field to the rank of captain and was put in command of Company "C," Texas Light Cavalry.[2] At the head of them throughout the campaign in Arkansas, he had earned the reputation for being an exceptional military raider and worthy contemporary of Turner Ashby and John Singleton "the Grey Ghost" Mosby, the South's other leading exponents of what would later become known as "commando" raids.[3] In addition to averting a scheme by a Union general to employ a virulent version of what was to be given the name, "mustard gas" following its use by Germans in World War I[4] and preventing a pair of pro-Northern fanatics from starting an Indian uprising which would have decimated much of Texas,[5] he had supported Belle "the Rebel Spy" Boyd on two of her most dangerous assignments.[6][6a]

At the conclusion of the War Between The States, Dusty became the *segundo* of the great OD Connected ranch—its

---

[1] *Details of some of Dustine Edward Marsden "Dusty" Fog's activities prior to his enrolment are given in:* Part Five, "A Time For Improvisation, Mr. Blaze," J.T.'S HUNDREDTH.

[2] *Told in:* YOU'RE IN COMMAND NOW, MR. FOG.

[3] *Told in:* THE BIG GUN, UNDER THE STARS AND BARS, Part One, "The Futility Of War," THE FASTEST GUN IN TEXAS *and* KILL DUSTY FOG!

[4] *Told in:* A MATTER OF HONOUR.

[5] *Told in:* THE DEVIL GUN.

[6] *Told in:* THE COLT AND THE SABRE *and* THE REBEL SPY.

[6a] *More details of the career of Belle "the Rebel Spy" Boyd can be found in:* THE BLOODY BORDER; BACK TO THE BLOODY BORDER—*Berkley Books, New York, August 1978 edition re-titled,* RENEGADE—THE HOODED RIDERS; THE BAD BUNCH; SET A-FOOT: TO ARMS! TO ARMS! IN DIXIE!; THE SOUTH WILL RISE AGAIN; THE QUEST FOR BOWIE'S BLADE; Part Eight, "Affair Of Honour," J.T.'S HUNDREDTH *and* Part Five, "The Butcher's Fiery End," J.T.'S LADIES.

brand being a letter O to which was attached a D—in Rio Hondo County, Texas. Its owner and his maternal uncle, General Jackson Baines "Ole Devil" Hardin, C.S.A., had been crippled in a riding accident and was confined to a wheel-chair.[7] [7a] This placed much responsibility, including the need to handle an important mission—with the future relationship, between the United States and Mexico at stake—upon his young shoulders.[8] While carrying out the assignment, he met Mark Counter and the Ysabel Kid. Not only did they do much to bring it to a successful conclusion, they became his closest friends and leading lights of the ranch's floating outfit.[9] After helping to gather horses to replenish the ranch's depleted remuda,[10] he was sent to assist Colonel Charles Goodnight[11] [11a] [11b] on the trail drive to Fort Summer, New Mexico, which did much to help Texas recover from the impoverished conditions

[7] *Told in,* Part Three, "The Paint," THE FASTEST GUN IN TEXAS.

[7a] *Further information about the General's earlier career is given in the* Ole Devil Hardin *and Civil War series. His death is recorded in,* DOC LEROY, M.D.

[8] *Told in:* THE YSABEL KID.

[9] *"Floating Outfit": a group of four to six cowhands employed by a large ranch to work the more distant sections of the property. Taking food in a chuck wagon, or "greasy sack" on the back of a mule, they would be away from the ranch house for long periods and so were selected for their honesty, loyalty, reliability and capability in all aspects of their work. Because of General Hardin's prominence in the affairs of Texas, the OD Connected's floating outfit were frequently sent to assist such of his friends who found themselves in difficulties or endangered.*

[10] *Told in:* .44 CALIBRE MAN *and* A HORSE CALLED MOGOLLON.

[11] *Rancher and master cattleman Charles Goodnight never served in the Army. The rank was honorary and granted by his fellow Texans in respect for his abilities as a fighting man and leader.*

[11a] *In addition to playing an active part in the events recorded in the books referred to in Footnotes 13 and 14, Colonel Goodnight makes "guest" appearances in:* Part One, "The Half Breed," THE HALF BREED; *its "expansion,"* WHITE INDIANS *and* IS-A-MAN.

[11b] *Although Dusty Fog never received higher official rank than Captain, in the later years of his life, he too was given the honorific, "Colonel" for possessing the same qualities.*

left by the War.[12] With that achieved, he had been equally successful in helping Goodnight convince other ranchers it would be possible to drive large herds of longhorn cattle to the railroad in Kansas.[13]

Having proven himself to be a first class cowhand, Dusty went on to become acknowledged as a very competent trail boss,[14] roundup captain,[15] and town taming lawman.[16] Competing in the first Cochise County Fair in Arizona, against a number of well known exponents of very rapid drawing and accurate shooting with revolvers, he won the title, "The Fastest Gun In The West."[17] In later years, following his marriage to Lady Winifred Amelia "Freddie Woods" Besgrove-Woodstone,[18] he became a noted diplomat.

Dusty never found his lack of stature an impediment to his achievements. In fact, he occasionally found it helped him to achieve a purpose.[19] To supplement his natural strength,[20] also

[12] *Told in:* GOODNIGHT'S DREAM—*Bantam Books, U.S.A. July 1974 edition re-titled,* THE FLOATING OUTFIT, *despite our already having had a volume of that name published by Corgi Books, U.K., see Footnote 19*—and FROM HIDE AND HORN.

[13] *Told in:* SET TEXAS BACK ON HER FEET—*although Berkley Books, New York re-titled their October, 1978 edition* VIRDIDIAN'S TRAIL, *they reverted to the original title when re-issuing the book in July, 1980*—and THE HIDE AND TALLOW MEN.

[14] *Told in:* TRAIL BOSS.

[15] *Told in:* THE MAN FROM TEXAS.

[16] *Told in:* QUIET TOWN, THE MAKING OF A LAWMAN, THE TROUBLE BUSTERS, THE GENTLE GIANT, THE SMALL TEXAN *and* THE TOWN TAMERS.

[17] *Told in:* GUN WIZARD.

[18] *Lady Winifred Besgrove-Woodstone appears as "Freddie Woods" in:* THE TROUBLE BUSTERS; THE MAKING OF A LAWMAN; THE GENTLE GIANT; BUFFALO ARE COMING!; THE FORTUNE HUNTERS; WHITE STALLION, RED MARE; THE WHIP AND THE WAR LANCE *and Part Five,* "The Butcher's Fiery End," J.T.'S LADIES. *She also "guest" stars under her married name, Mrs. Freddie Fog, in:* NO FINGER ON THE TRIGGER.

[19] *Three occasions when Dusty Fog utilized his small size to his advantage are described in:* KILL DUSTY FOG!; *Part One,* "Dusty Fog And The Schoolteacher," THE HARD RIDERS; *its "expansion,"* MASTER OF TRIGGERNOMETRY

perhaps with a desire to distract attention from his small size, he had taught himself to be completely ambidextrous.[21] Possessing perfectly attuned reflexes, he could draw either, or both, his Colts—whether the 1860 Army Model,[22] or their improved "descendant," the fabled 1873 Model "Peacemaker"[23]—with lightning speed and shoot most accurately. Furthermore, Ole Devil Hardin's "valet," Tommy Okasi, was Japanese and a trained Samurai warrior.[24] From him, as was the case with the General's "granddaughter," Elizabeth "Betty" Hardin,[25] [25a] Dusty learned ju-jitsu and Karate. Neither

and Part One, "The Phantom Of Gallup Creek," THE FLOATING OUTFIT.

[20] *Two examples of how Dusty Fog exploited his exceptional physical strength are given in:* MASTER OF TRIGGERNOMETRY *and* THE PEACEMAKERS.

[21] *The ambidextrous prowess was in part hereditary. It was possessed and exploited with equal success by Freddie and Dusty's grandson, Alvin Dustine "Cap" Fog who also inherited his grandfather's physique of a Hercules in miniature. Alvin utilized these traits to help him be acknowledged as one of the finest combat pistol shots in the United States during the Prohibition era and to earn his nickname by becoming the youngest man ever to hold rank of Captain in the Texas Rangers. See the* Alvin Dustine "Cap" Fog *series for further details of his career.*

[22] *Although the military sometimes claimed derisively it was easier to kill a sailor than a soldier, the weight factor of the respective weapons had caused the United States' Navy to adopt a revolver of .36 calibre while the Army employed the larger .44. The reason was that the weapon would be carried on a seaman's belt and not—handguns having been originally and primarily developed for use by cavalry—on the person or saddle of a man who would be doing most of his travelling and fighting from the back of a horse. Therefore, .44 became known as the "Army" calibre and .36, the "Navy."*

[23] *Details about the Colt Model P of 1873, more frequently known as "the Peacemaker" can be found in those volumes following* THE PEACEMAKERS *in our list of Floating Outfit* series' titles in chronological sequence.*

[24] *"Tommy Okasi" is an Americanised corruption of the name given by the man in question, who had left Japan for reasons which the Hardin, Fog and Blaze families refuse to divulge even at this late date, when he was rescued from a*

form of unarmed combat had received the publicity they would be given in later years and were little known in the Western Hemisphere at that time. Therefore, Dusty found the knowledge useful when he had to fight with bare hands against larger, heavier and stronger men.

derelict vessel in the China Sea by a ship under the command of General Hardin's father.

[25] *The members of the Hardin, Fog and Blaze families cannot—or will not—make any statement upon the exact relationship between Elizabeth "Betty" and her "grandfather," General Hardin.*

[25a] *Betty Hardin appears in:* Part Five, "A Time For Improvisation, Mr. Blaze," J.T.'S HUNDREDTH; Part Four, "It's Our Turn To Improvise, Miss Blaze," J.T.'S LADIES; KILL DUSTY FOG!; THE BAD BUNCH: McGRAW'S INHERITANCE; Part Two, "The Quartet," The HALF BREED; THE RIO HONDO WAR *and* GUNSMOKE THUNDER.

With his exceptional good looks and magnificent physical development,[1] [1a] [1b] [1c] Mark Counter presented the kind of appearance many people expected of a man with the reputation gained by his *amigo*, Captain Dustine Edward Marsden "Dusty" Fog. It was a fact of which they took advantage when the need arose.[2] On one occasion, it was also the cause of the blond giant being subjected to a murder attempt although the Rio Hondo gun Wizard was the intended victim.[3]

While serving as a lieutenant under the command of General Bushrod Sheldon in the War Between the States, Mark's merits as an efficient and courageous officer had been overshadowed by his unconventional taste in uniforms. Always something of a dandy, coming from a wealthy family had allowed him to indulge in his whims. Despite considerable op-

---

[1] *Two of Mark Counter's grandsons, Andrew Mark "Big Andy" Counter and Ranse Smith inherited his good looks and exceptional physique as did two great-grandsons, Deputy Sheriff Bradford "Brad" Counter and James Allenvale "Bunduki" Gunn. Unfortunately, while willing to supply information about other members of his family, past and present, "Big Andy" has so far declined to allow publication of any of his own adventures.*

[1a] *Some details of Ranse Smith's career as a peace officer during the Prohibition era are recorded in:* THE JUSTICE OF COMPANY "Z" *and* THE RETURN OF RAPIDO CLINT AND MR. J.G. REEDER.

[1b] *Brad Counter's activities are described in:* Part Eleven, "Preventive Law enforcement," J.T.'S HUNDREDTH *and the* Rockabye County *series, covering aspects of law enforcement in present day Texas.*

[1c] *Some of James Gunn's life story is told in:* Part Twelve, "The Mchawi's Powers," J.T.'s HUNDREDTH *and the* Bunduki *series. His nickname arose from the Swahili word for a hand held firearm of any kind being, "bunduki" and gave rise to the horrible pun that when he was a child he was, "Toto ya Bunduki," meaning "Son of a Gun."*

[2] *One occasion is recorded in:* THE SOUTH WILL RISE AGAIN.

[3] *The incident is described in:* BEGUINAGE.

position and disapproval from hide-bound senior officers, his adoption of a "skirtless" tunic in particular has come to be much copied by the other rich young bloods of the Confederate States' Army.[4] Similarly in later years, having received an independent income through the will of a maiden aunt,[5] his taste in attire had dictated what the well dressed cowhand from Texas would wear to be in fashion.

When peace had come between the North and the South, Mark had accompanied Sheldon to fight for Emperor Maximilian in Mexico. There he had met Dusty Fog and the Ysabel Kid. On returning with them to Texas, he had received an offer to join the floating outfit of the OD Connected ranch. Knowing his two older brothers could help his father, Big Ranse, to run the family's R Over C ranch in the Big Bend country—and considering life would be more enjoyable and exciting in the company of his two *amigos*—he accepted.

An expert cowhand, Mark had become known as Dusty's right bower.[6] He had also gained acclaim by virtue of his enormous strength. Among other feats, it was told how he used a tree-trunk in the style of a Scottish caber to dislodge outlaws from a cabin in which they had forted up,[7] and broke the neck of a Texas longhorn steer with his bare hands.[8] He had acquired further fame for his ability at bare handed roughhouse brawling. However, due to spending so much time in the company of the Rio Hondo gun wizard, his full potential as a gun fighter received little attention. Nevertheless, men who were competent to judge such matters stated that he was second only to the small Texan when it came to drawing fast

---

[4] The Manual of Dress Regulations for the *Confederate States' Army* stipulated that the tunic should have "a skirt extending half way between hip and knee."

[5] The legacy also caused two attempts to be made upon Mark's life, see: CUT ONE, THEY ALL BLEED and Part Two, "We Hang Horse Thieves High," J.T.'S HUNDREDTH.

[6] "Right bower"; second in command, derived from the name given to the second highest trump card in the game of euchre.

[7] Told in: RANGELAND HERCULES.

[8] Told in: THE MAN FROM TEXAS, this is a rather "pin the tail on the donkey" title used by our first publishers to replace our own, ROUNDUP CAPTAIN which we considered far more apt.

and shooting accurately with a brace of long barrelled Colt revolvers.[9]

Many women found Mark irresistible, including Martha "Calamity Jane" Canary.[10][10a] However, in his younger days, only one—the lady outlaw, Belle Starr—held his heart.[11][11a][11b] It was not until several years after her death that he courted

[9] *Evidence of Mark Counter's competence as a gun fighter and his standing compared to Dusty Fog is given in:* GUN WIZARD.

[10] *Martha "Calamity Jane" Canary's meetings with Mark Counter are described in:* Part One, "The Bounty On Belle Starr's Scalp," TROUBLED RANGE; *its "expansion,"* CALAMITY, MARK AND BELLE; Part One, "Better Than Calamity," THE WILDCATS; *its "expansion,"* CUT ONE, THEY ALL BLEED; THE BAD BUNCH; THE FORTUNE HUNTERS; THE BIG HUNT *and* GUNS IN THE NIGHT.

[10a] *Further details about the career of Martha Jane Canary are given in the* Calamity Jane *series, also:* Part Seven, "Deadwood, August the 2nd, 1876," J.T.'S HUNDREDTH; Part Six, "Mrs. Wild Bill," J.T.'S LADIES *and she makes a "guest" appearance in:* Part Two, "A Wife For Dusty Fog," THE SMALL TEXAN.

[11] *How Mark Counter's romance with Belle Starr commenced, progressed and ended is told in:* Part One, "The Bounty On Belle Starr's Scalp," TROUBLED RANGE; *its "expansion,"* CALAMITY, MARK AND BELLE; THE BAD BUNCH; RANGELAND HERCULES; THE CODE OF DUSTY FOG; Part Two, "We Hang Horse Thieves High," J.T.'S HUNDREDTH; THE GENTLE GIANT; Part Four, "A Lady Known As Belle," THE HARD RIDERS *and* GUNS IN THE NIGHT.

[11a] *Belle Starr "stars"—no pun intended—in:* WANTED; BELLE STARR. *She also makes "guest" appearances in:* THE QUEST FOR BOWIE'S BLADE; Part One, "The Set-Up," SAGEBRUSH SLEUTH; *its "expansion,"* WACO'S BADGE *and* Part Six, "Mrs. Wild Bill," J.T.'S LADIES.

[11b] *We are frequently asked why it is the "Belle Starr" we describe is so different from a photograph which appears in various books. The researches of the world's foremost fictionist geanologist, Philip Jose Farmer—author of, amongst numerous other works, TARZAN ALIVE, A Definitive Biography of Lord Greystoke and DOC SAVAGE, His Apocalyptic Life—with whom we consulted have established the lady about whom we are writing is not the same person as another equally famous bearer of the name. However, the Counter family have asked Mr. Farmer and ourselves to keep her true identity a secret and this we intend to do.*

and married Dawn Sutherland, who he had first met on the trail drive taken by Colonel Charles Goodnight to Fort Sumner, New Mexico.[12] The discovery of oil on their ranch brought an added wealth to them and this commodity now forms the major part of the present members of the family's income.[13]

Recent biographical details we have received from the current head of the family, Andrew Mark "Big Andy" Counter, establish that Mark was descended on his mother's side from Sir Reginald Front de Boeuf, notorious as lord of Torquilstone Castle in Medieval England[14] and who lived up to the family motto, *Cave Adsum*.[15] However, although a maternal aunt and her son, Jessica and Trudeau Front de Boeuf, behaved in a way which suggested they had done so,[16] the blond giant had not inherited the very unsavoury character and behaviour of his ancestor.

[12] *Told in:* GOODNIGHT'S DREAM *and* FROM HIDE AND HORN.

[13] *This is established by inference in:* Case Three, "The Deadly Ghost," YOU'RE A TEXAS RANGER, ALVIN FOG.

[14] *See:* IVANHOE, *by Sir Walter Scott.*

[15] *"Cave Adsum"; roughly translated from Latin, "Beware, I am Here."*

[16] *Some information about Jessica and Trudeau Front de Boeuf can be found in:* CUT ONE, THEY ALL BLEED *and* Part Three, "Responsibility To Kinfolks," OLE DEVIL'S HANDS AND FEET.

APPENDIX THREE

Raven Head, only daughter of Chief Long Walker, war leader of the *Pehnane*—Wasp, Quick Stinger, Raider—Comanche's Dog Soldier lodge and his French Creole *pairaivo*,[1] maried an Irish-Kentuckian adventurer, Big Sam Ysabel, but died giving birth to their first child.

Baptized "Loncey Dalton Ysabel," the boy was raised after the fashion of the *Nemenuh*.[2] With his father away from the camp for much of the time, engaged upon the family's combined businesses of mustanging—catching and breaking wild horses[3]—and smuggling, his education had largely been left in the hands of his maternal grandfather.[4] From Long Walker, he learned all those things a Comanche warrior must know: how to ride the wildest freshly caught mustang, or make a trained animal subservient to his will while "raiding"—a polite name for the favourite pastime of the male *Nemenuh*, stealing horses—to follow the faintest tracks and just as effectively conceal signs of his own passing,[5] to locate hidden enemies, or keep out of sight himself when the need arose; to move in silence on the darkest of nights, or through the thick-

[1] "Pairaivo": *first, or favourite wife. As is the case with the other Comanche terms, this is a phonetic spelling.*

[2] "Nemenuh"; *"the People," the Comanches' name for themselves and their nation. Members of other tribes with whom they came into contact called them, frequently with good cause, the "Tshaoh," the "Enemy People."*

[3] *A description of the way in which mustangers operate is given in:* .44 CALIBRE MAN *and* A HORSE CALLED MOGOLLON.

[4] *Told in:* COMANCHE.

[5] *An example of how the Ysabel Kid could conceal his tracks is given in:* Part One, "The Half Breed," THE HALF BREED.

est cover; to know the ways of wild creatures[6] and, in some cases, imitate their calls so well that others of their kind were fooled.[7]

The boy proved a most excellent pupil at all the subjects. Nor were practical means of protecting himself forgotten. Not only did he learn to use all the traditional weapons of the Comanche,[8] when he had come into the possession of fire-arms, he had inherited his father's Kentuckian skill at shooting with rifle and, while not *real* fast on the draw—taking slightly over a second to bring his Colt Second Model of 1848 Dragoon revolver and fire, whereas a tophand could practically halve that time—he could perform passably with it. Furthermore, he won his *Nemenuh* "Man-name," *Cuchilo,* Spanish for "Knife," by his exceptional ability at wielding one. In fact, it was claimed by those best qualified to judge that he could equal the alleged designer in performing with the massive and special type of blade which bore the name of Colonel James Bowie.[9, 9a, 9b, 9c]

<hr />

[6] *Two examples of how the Ysabel Kid's knowledge of wild animals were turned to good use are given in:* OLD MOCCASINS ON THE TRAIL *and* BUFFALO ARE COMING!

[7] *An example of how well the Ysabel Kid could impersonate the call of a wild animal is recorded in:* Part Three, "A Wolf's A Knowing Critter," J.T.'S HUNDREDTH.

[8] *One occasion when the Ysabel Kid employed his skill with traditional Comanche weapons is described in:* RIO GUNS.

[9] *Some researchers claim that the actual designer of the knife which became permanently attached to Colonel James Bowie's name was his oldest brother, Rezin Pleasant. Although it is generally conceded the maker was James Black, a master cutler in Arkansas, some authorities state it was manufactured by Jesse Cliffe, a white blacksmith employed by the Bowie family on their plantation in Rapides Parish, Louisiana.*

[9a] *What happened to James Bowie's knife after his death in the final assault of the siege of the Alamo Mission, San Antonio de Bexar, Texas, on March the 6th, 1836, is told in:* GET URREA *and* THE QUEST FOR BOWIE'S BLADE.

[9b] *As all James Black's knives were custom made, there were variations in their dimensions. The specimen owned by*

Joining his father in smuggling expeditions along the Rio Grande, the boy became known to the Mexicans of the border country as *Cabrito*—the Spanish name for a young goat—a nickname which arose out of hearing white men refer to him as the "Ysabel Kid," but it was spoken *very* respectfully in that context. Smuggling was not an occupation to attract the meek and mild of manner, yet even the roughest and toughest of the bloody border's denizens came to acknowledge it did not pay to rile up Big Sam Ysabel's son. The education received by the Kid had not been calculated to develop any over-inflated belief in the sanctity of human life. When crossed, he dealt with the situation like a *Pehnane* Dog Soldier—to which war lodge of savage and *most* efficient warriors he had earned initiation—swiftly and in an effectively deadly manner.

During the War Between The States, the Kid and his father had commenced by riding as scouts for Colonel John Singleton "the Grey Ghost" Mosby. Soon, however, their specialized knowledge and talents were diverted to having them collect and deliver to the Confederate States' authorities in Texas supplies which had been purchased in Mexico, or run through the blockade by the United States' Navy into Matamoros. It

the Ysabel Kid had a blade eleven and a half inches in length, two and a half inches wide and a quarter of an inch thick at the guard. According to William "Bo" Randall, of Randall-Made Knives, Orlando, Florida—a master cutler and authority upon the subject in his own right—James Bowie's knife weighed forty-three ounces, having a blade eleven inches long, two and a quarter inches wide and three-eighths of an inch thick. His company's Model 12 "Smithsonian" bowie knife—one of which is owned by James Allenvale "Bunduki" Gunn, details of whose career can be found in the Bunduki series—is modelled on it.

[9c] One thing all "bowie" knives have in common, regardless of dimensions, is a "clip" point. The otherwise unsharpened back of the blade joins and becomes an extension of the main cutting surface in a concave arc, whereas a "spear" point—which is less utilitarian—is formed by the two sides coming together in symmetrical curves.

was hard and dangerous work,[10] but never more so than the two occasions when they became engaged in assignments with Belle "the Rebel Spy" Boyd.[11]

Soon after the War ended, Sam Ysabel was murdered. While hunting down the killers, the Kid met Captain Dustine Edward Marsden "Dusty" Fog and Mark Counter. When the mission upon which they were engaged was brought to its successful conclusion, learning the Kid no longer wished to go on either smuggling or mustanging, the small Texan offered him employment at the OD Connected ranch. It had been in the capacity as scout rather than ordinary cowhand that he was required and his talents in that field were frequently of the greatest use as a member of the floating outfit.

The acceptance of the job by the Kid was of the greatest benefit all around. Dusty acquired another loyal friend who was ready to stick to him through any kind of peril. The ranch obtained the services of an extremely capable and efficient fighting man. For his part, the Kid was turned from a life of petty crime—with the ever present danger of having his illicit activities develop into serious law breaking—and became a useful and law abiding member of society. Peace officers and honest citizens might have found cause to feel grateful for that. His *Nemenuh* upbringing would have made him a terrible and murderous outlaw if he had been driven into a life of violent crime.

Obtaining his first repeating rifle—a Winchester Model of 1866, although at first known as the "New Improved Henry," nicknamed the "Old Yellowboy" because of its brass frame— while in Mexico with Dusty and Mark, the Kid had soon become an expert in its use. At the First Cochise County Fair in Arizona, despite circumstances compelling him to use a weapon with which he was not familiar,[12] he won the first prize in the rifle shooting competition against stiff opposition. The prize was one of the legendary Winchester Model of 1873

[10] *An occasion when Big Sam Ysabel went on a mission without his son is recorded in:* THE DEVIL GUN.

[11] *Told in:* THE BLOODY BORDER *and* BACK TO THE BLOODY BORDER.

[12] *The circumstances are described in:* GUN WIZARD.

rifles which qualified for the honoured designation, "One Of A Thousand."[13]

It was, in part, through the efforts of the Kid that the majority of the Comanche bands agreed to go on the reservation, following attempts to ruin the signing of the treaty.[14] It was to a large extent due to his efforts that the outlaw town of Hell was located and destroyed.[15] Aided by Annie "Is-A-Man" Singing Bear—a girl of mixed parentage who gained the distinction of becoming accepted as a *Nemenuh* warrior[16]—he played a major part in preventing the attempted theft of Morton Lewis' ranch provoking trouble with the *Kweharehnuh* Comanche.[17] To help a young man out of difficulties caused by a gang of card cheats, he teamed up with the lady outlaw, Belle Starr.[18] When he accompanied Martha "Calamity Jane" Canary to inspect a ranch she had inherited, they became involved in as dangerous a situation as either had ever faced.[19]

Remaining at the OD Connected ranch until he, Dusty and Mark met their deaths whilst on a hunting trip to Kenya

[13] *When manufacturing the extremely popular Winchester Model of 1873 rifle—which they claimed to be the "Gun Which Won The West"—the makers selected all those barrels found to shoot with exceptional accuracy to be fitted with set triggers and given a special fine finish. Originally, these were inscribed, "1 of 1,000," but this was later changed to script, "One Of A Thousand." However, the title was a considerable understatement. Only one hundred and thirty-six out of a total production of 720,610 qualified for the distinction. Those of a grade lower were to be designated, "One Of A Hundred," but only seven were so named. The practice commenced in 1875 and was discontinued three years later because the management decided it was not good sales policy to suggest different grades of gun were being produced.*

[14] *Told in:* SIDEWINDER.

[15] *Told in:* HELL IN THE PALO DURO *and* GO BACK TO HELL.

[16] *How Annie Singing Bear acquired the distinction of becoming a warrior and won her "man-name" is told in:* IS-A-MAN.

[17] *Told in:* WHITE INDIANS.

[18] *Told in:* Part Two, "The Poison And The Cure," WANTED! BELLE STARR.

[19] *Told in:* WHITE STALLION, RED MARE.

shortly after the turn of the century, his descendants continued to be associated with the Hardin, Fog and Blaze clan and the Counter family.[20]

---

[20] *Mark Scrapton, a grandson of the Ysabel Kid, served as a member of Company "Z," Texas Rangers, with Alvin Dustine "Cap" Fog and Ranse Smith—respectively grandson of Captain Dustine Edward Marsden "Dusty" Fog and Mark Counter—during the Prohibiton era. Information about their specialized duties is given in the* Alvin Dustine "Cap" Fog *series.*

Left an orphan almost from birth by an Indian raid and acquiring the only name he knew from the tribe involved,[1] Waco was raised as one of a North Texas rancher's large family.[2] Guns were always part of his life and his sixteenth birthday saw him riding with the tough, "wild onion" crew of Clay Allison. Like their employer, the CA cowhands were notorious for their wild and occasionally dangerous behaviour. Living in the company of such men, all older than himself, the youngster had become quick to take offence and well able, eager even, to prove he could draw his revolvers with lightning speed and shoot very accurately. It had seemed only a matter of time before one shootout too many would see him branded as a killer and fleeing from the law with a price on his head.

Fortunately for Waco and—as was the case with the Ysabel Kid—law abiding citizens, that day did not come!

From the moment Dusty Fog saved the youngster's life during a cattle stampede, at some considerable risk to his own, a change for the better had commenced.[3] Leaving Allison, with the blessing of the "Washita curly wolf," Waco had become a member of the OD Connected ranch's floating outfit. The other members of that elite group treated him like a favourite younger brother and taught him many useful lessons. Instruction in bare handed combat was provided by Mark Counter. The Kid showed him how to read tracks and other secrets of the scout's trade. From a friend who was a professional gambler, Frank Derringer,[4] had come information about

[1] Alvin Dustine "Cap" Fog informs us that at his marriage to Elizabeth "Beth" Morrow, Waco used the surname of his adoptive family, "Catlin."

[2] How Waco repaid his obligation to the family which raised him is told in: WACO'S DEBT.

[3] Told in: TRIGGER FAST.

[4] Frank Derringer appears in: QUIET TOWN, THE MAKING OF A LAWMAN, THE TROUBLE BUSTERS, THE GENTLE GIANT and COLD DECK, HOT LEAD.

the ways of honest and dishonest followers of his chosen field of endeavour. However, it was from the Rio Hondo gun wizard that the most important advice had come. *When*, he already knew well enough *how*, to shoot. Dusty had also supplied training which, helped by an inborn flair for deductive reasoning, turned him into a peace officer of exceptional merit. After serving in other official capacities,[5] then with the Arizona Rangers[6]—in the company of Marvin Eldridge "Doc" Leroy[7]—and as sheriff of Two Forks County, Utah,[8] he was eventually appointed a United States' marshal.[9]

[5] *Told in:* THE MAKING OF A LAWMAN; THE TROUBLE BUSTERS; THE GENTLE GIANT; Part Five, "The Hired Butcher." THE HARD RIDERS; Part Four, "A Tolerable Straight Shooting Gun," THE FLOATING OUTFIT; Part Two, "The Invisible Winchester," OLE DEVIL'S HANDS AND FEET; THE SMALL TEXAN *and* THE TOWN TAMERS.

[6] *During the 1870's the Governor of Arizona formed this particular law enforcement agency to cope with the threat of serious organized law breaking in his Territory. A similar decision was taken by a later Governor and the Arizona Rangers were brought back into being. Why it was considered necessary to appoint the first force, how it operated and was finally disbanded is recorded in the* Waco *series and Part Six, "Keep Good Temper Alive,"* J.T.'S HUNDREDTH.

[7] *At the period of this narrative, although having acquired a reputation for knowledge in medical matters, Marvin Eldridge "Doc" Leroy had not yet been able to attain his ambition of following his father's footsteps by becoming a qualified doctor. How he did so is recorded in:* DOC LEROY, M.D.

[8] *Told in:* THE DRIFTER, *which also describes how Waco first met Elizabeth "Beth" Morrow.*

[9] *Told in:* HOUND DOG MAN.

Throughout the years we have been writing, we have frequently received letters asking for various terms we employ to be explained in greater detail. While we do not have the slightest objection to such correspondence and always reply, we have found it saves much time consuming repetition to include those most frequently requested in each new title. We ask our "old hands," who have seen these items many times in the past, to remember there are always "new chums" coming along who have not and to bear with us. J.T.E.

1. We strongly suspect the trend in movies and television series made since the mid-1950's wherein all cowhands are portrayed as heavily bearded, long haired and filthy arose less from a desire on the part of the productions companies to create "realism" than because there were so few actors available—particularly to play "supporting" roles—who were short haired and clean shaven. Another factor was because the "liberal" elements who were starting to gain control over much of the media seem to obtain some form of "ego trip" from showing dirty conditions, filthy habits and unkempt appearances. In our extensive reference library, we cannot find even a dozen photographs of actual *cowhands*—as opposed to civilian scouts for the Army, old time mountain men, or gold prospectors—with long hair and bushy beards. In fact, our reading on the subject and conversations with friends living in the Western States of America have led us to the conclusion that the term "long hair" was one of opprobrium in the Old West and Prohibition eras just as it still tends to be today in cattle raising country.

2. Introduced in 1873 as the Colt Model P "Single Action Army" revolver—although with a calibre of .45 instead of the erstwhile traditional .44—was more generally known as "the Peacemaker." Production continued until 1941, when it was taken out of the line to make way for the more modern weapons required for use in World War II.

2a. Between 1873 and 1941, over three hundred and fifty thousand were manufactured in practically every hand gun calibre from .22 Short Rimfire to .476 Eley; with the exception of the .41 and .44 Magnums, which were not developed commercially during the original production period. However, the majority fired either .45 or .44-40. The latter, given the designation, "Frontier Model," handled the same cartridges as the Winchester Model of 1873 rifle and carbine.

2b. The barrel lengths of the Model P could be from three inches in the "Storekeeper" Model, which did not have an extractor rod for dislodging spent cartridge cases from the cylinder, to the sixteen inches for what became known to the public and firearms collectors as the "Buntline Special." The latter was also offered with an attachable metal "skeleton" butt stock so it could be used as an extemporized carbine. The main barrel lengths were: Cavalry, seven and a half inches; Artillery, five and a half inches; Civilian, four and three-quarter inches.

2c. Popular demand, said to have resulted from the upsurge of action-escapism-adventure Western series being shown on television, brought the Peacemaker back into production in 1955 and it is still in the line. During this period, because of interest arising from the use of such a weapon by actor Hugh O'Brian starring in the WYATT EARP series, Colt for the first time produced and gave a Model the name, "Buntline special," albeit with a barrel only twelve and a half inches in length.

3. We consider at best specious—at worst, a snobbish attempt to "put down" the myth and legends of the Old West—the frequently repeated assertion that the gun fighters of that era could not "hit a barn door at twenty yards." While willing to concede that the average person then, as now, would not have much skill in using a handgun, knowing his life would depend upon it, the professional *pistolero* on either side of the law expended time, money and effort to acquire proficiency. Furthermore, such a man did not carry a revolver to indulge in shooting at *anything* except at close range. He employed it as a readily accessible *weapon* which would incapacitate an enemy, preferably with the first shot, at close quarters, hence the preference for a cartridge of heavy calibre.

3a. With the exception of .22 calibre handguns intended for casual pleasure shooting, those specially designed for Olympic style "pistol" matches, the Remington XP100—one of which makes an appearance in: Case Two, "A Voice From The Past," THE LAWMEN OF ROCKABYE COUNTY—designed for "varmint" hunting at long distance, or medium to heavy calibre automatic pistols "accurized" and in the hands of a proficient exponent of moder "combat" shooting, a handgun is a short range *defensive* and not an *offensive* weapon. Any Old West gun fighter, or peace officer in the Prohibition era and present times expecting to have to shoot at distance beyond about twenty *feet* would take the precaution of arming himself with a shotgun or a rifle.

4. "Make wolf bait," one term meaning to kill. Derived from the practice in the Old West, when a range was infested by stock killing predators—not necessarily just wolves, but coyotes, the occasional jaguar in southern regions, black and grizzly bears—of slaughtering an animal and, having poisoned the carcase, leaving it to be devoured by the carnivores.

5. "Up to the Green River": to kill, generally with a knife. First produced on the Green River, at Greenfield, Massachusetts, in 1834, a very popular type of general purpose knife had the inscription, "J. Russell & Co./Green River Works" on the blade just below the hilt. Therefore any edged weapon thrust into an enemy "up to the Green River" would prove fatal whether it bore the inscription or not.

6. "Light a shuck," a cowhand term for leaving hurriedly. Derived from the habit in night camps on "open range" roundups and trail drives of supplying "shucks"—dried corn cobs—to be lit and used for illumination by anybody who had to leave the campfire and walk about in the darkness. As the "shuck" burned away very quickly, a person needed to hurry if wanting to benefit from its illumination.

7. The sharp toes and high heels of boots worn by cowhands were functional rather than merely decorative. The former could find and enter, or be slipped free from, a stirrup iron very quickly in an emergency. Not only did the latter offer a firmer brace against the stirrups, they could be spiked into the ground to supply added holding power when roping on foot.

8. Americans in general used the word, "cinch," derived from the Spanish, *"cincha,"* to describe the short band made from coarsely woven horse hair, canvas, or cordage and terminated at each end with a metal ring which—together with the *latigo* —is used to fasten the saddle on the back of a horse. However, because of the word's connections with Mexico, Texans tended to employ the term, "girth," usually pronouncing it as "girt." As cowhands from the Lone Star State fastened the end of the lariat to the saddlehorn, even when roping half wild

longhorn cattle or free-ranging mustangs, instead of relying upon a "dally" which could be slipped free almost instantaneously in an emergency, their rigs had double girths.

9. "Chaps": leather overalls worn by American cowhands as protection for the legs. The word, pronounced, "shaps," is an abbreviation for the Spanish, *"chaperejos,"* or *chaparreras,"* meaning "leather breeches." Contrary to what is frequently shown in Western movies, no cowhand ever kept his chaps on when their protection was not required. Even if he should arrive in a town with them on, he would remove and either hang them over his saddle, or leave them behind the bar in his favourite saloon for safe keeping until his visit was over.

10. "Hackamore": an Americanised corruption of the Spanish word, *"jaquima,"* meaning "headstall." Very popular with Indians in particular, it was an ordinary halter, except for having reins instead of a leading rope. It had a headpiece something like a conventional bridle, a brow band about three inches wide which could be slid down the cheeks to cover the horse's eyes, but no throat latch. Instead of a bit, a *"bosal"*—a leather, rawhide, or metal ring around the head immediately above the mouth—was used as a means of control and guidance.

11. "Right as the Indian side of a horse"; absolutely correct. Derived from the habit of Indians mounting from the right, or "off" and not the left, or "near" side as was done by people of European descent and Mexicans.

12. "Mason-Dixon line," erroneously called the "Mason-Dixie line." The boundary between Pennsylvania and Maryland, as surveyed from 1763–67 by the Englishmen, Charles Mason and Jeremiah Dixon. It became considered as the dividing line separating the Southern "Slave" and Northern "Free" States.

13. "New England": the North East section of the United States—including Massachusetts, New Hampshire, Connecticut, Maine, Vermont and Rhode Island—which was first settled by people primarily from the British Isles.

14. "Gone to Texas": on the run from the law. During the white colonization period, which had commenced in the early 1820's, many fugitives from justice in America had fled to Texas and would continue to do so until annexation by the United States on February the 16th, 1846. Until the latter became a fact, they had known there was little danger of being arrested and extradited by the local authorities. In fact, like

Kenya Colony from the 1920's to the outbreak of World War II—in spite of the number of honest, hard working and law abiding settlers genuinely seeking to make a permanent home there—Texas had gained a reputation for being a "place in the sun for shady people."

15. "Summer name": an alias. In the Old West, the only acceptable way to express doubt about the identity which was supplied when being introduced to a stranger was to ask, "Is that your *summer* name?"

16. In the Old West, the jurisdictional powers of various types of law enforcement agencies were established as follows. A town marshal, sometimes called "constable" in smaller communities, and his deputies were confined to the town or city which hired them. A sheriff—who was generally elected into office for a set period of time—and his deputies were restricted to their own county. However, in less heavily populated areas, he might also serve a marshal of the county seat. Texas and Arizona Rangers could go anywhere within the boundaries of their respective States, but technically were required to await an invitation from the local peace officers before participating in an investigation. Although a United States Marshal and Deputy U.S. Marshal had jurisdiction everywhere throughout the country, their main function was the investigation of "Federal" crimes. Information about the organization and duties of a modern day Texas sheriff's office can be found in the *Rockabye County* series.

16a. As we explained in our *Alvin Dustine 'Cap' Fog* series, by a special dispensation of the Governor during the Prohibition era, Company 'Z' of the Texas Rangers were allowed to initiate operations without requesting permission under certain circumstances. During the late 1870's, the Governor of Arizona formed a similar force to cope with law breaking in the State. A similar decision was taken by a later Governor and the Arizona Rangers were brought back into being. Why it was considered necessary to organize the first force, how it operated and was finally disbanded is recorded in the *Waco* series and Part Four, "Keep Good Temper Alive," J.T.'S HUNDREDTH.

17. "Burro": in this context, a small wooden structure like the roof of a house upon which a saddle would be rested when not in use. Being so dependent upon his rig, a cowhand preferred to use a burro when one was available instead of laying it

down or hanging it by a stirrup.

17a. Despite the misconception created by Western movies—
even the late and great John Wayne being an offender—a
cowhand would *never* toss down his saddle on its skirts. If no
burro was available, he would either lay it on its side, or stand
it on its head, somewhere it would be safely clear of anybody
inadvertantly stepping upon it.

★★★★★★★★★★★★★★★★★★

The Biggest, Boldest, Fastest-Selling Titles in Western Adventure!

★★★★★★★★★★★★★★★★★★

CHARTER'S MOST WANTED LIST